"How about it, barkeep?" Saber asked. "Can I count on you to keep your mouth shut?"

"As God is my witness," Mort declared.

Saber grinned. His right hand came up from under the table holding his Colt. He fired once. Mort's body and the chair crashed to the floor, and Saber placed the revolver on the table and picked up his fork. "Never trust anyone with religion, boys. They're liable to turn on you no matter how much you pay them."

"What do we do with the body?" Twitch asked.

"The same thing you did with Hank's. The coyotes and buzzards hereabouts will be fat and sassy come tomorrow."

Twitch motioned. "And the saloon? Do we burn it to the ground when we're done eatin'?"

"You do not. I've always wanted to have my own waterin' hole. We'll stick around until Dunn and Hijino have stirred up a hornet's nest. Then we'll crush the hornets just like this." Saber slammed his fist down on the fly that had landed next to his plate.

Ralph Compton

Rio Largo

A Ralph Compton Novel
by David Robbins

A SIGNET BOOK

SIGNET
Published by New American Library, a division of
Penguin Group (USA) Inc., 375 Hudson Street,
New York, New York 10014, USA
Penguin Group (Canada), 90 Eglinton Avenue East, Suite 700, Toronto,
Ontario M4P 2Y3, Canada (a division of Pearson Penguin Canada Inc.)
Penguin Books Ltd., 80 Strand, London WC2R 0RL, England
Penguin Ireland, 25 St. Stephen's Green, Dublin 2,
Ireland (a division of Penguin Books Ltd.)
Penguin Group (Australia), 250 Camberwell Road, Camberwell, Victoria 3124,
Australia (a division of Pearson Australia Group Pty. Ltd.)
Penguin Books India Pvt. Ltd., 11 Community Centre, Panchsheel Park,
New Delhi—110 017, India
Penguin Group (NZ), cnr Airborne and Rosedale Roads, Albany,
Auckland 1310, New Zealand (a division of Pearson New Zealand Ltd.)
Penguin Books (South Africa) (Pty.) Ltd., 24 Sturdee Avenue,
Rosebank, Johannesburg 2196, South Africa

Penguin Books Ltd., Registered Offices:
80 Strand, London WC2R 0RL, England

First published by Signet, an imprint of New American Library,
a division of Penguin Group (USA) Inc.

First Printing, September 2006
10 9 8 7 6 5 4 3 2 1

Copyright © The Estate of Ralph Compton, 2006
All rights reserved

 REGISTERED TRADEMARK—MARCA REGISTRADA

Printed in the United States of America

THE IMMORTAL COWBOY

This is respectfully dedicated to the "American Cowboy." His was the saga sparked by the turmoil that followed the Civil War, and the passing of more than a century has by no means diminished the flame.

True, the old days and the old ways are but treasured memories, and the old trails have grown dim with the ravages of time, but the spirit of the cowboy lives on.

In my travels—to Texas, Oklahoma, Kansas, Nebraska, Colorado, Wyoming, New Mexico, and Arizona—I always find something that reminds me of the Old West. While I am walking these plains and mountains for the first time, there is this feeling that a part of me is eternal, that I have known these old trails before. I believe it is the undying spirit of the frontier calling, allowing me, through the mind's eye, to step back into time. What is the appeal of the Old West of the American frontier?

It has been epitomized by some as the dark and bloody period in American history. Its heroes—Crockett, Bowie, Hickok, Earp—have been reviled and criticized. Yet the Old West lives on, larger than life.

It has become a symbol of freedom, when there was always another mountain to climb and another river to cross; when a dispute between two men was settled not with expensive lawyers, but with fists, knives, or guns. Barbaric? Maybe. But some things never change. When the cowboy rode into the pages of American history, he left behind a legacy that lives within the hearts of us all.

—*Ralph Compton*

Chapter 1

The first rider came from the north. He appeared at Wolf Pass from out of the vastness of the wild and rugged Nacimiento Mountains.

Mort Decker was emptying a spittoon in the dawn light when he glanced up and spied the man and horse in deep shadow at the edge of the clearing. Instantly, Mort stiffened. He was not wearing his revolver, and his scattergun was under the bar. He relaxed when he saw it wasn't an Indian but he was upset with himself. Carelessness could get a man killed.

The rider just sat there.

Mustering a friendly smile, Mort raised a hand in greeting.

The rider did not respond.

Mort tensed up again. The newspapers and the politicians liked to crow that much of the West was settled and civilized, but that did not apply to New Mexico Territory. Wolves of the human variety were all too common; hostiles and outlaws were as thick as fleas on a bluetick hound. Kit Carson had whipped the Navajos, but small war parties of young hotheads acted up on occasion. The Apaches were still to be feared, too, especially with Geronimo on the loose. Then there were the white bad men, killers, and cutthroats of every stripe.

It was no wonder, then, that some folks said it was crazy of Mort to build his saloon so far off the safe and beaten path. But Mort never had cottoned to towns and cities, never had liked being up to his armpits in people and having to abide by a host of laws. His saloon enabled him to make a living, yet sometimes entire weeks went by when he did not see another soul. He liked it like that.

Now, lowering his arm, Mort turned and went back inside. His saloon was the only one in the Nacimientos. It granted him a certain immunity from the high-line riders, an immunity Mort did not take for granted. He set the spittoon down and went around the bar. Placing his hand on the scattergun, he waited.

The clomp of hooves announced the rider's arrival. Mort envisioned the man wrapping his reins around the hitch rail. Spurs jangled, and a silhouette filled the doorway. Really filled it. Mort had not realized how big the man was: shoulders as broad as a bull's, a chest a grizzly would envy.

The big man strode to the bar and leaned on an elbow. He wore typical cowboy garb: a high-crowned hat, a brown shirt, Levi's, and batwing chaps. Strapped around his waist was a black-handled Colt. Nothing unusual in any respect, yet Mort could not shake the feeling that this cowboy was more than he seemed.

"Mornin', mister. You spooked me out there. I don't often get customers this early."

"Whiskey," the man said.

Mort reached for a bottle.

"I hate watered-down bug juice," the man casually commented. "The last barkeep who pulled that on me lost all his front teeth and an ear, besides."

"Oh?" Mort reached for a different bottle. He opened it and filled a glass, all the while thinking furiously. Yes, it was common practice for saloons to water their drinks. Most folks accepted it and did not raise a fuss. He placed the glass in front of the big man and held out his palm. "That will be two bits."

The rider fished in a shirt pocket and slapped a coin into Mort's palm. In a smooth motion he upended the glass, gulped the contents in a single swallow, then wriggled the empty glass under Mort's nose. "Bring the bottle and leave it."

His ears burning with annoyance, Mort did as he was told. He recognized the signs. The flinty eyes. The hard features. The whipcord steel that lurked under the surface, waiting to spring at the least little provocation. He had encountered lobos like this rider before.

To cover his nervousness, Mort busied himself cleaning glasses. The rag he used needed washing, but his customers were generally not finicky.

"How long have you been here?"

Mort looked up. The rider was regarding him with an intensity Mort found disturbing. He hoped to God the man didn't intend to rob him. Mort always dreaded that happening, and liked to imagine himself defending his property and his life with his guns blazing. But he did not make a try for his scattergun. A tiny voice at the back of his mind warned that if he did, he would be dead before he touched it. Clearing his throat, he answered, "Since five o'clock."

"No, I meant your place here," the man said, gesturing at the ceiling and walls.

"Oh. Pretty near four years now, I reckon," Mort responded, and stressed the fact that if he were to be bucked out in gore, it would anger some people, by saying, "I have the only whiskey mill in these mountains." Maybe anger them enough to treat the culprit to a hemp social.

The rider chugged whiskey and let out a contented sigh. "You must know all there is to know about these parts."

Some of Mort's confidence returned. "That I do, friend. I daresay there isn't a gent for a hundred miles around that I haven't met, or a place I haven't been." He was exaggerating, but what was the harm?

Those flinty eyes fixed on him like the piercing eyes of a hawk on prey. "I'm new hereabouts. Maybe you wouldn't mind givin' me the lay of the land."

Encouraged, Mort moved closer. "There's not much to it. Follow the trail ten miles to the southeast and you'll come to the Sweet Grass Valley. The old Spanish called it the Rio Largo Valley, after the Rio Largo river, but a lot of the Spanish names aren't used anymore."

"I hear tell it's prime grazin' land," the rider remarked.

"Is it ever," Mort confirmed. "Between the Circle

T and the DP, there must be thirty thousand head or more."

"Those would be the two ranches I've heard about," the rider said. "Are there any others?"

Mort chuckled. "I'd like to see someone else try to horn in. Kent Tovey and Dar Pierce would fix their hash, pronto."

"Tell me about the outfits," the rider goaded. "I'm lookin' to hire on."

Warming to the topic, Mort leaned back. "The Rio Largo sort of divides the valley in half. The Circle T owns all the land north of the river; the DP has all the land south of it."

"Sort of? Are they about the same size?"

"The Circle T is bigger."

"Which ranch was here first?"

"The DP. Dar Pierce was with General Taylor during the Mexican War. When the troops pulled out, he stayed on and got himself hitched to a pretty Mexican gal by the name of Juanita."

The rider was about to take another swig. "You wouldn't catch me marryin' no greaser."

Mort smothered a flash of anger. "Juanita Pierce is a genuine lady. And I wouldn't go sayin' that about greasers between here and San Pedro, or the DP boys might get wind of it and come callin'."

"They don't worry me none," the rider said flatly.

"They should. They're a salty bunch. Insult their boss at your own risk."

The rider changed the subject. "What about the other spread? The Circle T? The owner's name is Tovey, did you say?"

Mort nodded. "He comes from a well-to-do family back east. Brought in a few thousand head from Texas to start his herd years back, and now has one of the best spreads in the whole territory."

"But wasn't Pierce already here when Tovey came? Didn't Pierce mind a greenhorn waltzin' in and takin' over half the valley?"

"Dar Pierce isn't land hungry like some cattle barons. He's content with what he has. But don't let that fool you. He's one tough hombre."

The rider treated himself to another swallow and wiped his mouth with his sleeve. "You wouldn't happen to know if the Circle T is hirin' hands?"

"Not that I'm aware," Mort said. "It's late in the season, and there's never a shortage of punchers who want to sign on. Tovey pays really well and has a first-rate cook."

"Food's not important," the rider said.

Mort blinked in surprise. Never in his life had he heard a saddle stiff utter such bald-faced blasphemy. To the cow crowd, food was *everything*. There was a saying to the effect that cowboys lived by their stomachs. The outfits with the best cooks always attracted the best cowpokes.

The man patted the bottle. "How much? I need to be moseyin' on. Daylight's a wastin'."

"Four dollars," Mort said.

"That's a mite steep."

"Rotgut doesn't grow on trees," Mort said. "The cost of shippin' it out here is twice what the saloons in San Pedro pay, and I need to make a profit same as any other business."

The man paid and touched his hat brim. "I'm

obliged for the information.'' He wheeled on his high heels and strode away.

Mort was struck by a strange insight: The man hardly had any dust on his clothes.

Given the time of year—the middle of the summer—and given how dry it was, any rider who traveled any distance was bound to be covered with the stuff. Curious, Mort walked outside.

The big man had unwrapped the reins to a zebra dun, and was reaching for the saddle horn. A lithe swing, and the saddle creaked under him.

Neither the zebra dun nor the saddle, Mort noticed, were the least bit dusty. The rider had lied about how far he'd come. An interesting tidbit that in and of itself meant nothing. The world was full of liars. *Good riddance*, Mort thought. Aloud, he said, ''If you're ever again in this neck of the woods, feel free to stop in.''

The rider looked back. He was supposed to act friendly to dilute suspicion, so he smiled and touched his hat brim, feeling the fool as he did. Once beyond the clearing, he applied his spurs. The trail was well defined. He made good time. It was not yet noon when he reined up on the crest of the last of the foothills.

Sweet Grass Valley was everything he had been told: lush with the rich greenery that lent the valley its name, prime grazing land any rancher worthy of the title would give anything to own.

The rider slid a folded sheet of paper from his pocket. The hand-drawn map was crude, but the landmarks were plain. He reined north, and for the next hour and a half followed the edge of the hills. Careful to stick to cover, he came to a trail that saw less use. It wound around a low hill, and presently brought him within sight of a shack.

Gigging the zebra dun into some scrub oak, the rider dismounted and shucked his Winchester from the saddle scabbard. He levered a round into the chamber, then crouched and cat-footed in among pockets of dry brush to within a stone's throw of the shack. Two horses were in a small corral attached to the side. Inside, someone was whistling.

The rider squatted and tucked the Winchester to his shoulder. Patient by nature, it did not bother him that over half an hour passed before the door opened and out came a human broomstick carrying a bucket. Shirtless and hatless, the string bean walked past the corral and over near a stand of cottonwoods.

Only then did the rider spot the spring.

"Yes, sir," the thin man said over his shoulder to the horses in the corral. "Ten more days and I'll be shed of line duty. I can't wait. Not that I mind your company, but you are a poor substitute for the gals at the Lucky Star."

Keeping low, the rider circled toward his quarry. There was no breeze, so he did not need to worry about his scent giving him away to the horses.

The broomstick knelt and dipped the wooden bucket into the water. "That Maggie sure treats me nice. Last time I was there, she did me for half price. I thought I'd died and gone to heaven."

A break in the brush gave the rider a clear shot. He sighted down the barrel, then lowered the Winchester without firing. Rocks lined the spring—large rocks that would serve as well as a bullet, if not better. Quickly bending, he removed his spurs and set them beside his rifle.

The thin man was a chatterbox, which was to be expected. The job of the line rider was lonely work, and cowhands often developed the habit of talking to themselves.

The rider should know. He had been a cowpoke, once.

"I aim to repay the favor by buyin' Maggie a fancy gift," the broomstick was saying. "A new shawl, maybe. Or one of those pretty new bonnets with the bows and frills the females cotton to. It can't be a mirror. Ugly women hate mirrors, and she sure is powerful ugly."

As silently as a stalking Comanche, the rider crept toward the puncher. He placed each foot with care. The broomstick had a Remington on his hip, and while it was doubtful he used it for anything more than shooting snakes, the rider preferred not to tempt fate by giving the cowboy time to draw.

"Listen to me!" the thin cowpoke marveled. "You would think I was booze-blind, but I'm sober as a parson." He laughed at his own antics. "Maybe it's true what old Shonsey says. Maybe there comes a time when every man is more than willin' to step into a woman's loop if it means a warm bed the rest of his nights."

One of the horses nickered.

The rider froze. The animal had seen him. But the cowboy did not look around. The rider continued his cautious advance.

"I laughed at the notion when I was younger," the

puncher rambled on. "But life has a way of sweatin'
the fat out of a man's brain." Sloshing water over
the rim, he raised the bucket out of the spring. "Of
course, if I'd had any sense to begin with, I wouldn't
be nursemaidin' cows for a livin', would I?" He
began to rise.

By then the rider was close enough. A single
bound brought him to the rocks. He had already se-
lected the one he wanted. As large as a melon, with
a jagged edge, it was perfect. He had it in his hands
and over his head before the broomstick awoke to
his presence.

"What in tarnation?" the cowboy blurted, his eyes
widening. He clawed for his pistol, but it was much
too late and he was much too slow.

The rider brought the rock crashing down. It
caught the cowboy across the forehead, caving in his
skull and bursting his brain like overripe fruit. He
was dead before his body hit the ground.

Tossing the bloody rock into the spring, the rider
hoisted the body and pushed it into the water, head-
first. He deliberately left the puncher's boots sticking
out, so someone would spot them.

Hurrying into the brush, the rider replaced his
spurs and snatched up his Winchester. Retrieving the
zebra dun took only a few moments. The bottle he
had bought at the Wolf Pass Saloon was in one of
his saddlebags. Taking it out, the rider returned to
the spring, opened it, and laid it at the water's edge.
Satisfied with his handiwork, he swung onto the
zebra dun. As he rode past the corral, the horses
stared at him. He winked at them.

"I hope the rest are as easy."

Chapter 2

The second rider came from the south. He used the Old Spanish Trail, once part of a network of trails established by Spain's intrepid explorers and colonizers to take them to remote mines and missions.

The second rider was different from the first. Where the big man who stopped at Wolf Pass was dark and somber, the second rider was friendly and cheerful. Macario Hijino always smiled. He smiled every minute of every day. He smiled when he ate; he smiled when he talked; he smiled when he rode; he smiled when he walked. He smiled when he killed, too, and to Hijino, killing was the most enjoyable part of life. As a boy, he had liked to kill snakes and toads and scorpions and every other small creature he could catch, including, on several occasions, family cats. He saw it as only natural that once he grew into manhood he would continue to kill, and what did it matter if those he slew walked on two legs and called themselves human?

Hijino dressed to match his disposition. His sombrero was the best he could afford, worn tilted at the back to lend a certain dash to his appearance. His

Spanish-style saddle and bridle were decorated with silver, as was his hatband, his belt, and his chaparreras. An amigo once joked that Hijino was a living silver mine, and Hijino had to admit he did love his silver. He flashed in the sun with brilliant gleams of light, and made a striking impression on all he met. Hijino liked it that way.

Next to killing and silver, Hijino's other passions in life were his white caballo, Blanco, his pearl-handled Colt, and money. Hijino spent money like he was the richest man in all of Mexico. Only he was not rich, and in order to go on spending, he had to obtain money by any and all means he could. Some of those means were illegal, which was why the Mexican authorities were so eager to stand him in front of a firing squad.

On this bright, gorgeous morning, Hijino rode with the easy air of someone at home in the saddle. Hijino and his white horse moved as one, in fluid synchrony, as superb an example of a caballero and his caballo as could be found south or north of the border.

Presently Hijino came to a high ridge, and drew rein. The Rio Largo Valley unfolded before him like a flower unfolding to embrace the warmth of a new day. Hijino's smile widened. Somewhere over the horizon was the river that gave the valley its name. Between the mountains and the river were herds of cattle, looking like so many ants from Hijino's altitude.

Lightly tapping his Spanish spurs against his mount, Hijino followed the Old Spanish Trail down to his destination. He adjusted his sombrero, flicked a few specks of dust from his jacket, and rode out across the valley, smiling the whole while. Soon he came upon cattle—cows so plump, Hijino imagined that if he squeezed them, they would pop like pimples.

Soon, riders spotted him. Three broke from a herd and galloped to intercept him. Hijino reined up and waited, smiling his perpetual smile, his hands casually folded over his silver saddle horn.

The three slowed and spread out. Their Spanish heritage was evident in their features and their attire. They were dressed much like Hijino, only their clothes were plainer, as befitted men more interested in their work than in how they looked in a mirror. They came to a stop twenty feet out, and regarded him with wary interest.

Hijino did not feel threatened. He knew he could draw and shoot all three before they cleared their *pistolas* from their holsters. He was lightning with his Colt, and proud of it.

At last the man in the middle spoke. Young and handsome, he had an air of authority. "Do you speak English?" he asked in Spanish.

Puzzled by the question, Hijino gave the young one closer scrutiny. He had been mistaken. This one was not entirely Mexican by birth. Traces of gringo were apparent in the eyes, the hair, the face. "*Sí.* I speak several languages," Hijino amiably answered. "English is but one of them."

The young man pushed his sombrero back on his head. "Why are you on the DP?"

Hijino did not like the other's tone, but he did not show his resentment. He feigned ignorance. "What is that?"

"The best rancho in all of New Mexico," the young man said. "It is run by my father, Dar Pierce. I am Julio, his youngest son."

"Ah." Hijino continued his act. "In Mexico we do not name our ranchos after the letters of the alphabet."

"You are a vaquero, then?"

"*Sí, patrón.* A vaquero in need of work if any is to be had."

"The last I heard there is no shortage of ranchos in Mexico," Julio said with a wry grin.

Hijino was not deceived. The young one was fishing. Many men came north a step ahead of prison, or worse. "I am not a bandido, *patrón*," he said with as much sincerity as he could fake. "I am a simple worker of cows."

One of the other men, a moon-faced pumpkin whose fondness for food was all too apparent, chuckled good-naturedly and commented, "*Madre de Dios.* You must have blinded half the cows in Mexico, wearing all that silver."

All of them chuckled, and Hijino mentally patted himself on the back. "That is why I seek employment here in the north. All those blind cows had to be put out of their misery, and there is not enough work for an honest vaquero between the border and Mexico City."

The one who had spoken laughed. "An hombre after my own heart. I am Paco." He jerked a thumb at the third man. "This other one is Roman. Perhaps you have heard of him?"

"Should I?"

"Roman has more than a small reputation as a *pistolero*," Paco revealed. "When Señor Pierce needs cow thieves and outlaws disposed of, he always calls on Roman."

Hijino's interest perked. All the more so because Roman was not wearing a gun belt. Slight bulges under Roman's black jacket explained the mystery. "A pleasure to meet you," he said. "Maybe you will honor me some time by showing me how good you are. I am only a fair shot, myself," he lied.

Roman's right hand blurred, and a short-barreled, ivory-handled Colt appeared as if out of thin air.

"Is that good enough for you?" Paco chortled.

Hijino was impressed, but not overly so. It had been so long since he met anyone who could rival him that it was too much to expect he had met one now. He shammed mock amazement. "You must be the fastest *pistolero* in New Mexico."

Roman's hand blurred a second time, and the Colt disappeared under his black jacket. "Would that it were true."

"There is someone faster?"

It was Paco who replied. "*Sí*. His name is Jesco. He rides for the Circle T. Each year they finish first and second in the pistol competition."

"I am always second," Roman said.

"The what?" Hijino could not wait to meet this Jesco. He almost wished he had been sent to the Circle T.

"Each year the two ranches hold a rodeo," Paco explained. "There are roping and riding contests. Shooting matches, too. Jesco always wins the pistol match. He is not human, that one."

Julio Pierce stirred, and said in Spanish, "Enough about pistols and shooting. We are cowmen, and cows are what matter." He switched to English. "You are welcome to come with us to the ranch house, if you like. My father does the hiring, and he is always on the lookout for good men."

"I would be most grateful," Hijino assured him in Spanish. Something in Julio's expression compelled him to repeat it in English. He sensed he was being tested, although why it should be so important for their vaqueros to speak English, he could not begin to guess.

"Let us go, then." Julio reined to the north.

Gigging Blanco, Hijino came up next to the sorrel and paced it, saying offhandedly, "It seems to me that you have a most marvelous rancho, señor."

"It is my father's ranch, not mine," Julio said, and went on to proudly extol the DP's virtues.

Hijino was already familiar with them. Approximately ten thousand head of cattle, and all the water the ranch could need, thanks to the Rio Largo. The valley was an oasis of plenty in the midst of the semiarid mountains. Every blade of grass was worth its weight in gold, or, to be more exact, worth its weight in beef. Julio finished, and Hijino commented, "But surely you are part owner, being the son?"

For an instant a frown curled the young man's mouth. "I am but one of three sons. When my father dies, he will undoubtedly divide the ranch between us and our sisters."

Without thinking, Hijino blundered. He said, "Three brothers and two sisters. But one-fifth of something is better than nothing, eh?"

Julio shot him a sharp glance. "How did you know?"

"Señor?"

"That I have two sisters. I did not mention how many."

Hijino became conscious that Paco and Roman were staring at him. Suppressing a stab of nerves, he shrugged and said, "The name Pierce. I have heard it before. Your ranch is well spoken of on both sides of the border."

"Rightly so!" Paco unwittingly came to Hijino's rescue. "The DP turns out the finest cattle anywhere."

"I suppose my family is well known," Julio said, but he did not sound happy about it. "My brothers Steve and Armando have made many cattle drives into Mexico to sell our beef."

"Steve?" Hijino said.

"He takes more after our father than our mother," Julio said. "My father named him after his father. Armando is named after my mother's grandfather."

"Who are you named after?"

"I was a coin toss." Julio laughed lightly. "My father wanted to name me John, and my mother wanted to name me Julio. Since they could not agree, they had Berto toss a coin, and my mother won."

"Berto?"

"Our caporal. Our foreman. He has been with my father from the beginning. He is most capable."

So Hijino had heard. But he would jump that hur-

dle when he came to it. Now that he had actually
seen the valley with his own eyes, he was fully com-
mitted to his part in the plot, come what may.

Cattle were everywhere. Fat, contented cattle
worth a fortune in themselves. All of the cowhands
were of Hispanic extraction, an expected advantage
for Hijino. It was easier to turn people against one
another when race was the issue.

Bathed in sunshine, the hacienda could be seen
from a long way off. Small wonder, since the valley
floor was essentially a broad, flat plain, broken only
by the Rio Largo, which slashed the valley from the
northwest to the southeast.

The buildings were adobe, except for the stable.
They reminded Hijino of the ranchos he had worked
south of the border before he took to living outside
the law. Vaqueros and others bustled about at vari-
ous tasks. A heavyset blacksmith was fixing a wagon
wheel. Two other men were winching bales of hay
into the hayloft.

The *casa grande* was everything Hijino expected—
a magnificent house, as stately as it was imposing.
Julio rode straight to the portico and dismounted.
Almost immediately, an old servant came out to take
Julio's reins.

Since Paco and Roman stayed on their horses, Hijino did the same. He must be careful not to over-
step himself.

Two more men came out of the house. One was a
tall gringo with a bony face, his hair gray at the temples. He had a casual manner about him. He wore
common work clothes and a sombrero rather than a

typical gringo hat. He did not wear a revolver. *"Hola,* son," he said softly, and warmly embraced Julio.

Hijino was amused. *This* was the famous and feared Dar Pierce? The gringo who had braved countless hardships to build the DP from empty grassland? Hijino almost laughed. Then he noticed the second man studying him, and his instincts warned him that the hurdle was upon him sooner than he had imagined it would be.

The second man was a short, stocky Mexican, with a body as square as an adobe brick and a face that made Hijino think of a fox. Intelligence glistened in the man's dark eyes. To be under his gaze was like being under a magnifying glass. Hijino inwardly shook off the feeling that the man could see right through him.

Julio and Dar Pierce had exchanged words, and now Dar stepped to the end of the porch. "My son tells me you are looking for work."

"Sí, patrón," Hijino said with the utmost civility.

"He also tells me you speak English."

"Yes, I do. Quite well, señor. Is that important?" Hijino used the most perfect English of which he was capable.

"At most ranches, no," Dar said. "But at the DP all the hands speak both. It has to do with my wife and I being from two different cultures. I speak both and so does she."

"I see," Hijino said, although he did not really see at all.

"I happen to be in need of an experienced hand," Dar said. "But I never hire anyone without putting them to the test. You have a month to show your worth—at full pay, of course—and if you pass muster, you can stay on as long as you like."

"*Gracias*, señor. I mean, thank you, sir."

Dar motioned. "Save your gratitude. It won't be easy. My men earn their pay the hard way. They work for it." He nodded at the fox beside him. "My foreman, Berto, has the final say. It's him you must impress."

"I will try my best, señor," Hijino promised. He looked at Berto and resorted to his most charming smile, but it had no effect.

"The rules are simple," Berto said. "Do what I tell you to do when I tell you to do it. No drinking at the rancho unless it is a special occasion. No cursing, either, in the presence of the señora and the señoritas. Behave yourself and we will get along."

"I rarely drink," Hijino said, "and I never swear, señor."

"Never?" Berto repeated skeptically.

"I have my mother to thank. My father died when I was young and she raised me by herself. She was very religious. She went to church twice a day, and three times on Sunday." Hijino did not add that he grew so tired of her constant nagging to get him to go with her that one night he slit her throat and fed her to the hogs.

Chapter 3

"The socializing will be fun."

Kent Tovey gave rise to mild exasperation. "It's called a rodeo, dear," he responded across the breakfast table. "The men take it quite seriously." Of average height and build, there was nothing remarkable about him except his chin, which jutted like an anvil. He hated his chin as he hated few other things.

In the act of buttering a muffin, Nancy Tovey paused. "Too seriously, if you ask me. One of these years, the competition will end in violence. Mark my words."

"Don't I always listen to you?" Kent knew it was a mistake the moment he uttered the words.

"Don't patronize me. You know how I detest being patronized. Just because I was born and raised in New York does not make me ignorant. And need I remind you that you were born there, too?"

Kent sighed and sat back. His wife of three decades taxed his self-control at times. No, he did not need to be reminded. He remembered his upbringing vividly; the pleasant years of growing up in New York City, the decision to follow in his father's footsteps and go into business, the mercantile he ran until a chance encounter filled his head with visions of the fabulous opportunities awaiting the intrepid on the frontier. His move to Texas, and then, years later, uprooted to New Mexico Territory. Now here he was, in his forties and the owner of one of the largest and most profitable ranches in the Southwest. A success by any measure.

There were those who had warned Kent he would fail. His father, for instance, labeled leaving New York foolhardy. "What do you know about cows? You were reared in the city, not on a farm."

Kent had a pat answer. "What I don't know, I will learn. I will do as I have done with the mercantile, and only hire the best men for the job. Their experience will compensate for mine until mine matches theirs."

His wife had objected, too. Nancy came from a wealthy family. She had been reared in the lap of luxury. That she fell in love with him and elected to marry him was a constant source of wonderment to Kent. She did not seem to understand that his decision to strike out west and make his fortune was in part motivated by his desire to give her the many things he could not give her as mercantile manager. "Bold dreams call for bold risks," he had told her.

She had clucked in the annoying way she had, and replied, "I took you for better or worse, so where you go, I go. But if I end up in a boardinghouse ridden with lice and rodents, I will never let you hear the end of it."

That was his Nance, as she liked to be called, always speaking her mind, and tact be damned. Kent loved her, sincerely and truly loved her, but there were moments when he sincerely and truly longed to throttle her. Now, forking scrambled eggs into his mouth and chewing, he gave thought to the preparations for the rodeo. "I must consult with Clayburn and Jesco today."

"He scares me," Nance said.

"Who?" Kent asked in surprise.

"Well, it certainly wouldn't be Walt Clayburn." Nance fluffed her light brown hair. For her age she was remarkably attractive. She had an oval face, full lips, and green eyes—the loveliest eyes Kent had ever looked into. Her dress came all the way from Denver, her shoes from Saint Louis. She insisted on wearing the latest fashions. Queen of the Circle T, people called her, and the title fit. "Walt is the nicest man who ever drew breath. He always treats me with the utmost respect."

Kent agreed. But then, his foreman was wise to the wiles of men *and* women, and treated females with the same regard he treated cattle. "You're afraid of John Jesco?"

"Don't make it sound so preposterous. He is an enigma, that one. He hardly ever speaks to me. And he's killed. Shot others in cold blood."

Exasperation blossomed into anger, and Kent set down his fork. "I will thank you never to talk like that about him again. Jesco is quiet by nature, and shy around women. As for the shootings, he had no choice. I've had all the details from Clayburn."

"Suppose you share them."

"Really, now," Kent said. "Breakfast is hardly the time to discuss bloodletting."

"You're the one who claims it was justified," Nance said. "Prove it."

When she took that tone, what choice did Kent have? "Jesco has shot four men that I know of. There are rumors of several more, but he never talks about them and no one would presume to delve into his past. That's just not done."

Nance sniffed in distaste. "Yes, more of that crude Western etiquette I am forced to live by."

"Honestly," Kent said. After all this time, he thought she would have adjusted.

"Go on."

"All of Jesco's shootings were done in self-defense. The first time, a saloon girl was involved. She fancied him, and the other man took exception."

"Yes, I can see where a backward waif might be smitten by those exceptional good looks of his."

A thought struck Kent. The thought that maybe his wife's unease did not stem from fear so much as another emotion. Apparently, she did not realize how much her comment revealed. "Anyway, the other fellow drew on Jesco, and would have shot him down if Jesco had not been so quick."

"You say that with a degree of pride."

"Why shouldn't I? Out here a man's worth is not always judged by how much money he has or how much land he owns. Jesco does us a service by staying with the Circle T. His reputation serves to discourage troublemakers."

"As if anyone in their right mind would dare try to do us harm," Nance scoffed. "You have nearly thirty hands riding for you. A small army. You don't need a man like John Jesco."

"But that's where you're wrong, dear," Kent took delight in pointing out. "Most of our hands are plain and simple cowboys. They've never shot anyone in their life. Oh, they wear six-shooters, but those are tools of their trade, like their ropes and their spurs, useful for disposing of rattlesnakes and coyotes. Jesco is different. He is gun-savvy, as they say, and he is loyal to the brand, which makes him an important asset."

"I still don't see where it is anything to be proud of. Killing is killing. The day we start to place killers on pedestals is the day this country teeters on the precipice."

Kent did not say anything. She was judging Western ways by Eastern standards, a failing of hers. He was to blame. He sheltered her from the harsher realities of life. Her view of the West had been limited to the view out the window of their house in Dallas when they lived in Texas, and now by her standing as co-owner of the Circle T. She never actually had to live among the common folk and see the world through their eyes.

"All that silliness aside, I look forward to seeing Juanita again. It has been over a month, and I do so miss her." Nance's brow furrowed. "Odd, isn't it, that we should be so close? I mean, she comes from a poor family in a small village somewhere in Mexico, and I was raised in a mansion on the banks of the Hudson."

"Juanita Pierce is a walking, breathing bouquet of roses," Kent said.

Nance's furrows deepened. "I had no idea you felt so highly about her. But for once we agree. She is a saint, if ever there was one. I often wonder how hard it must be for her, married to a man like Pierce."

Kent did not hide his indignation. "What in the world are you talking about? He dotes over her. They get along marvelously, like two peas in a pod."

"Well, she is considerably younger."

"So? Dar gives her everything she wants. He even modeled his ranch after the Mexican variety because she misses Mexico so much. How much more must he do to prove his love for her?"

"Sometimes love is not enough," was Nance's reply.

Kent had endured enough foolishness for one meal. He finished and excused himself. The maid would clear his dishes.

Morning was Kent's favorite time of the day. After breakfast, he liked to sit in a rocking chair on the porch and gaze out over his domain while puffing on his beloved pipe.

The timber for the buildings had been hauled from the Nacimiento Mountains. Everything was painted white: the ranch house, the bunkhouse, the cookhouse, the stable, the blacksmith shop, the chicken coop, the sheds, the outbuildings, everything. The hands liked to joke about how neat and tidy Kent insisted the ranch be, but Kent did not relent. He managed the ranch as he had managed the mercantile, as a model of efficiency. That was the secret to reaping profits year after year, and Kent was not in the cattle business to lose money.

Shonsey, the cook, once made a comment within Kent's hearing about how the Almighty was riled because Kent ran the Circle T better than the Almighty ran heaven. "Any day now St. Peter will show up askin' for work."

Hardly had the remembrance entered his head than Kent saw his foreman and another man approach.

Walt Clayburn lived, breathed, and ate cows. He got his start as a puncher working outfits in Texas. By the time Kent met him in Dallas, Clayburn was foreman of a small ranch. Clayburn leaped at the offer to join Kent's drive to New Mexico and become foreman of the Circle T.

Clayburn never gave Kent a single occasion to regret the decision. The Circle T operated as smoothly as a well-oiled steam engine, and that was largely due to Walt. Kent trusted him implicitly.

Today Clayburn was dressed as he nearly always was, in a dusty gray hat, a store-bought shirt, scuffed brown leather vest, Levi's and boots. He seldom wore a pistol. His brown eyes were framed by black bangs. He had a big nose but a small mouth. "Mornin', Mr. Tovey," he said with a smile as he stopped at the bottom of the steps.

"Will I ever persuade you to stop being so formal?" Kent asked. "You can call me by my first name if you like. If I've mentioned that once, I must have told you a thousand times."

"Sorry, Mr. Tovey, but old habits are hard to break, and I was bred to treat my employers with respect." Clayburn nodded at the newcomer. "This here is Lafe Dunn. He's lookin' for work."

Kent puffed on his pipe. He always let Clayburn

handle the hiring, but Clayburn always insisted on getting his approval. "As always, I will rely on your judgment."

"Thank you, sir. We are a hand short since Wilson went and busted his skull up at the line shack." Clayburn sadly shook his head. "I never will understand what he was doin' with that bottle. He wasn't much of a drinker."

Kent did not understand it, either. Ed Wilson had been at the Circle T for six years, as dependable a cowhand as any. For him to get drunk and fall on that rock in the spring had come as a shock.

"If Dunn works out," Clayburn was saying, "he can take Wilson's place."

Kent had not paid much attention to the new cowboy, but he did so now. Dunn was as tall as Jesco, the tallest man in the outfit, but with a more muscular build. Dunn's eyes were dark, virtually black, and had a predatory aspect that reminded Kent of a hawk one of the hands found with a broken wing and nursed back to health. "I take it you have done ranch work before?"

Dunn nodded.

"I pay top dollar, but I demand top work," Kent went through the ritual. "I'm not as strict as my good friend Dar Pierce, in that I do not expect you to be a paragon of virtue." Kent wagged the pipe at him. "But in my presence and that of Mrs. Tovey, my hands are required to show due respect. Is that understood?"

Again Dunn nodded.

"Have you lost your voice?" Clayburn asked.

"Yes, sir, I understand," Dunn finally spoke. He

had a deep voice with a slight rasp. "I'm not much of a talker, is all."

"That's perfectly all right," Kent assured him. "It's your roping and riding skills that count. You will be paid forty-five dollars a month, which I'm sure you'll agree is more than fair. You are entitled to two Saturdays off a month, at the foreman's discretion."

"Any questions?" asked Clayburn.

"None that I can think of," Dunn said.

Kent had one. "How do you feel about Mexicans, Mr. Dunn?"

"Sir?"

"Dar Pierce has a Mexican wife. They often pay us visits. His punchers are Mexican. They sometimes cross onto our side of the river after cattle that have strayed across the Rio Largo. You will also run into them in San Pedro. Are you comfortable with that?"

Dunn cocked his head. "Comfortable how, sir?"

"In being around them. We hold an annual rodeo. This year it is the Circle T's turn to host the event, and many of them will be here." Kent began to rock back and forth. "I do not hire bigots, Mr. Dunn. If you are one of those who regards anyone with Mexican blood as a 'greaser' or a 'chili-eater,' say so now and you may leave with no hard feelings."

"Not me, sir. I've been around them all my life. They're no different than anyone else."

"I am gratified to hear that."

The screen door opened and out came Nance. "Good morning, Walt," she said merrily. "Care to partake of some coffee? We have half a pot left from breakfast."

"Thank you, ma'am, but no," Clayburn replied. "I

have too much work to do." He glanced at their new man. "Go pick a bunk and store your war bag. I'll be along shortly."

Dunn touched his hat brim to Nancy, and departed.

"Fortuitous, him showing up when he did," Kent commented. "Otherwise it might have taken us two or three weeks to find someone to take Wilson's place."

Nance gracefully sank into the other rocking chair. "I need someone to take me into San Pedro in a few days. There are things we need for the celebration."

"I'll have Jesco do it, ma'am," Clayburn said.

"I wouldn't want to tear him from his work." Nance fluttered her lips. "Why not ask the new man? He seemed nice enough."

"Whatever you say, ma'am."

"It's settled, then." Nance smiled sweetly at Kent, and said with sugary delight, "See how agreeable I can be?"

Chapter 4

Trella Pierce was upset. She stood in front of the full-length mirror in her bedroom, and did not like what she saw. Her lustrous black hair fell to her waist in a straight line. Not a curl anywhere, which in Trella's estimation was so unfair. Her sister, Dolores, had curls to spare.

Nor did Trella like that while she had the pear shape of her mother's face, and her mother's arched eyebrows and small nose, she had her father's thin lips. Hideous lips, in Trella's opinion, lips men would find revolting.

But Trella's major complaint was that unlike her full-busted mother and sister, she was flat-chested. Nature had been cruel in giving her the mind of a girl in the body of a boy. Both her mother and her sister assured her that she would eventually fill out, but here Trella was, sixteen years old, and she had walnuts for breasts where her mother and sister had melons.

"I am ugly as sin," Trella said aloud. Smoothing her blouse, she left her room and went down the long, cool hallway to the kitchen. The sounds and smells of breakfast reached her before she got there.

Meals in the Pierce casa were a family affair. No one was excused. Sometimes her brothers were out on the range, but that was the only exception allowed.

Sunshine streamed in through the windows. Her father was at the head of the table, her mother and sister on the right, her brothers on the left. Trella claimed her usual chair next to Dolores.

"Well, look who it is," Steve said with a grin. "We thought maybe you were sleeping in until noon." Of all the brothers, he looked most like their father. He preferred to dress in American-style clothes, not Mexican, and although fluent in English and Spanish, as they all were, he seldom spoke the latter unless he had to.

"I hope a horse steps on you today," Trella retorted.

"Your brother has a point, daughter," Juanita said. "Breakfast started ten minutes ago. Do us the courtesy of being on time." As always, she was the perfect portrait of poise and elegance.

Dolores could not resist adding her opinion. "My darling sister probably could not decide what to wear. The maid told me that she changes her clothes five or six times each morning and leaves them scattered about her room."

Dar looked at them over his coffee cup. "That maid has a name. And, Trella, how many times must I remind you to pick up after yourself? Just because we have servants does not give you an excuse to be lazy."

"Yes, father," Trella said dutifully. Under the table, she kicked Dolores.

The breakfast conversation bored her. Steve and Armando talked about horses and the bull they were taking to the rodeo. Julio asked if he would be permitted to ride the bull this year, and her father said they would see.

Trella felt sorry for Julio. He was a year older than she, and straining at the bit to be a man.

"You let Steve and Armando ride the bull when they were my age. I do not understand why I can't."

Dar was spooning raisins into a bowl of oatmeal. He never had oatmeal without raisins. "Did I say you couldn't? No, son. But the bull this year is new and untested. If it has a vicious temperament you might want to hold off."

"I will not be treated like a child," Julio sulked.

"When do I ever do that?" Dar asked in mild reproach. He never got angry, their father. He was always reasonable and calm and in complete control of himself and all around him.

"You do, and don't realize it," Julio would not relent. "Even some of the vaqueros have noticed. Just the other day, Hijino asked why it is that you never let me break any of the mustangs."

"What business is it of his?" Steve asked.

"That one has a mouth on him," Armando said. In contrast to Steve, he, like Julio, always wore Mexican clothes. Of the three brothers he was the most level-headed. In that respect, he took after their father, although his features were more like their mother's. "He is always talking. Some of the men wish he would talk less."

That earned an, "Oh?" from their father.

"He is a good worker, though," Armando quickly

amended. "He rides like he was born to the saddle, and I have never seen anyone better with a rope."

"Look at how he dresses," Steve said. "He is in love with himself, and with his own voice. He is always going on and on about how everything Mexican is better than everything north of the border."

"One of those, is he?" Dar said. "Does he also look down his nose at the people north of the border?"

Armando answered. "Not that we are aware, no, father."

"I will have a talk with Berto anyway," Dar said.

Trella had heard enough. "I think Hijino is nice," she made bold to interject. She also thought the new vaquero was uncommonly handsome, and liked how he flattered her with his comments and his eyes. She had dreamed about him the other night. In it, he saved her from bandits and she rode off into the sunset with him on his wonderful white horse. It was a silly dream, but it made her feel all warm inside when she remembered it the next day.

"Everyone is nice to you pretty girls," Armando said. "You are the darlings of the rancho."

"I do not ask to be." Trella resented being treated as a *girl*. She was a *woman*, whether anyone else agreed or not. In a sullen mood, she ate her breakfast in silence, barely listening to the others.

Afterward, her father went to find Berto. Steve, Armando, and Julio had work to do. Juanita had to begin packing for the trip to the Circle T. Dolores practiced on the piano.

Left on her own, Trella strolled outdoors. She breathed deep of the morning air, and bent her steps toward the stable. She had done so frequently of late, always with the hope of seeing the man she now saw standing by the corral. He was practicing with his rope, throwing the loop over a gatepost.

"*Buenos días, señorita.*"

"*Buenos días, Hijino,*" Trella said. Her hands clasped behind her back so her bosom, such as it was, jutted against her blouse, Trella leaned against the rails.

"How do you do it?" Hijino asked.

"Do what?"

"Always look so pretty. In Mexico City you would have caballeros groveling at your feet to win your favor."

"I would not," Trella said, secretly pleased by the flattery. She did not want him to know that, though, so she said, "Shouldn't you be off tending cattle?"

"Why, señorita, you stab me in the heart. Can it be you do not enjoy my company? I enjoy yours."

Trella could not get over how handsome he was. That he showed an interest in her seemed too good to be true. "If my father heard you say that, he would be cross with you."

"Your father has not said two words to me since the day I was hired," Hijino said. "He has forgotten I exist."

"That's what you think," Trella remarked. "You were brought up at breakfast today."

Hijino's arms froze in midswing. "I was?"

"*Sí.* Armando says you talk too much," Trella teased. "And Steve thinks you are too critical of norteamericanos. You had better learn to hold your tongue, or you will find yourself out of a job."

"Thank you for telling me. I will be more careful from now on. I will walk on eggs with my mouth."

Trella laughed. "What a strange way to put it. Just don't talk about how much better Mexico is than the United States."

"So that was it." With a deft flick, Hijino tossed his rope over the post. "I can not help it if I love the country I am from. Have you ever been there?" He did not wait for her to answer. "If you have, then you must feel as I do. Mexico is special. Its people are special. They are more of the earth. More natural. They are not like these norteamericanos who are only interested in hoarding pesos, and who treat the land like it is their personal possession to scar as they wish."

His passion stirred Trella. "Perhaps that is true of some norteamericanos, but not my father."

"No, señorita, not your *padre*. And why is that, do you think? I think it is because in his great love for your *madre*, he has become more like us. More like you and me. More *mejicano* than norteamericano."

Trella had never thought of it like that. "He has always told me to embrace both ways of life."

"Yet he lives more like a Mexican than that gringo across the river," Hijino pointed out.

Straightening, Trella glanced nervously about. "Don't let anyone hear you say that ever again. They might think you do not like gringos." It worried her that he might be fired.

"I have nothing against most gringos," Hijino said. "Only the ones who call us greasers, whether to our face or behind our backs." He leaned toward her and lowered his voice. "I have heard that some of the gringo cowboys do just that."

"I do not believe it."

Hijino sighed. "You do not want to believe it. If you will forgive my bluntness, you are as blind as your *padre* and *madre*."

"How dare you," Trella said. She would not stand for having her parents insulted. Ever.

"Hear me out," Hijino requested. "If I am wrong, I apologize. But did your father not settle here first? Was not this whole valley his by right? Yet Kent Tovey came and took half of it away without paying your father a cent, I hear. Tovey brought in his cattle and his cowboys, and now his ranch is bigger than your father's. He has more cows, more men. He is richer, and grows richer every year. At your father's expense."

"You mistake his motives," Trella said. "Kent Tovey is a good friend."

"Is he really? What if your father had refused to let him settle here? Do you think this Tovey would have turned around and gone back to Texas?" Hijino shook his head. "A rattlesnake is nice enough until you step on it, but I would still not want to have one for a neighbor."

"Enough," Trella said sharply.

"As you wish." Hijino gave a courteous bow. "But I warn you, señorita. If this Tovey is ever crossed, he will show his true nature, and your father will regret being so kind."

Trella stamped her foot. "Stop it, I say! You fill my head with ideas that should not be there. The Toveys would never turn on us." She had more to say, but a stocky figure had appeared at the corner of the stable. Alarm spiked through her. She wondered how much he had overheard.

"Is everything all right, señorita?" Berto asked.

"Everything is fine," Trella answered.

Hijino acted as if he did not have a care in the world. He smiled at the foreman and tossed his loop again. "I have been showing her how to rope a cow."

"How considerate of you," Berto said dryly. "But you were hired to work with *real* cows. Saddle your horse and join Paco and Roman. They leave in fifteen minutes to search the foothills to the east for strays."

"I will be ready in five minutes." Hijino doffed his sombrero to Trella and jingled off.

Berto turned to Trella. "Forgive my lack of manners, but what did he say to you, señorita?"

"We talked about the rodeo and other things. Nothing of any importance." Trella could not bring herself to reveal the truth and get Hijino into trouble. "Why do you ask?"

"I am growing not to like that one, señorita. Hiring him might have been a mistake, but it is a mistake easily remedied."

"You will not fire him on my account," Trella said. "He always behaves as a caballero should."

"Is that so, señorita?"

Trella divined that Berto did not believe her, but he thought too highly of her father and was too polite to say so to her face. "I must go in." She started to leave, but Berto shocked her by placing a hand on her arm. He had never touched her before, not in all the years she knew him.

"Forgive me, señorita, but I feel it is my duty to warn you."

It is a day for warnings, Trella thought. "Warn me about what?" As if she could not guess.

Berto nodded in the direction Hijino had gone. "He is young and handsome. It is no mystery why you like his company." She went to respond, but Berto held up his hand. "Do not deny it. I have seen you talking to him before. That is your right. But for your sake, and your father's, do not become too attached. He is a drifter. We know nothing about him. You invite unhappiness by being so friendly."

"And you presume too much."

"*Sí*. I do. But only because of the great affection I bear you and your family. I do not want you to come to harm."

"Oh, please," Trella angrily countered. "What harm could he do? The idea is preposterous." Simmering with indignation, she marched stiffly toward the house. She had half a mind to complain to her father. But he would want to know why she was spending so much time with Hijino, and might forbid her to see him. She couldn't have that. Because Berto was right. She liked Hijino, liked him a lot, liked him more than she had ever liked any other man. So what if he said things he shouldn't? He was so handsome!

Trella remembered her dream. *What if it was an omen?* she asked herself. Was it possible he could grow to care for her as she cared for him? She wondered what it would be like to kiss him.

Trella was glad she had warned Hijino to be careful. She would do all in her power to see that he stayed on at the DP. The prospect made her tingle.

Chapter 5

Mort Decker was engaged in a battle of wits with a fly, and the ornery fly was winning. Five times Mort tried to swat it with his broom, and five times he missed. Now it was at the window, buzzing noisily as if to mock him.

"The same to you, you bug-eyed bastard," Mort growled, and advanced with the broom held high. He hated flies. He had always hated flies. Their fondness for everything from rancid food to manure disgusted him. Flies were foul creatures, as senseless in the scheme of things as mosquitos and ticks. Mort hated them, too.

"No one can convince me the Almighty wasn't drunk when he whipped up creation," Mort declared for the fly's benefit. He had given it a lot of thought over the years, and it was the only thing that explained all the pain and suffering in the world. Either that, or the Lord didn't give a tinker's damn.

Mort swung, and missed yet again. The fly taunted him by flying past his face and over to the bar. Mort wagged his broom. "You're dead! Do you hear me? Just you wait!"

The fly alighted on the glass of ale Mort had been sipping. Incensed, he was about to rush headlong into the fray when hooves clattered noisily in Wolf Pass. His first thought, as always, was of Indians. Rushing behind the bar, he grabbed his scattergun and hurried to the front door. He had propped the door open earlier, which was how the fly got in. About to step outside, he stopped cold as a line of riders swept out of the forest and crossed the clearing.

Mort almost slammed and bolted the door. But some of them had seen him. Quickly backpedaling, he replaced the shotgun. It would not do to have them think he did not want them there. His heart raced, and he broke out in a cold sweat. It took every iota of self-control he possessed to smile and say calmly, "Howdy, gents," as the first of the eight riders tramped inside.

Their leader did not return the greeting. He wore grimy clothes that matched his grimy looks. A perpetual grimace twisted his ferret face. From his right eyebrow to his chin zigzagged a bright scar. Rumor had it a settler took exception to the ferret-faced man raping the settler's wife, so the settler, who had served in the Union cavalry during the war, took a saber to him. That was the day Rufus Jenks acquired the nickname by which he was widely known throughout New Mexico Territory and several adjoining states: Saber.

Next to enter was a vicious killer called Creed. He wore a wide-brimmed black hat and a pair of pearl-handled Remingtons, the pale hue of the grips contrasting sharply with the dusky hue of his skin. He also wore a belt knife. Creed never smiled. His eyes were as flat and inhuman as a snake's.

After the black came Twitch, a sinewy back-shooter supposedly related somehow to Saber. He did not wear a gun belt, but had a pair of Colts tucked under a wide leather belt on the outside of a buckskin jacket. His handle stemmed from the constant nervous twitching of his mouth.

The rest were unfamiliar, but stamped in the same cruel mold. One look was enough to impress on Mort that they were not the kind any sane man trifled with. "What would you gentlemen like?"

Saber placed his hands on the counter, and snickered. "I don't see any gentlemen around here. Do you see any gentlemen, Creed?"

"Sure don't." Creed was not much of a talker. He stood with his hands loose at his sides, close to his Remingtons.

"If there was a gentleman here, I'd shoot him," Twitch said, his mouth doing its odd tic. "How about you, barkeep? Are you a gentleman?"

"Not me." Mort was dismayed at how his voice squeaked. Coughing, he steadied his nerves and smiled. "Same as the last time?"

"Last time?" Saber repeated.

"You and a couple of others stopped here about a year ago," Mort said. "It was late, pretty near midnight. You had a whiskey and asked if I could fix you somethin' to eat. I rustled up eggs and ham."

"By God, that's right," Saber said. "How is it you remember all that?"

Mort prided himself on his memory. He never forgot a face, or a drink that face ordered. "I have a knack."

"You don't say." Saber drummed his fingers on the counter, then glanced at Creed and nodded.

What was that about? Mort wondered. If only he had the gumption to announce he was closing for the day. He would take his rifle and go off into the mountains and not come back for a week or two. By then, they would be long gone.

"Set us up," Saber commanded. "Coffin varnish all around."

"Yes, sir." Mort had learned it was smart to be courteous to curly wolves. They were less apt to become riled over imagined slights. He set out glasses and filled each to the brim, making it a point to fill Saber's first. "Is that all?"

Saber asked a strange question. "I don't suppose you remember what I was wearin' that night, do you?"

Mort had to think about it. "The same hat as now, a flannel shirt, and brown pants. I didn't pay much attention to your boots."

"Amazin'."

"Thank you," Mort said, and did not understand why Creed and Twitch laughed. "Are you hungry? I shot a deer yesterday and have plenty of fresh meat. Potatoes, too, if you're partial."

"You're a regular marvel," Saber said. "Venison steak would please me considerable." He nodded at Creed and Twitch, and headed for a table. "Bring the bottle, boys. I'm fixin' to stay a while."

"Is that wise?" The question came from the oldest

of the eight outlaws, a grizzled slab of bone and gristle with a crooked nose and a cleft chin.

Everyone except Saber stood stock-still. He cocked his head and said, "What was that, Hank?"

"With what we're up to and all," Hank responded. "Is it wise for us to come out into the open like this?"

"Why, Hank," Saber said, as mildly as could be, "whatever do you mean?"

"The ranch business."

"I have no idea what you're talkin' about," Saber remarked, still as sugary as molasses. He grinned as he said it, and he was still grinning as he drew his Colt and shot Hank through the forehead. The slug blew out the back of Hank's skull, spraying hair, bone, and blood.

Mort nearly jumped out of his boots. He had witnessed shootings before, but never one so unexpected, so sudden. Usually it was between drunks who argued and shouted and worked themselves into a rage before resorting to their hardware. He held his breath, in the fear he would be next.

Saber holstered his Colt and continued to the table. "Some of you boys drag that jackass into the woods for the wild critters to feed on."

The bloodshed had no effect on the others. To them, the killing was a matter of course, as ordinary as swatting the fly that had eluded Mort.

"Barkeep, quit standin' there with your mouth hangin' open and rustle us up those steaks," Saber directed.

"Right away." Mort scampered to the kitchen. The back door beckoned, but if he ran they might burn his place to the ground to spite him. He kindled the embers in the stove, retrieved his butcher knife from a drawer, and went into the pantry to cut thick slabs from the haunch hanging in a corner. When he came out, he was startled to see Twitch over by the cupboard. "Somethin' I can do for you?"

Twitch chortled. "No. My cousin just wants me to keep you company. He figured you might get lonesome."

Mort did not like that, he did not like that at all, but he did not let on as he went about cooking their meal. He sliced potatoes, heaped them in a frying pan, and smothered them in butter. He put coffee on to brew. He also made toast.

"You do that real nice," Twitch said as Mort was spreading the jam. "If you were a woman, I'd marry you."

"Would you mind carryin' one of the trays?"

"Not so long as you go ahead of me."

A poker game was under way. At the other table, Saber and Creed were talking in hushed tones. They stopped when Mort set their tray down, and Saber sniffed several times.

"If it tastes as good as it smells, barkeep, you should be in Saint Louis runnin' a fancy restaurant."

"I don't like bein' around people that much," Mort admitted, and blanched, worried they would take it as some sort of insult.

"That makes two of us," Saber said. "I was knee-high to a yearlin' when I learned that most folks are as worthless as teats on a stallion."

With a loud crunch, Creed bit into a slice of toast. Whether he liked it or not was impossible to tell; the man never changed his expression.

"Why don't you join us?" Saber kicked out a chair. "You and me have some things to talk about."

"We do?" Mort noticed that Twitch had not sat down, but was a few yards away, his hands on his Colts. Icy fear stabbed through him.

Forking a piece of steak into his mouth, Saber chewed lustily, with his mouth open. "What do you want most in this world, barkeep?"

Bewilderment seized Mort. How did he answer something like that? What was Saber getting at? "The thing I want most is to go on breathin'."

Saber burst into hearty laughter. As if it were the most hilarious comment he'd ever heard, he smacked the table and howled. "Did you hear him, Creed? He's not as dumb as he looks."

Mort resented the insult, but sat awaiting developments. Twitch had come closer and now had only one hand on a Colt.

"Most people say that what they want most in this world is money," Saber said. His pale blue eyes bored into Mort. "How much do you have? Got it squirreled away, do you?"

The truth was, Mort had slightly over three hundred hidden in a jar under a floorboard behind the bar. But he answered, "I never make enough to set any aside. It's hand to mouth, day in, day out."

"I figured as much," Saber said. He speared a potato slice and popped it into his mouth. "How would you like to make a hundred dollars right here and now?"

"Who do I have to shoot?"

Again Saber cackled, and glanced at Creed. "I like this one. He tickles my funny bone." To Mort he

said, "Leave the shootin' to us, friend. The hundred
dollars is yours to forget we were ever here. Forget
you ever saw us, should anyone come askin'."

"That's all?" Mort speculated that maybe lawmen
were after them.

"To tell you the truth, I was considerin' whether to
buck you out in gore," Saber revealed while chomping.
"Your memory is too good for my comfort. But then I
got to thinkin' how it must be, tryin' to make ends
meet in this dump. You're miles from anywhere, and
customers must be few and far between."

"That they are," Mort conceded.

"A man like you could always use spendin'
money," Saber said. "Say, the hundred dollars now
and more later."

Mort's innards churned. "You plan to come back?"

"We're not leavin'. We'll make camp off a ways,
and from time to time we'll stop by. When that hap-
pens, it doesn't happen. Savvy?"

Apprehension coursed through Mort, and he asked
without thinking, "What could possibly interest you
down there?"

About to take another bite of steak, Saber's features
clouded. "I wouldn't be too nosy, were I you."

"It's just that there's nothin' down there but a couple of ranches—" Mort stopped. The hapless Hank
had said something about "ranch business" right before he was shot.

Saber sighed and lowered his fork to his plate.
"You see?" he said to Creed. "You try to do right
by some folks and they throw it in your face."

"What?" Mort said, aghast at the magnitude of his
blunder. "I never did any such thing."

"You certainly did. You've met them, haven't you? The Toveys and the Pierce clan?"

"I've seen them in San Pedro," Mort admitted. "Some of their punchers stop here every blue moon, usually when they're up in the mountains huntin', but that's about it." Mort was desperate to get back in Saber's good graces, so he added, "But I've never spoken to Kent Tovey or his missus, or the Pierces, neither."

"What about the cowboys and the vaqueros?"

"I've swapped pleasantries when they stop in for a drink, sure." Mort was so nervous, his knees began to tremble. He stilled them by sheer force of will. "Is it important? It's not like any of them are friends."

Saber drummed his fingers again, then looked at Creed. "What do you say? Should we be generous, or turn him into worm food?"

"Worm food," the black said.

"How about you?" Saber shifted toward Twtich.

"You're givin' us a say? Will wonders never cease. But since you asked," Twitch paused and smirked at Mort. "Look at this jasper. He's so scared, he's ready to wet himself. He wouldn't dare cross us."

"How about it, barkeep?" Saber asked. "Can I count on you to keep your mouth shut?"

"As God is my witness," Mort declared.

Saber grinned. His right hand came up from under the table holding his Colt. He fired once. Mort's body and the chair crashed to the floor, and Saber placed the revolver on the table and picked up his fork. "Never trust anyone with religion, boys. They're liable to turn on you no matter how much you pay them."

"What do we do with the body?" Twitch asked.

"The same thing you did with Hank's. The coyotes and buzzards hereabouts will be fat and sassy come tomorrow."

Twitch motioned. "And the saloon? Do we burn it to the ground when we're done eatin'?"

"You do not. I've always wanted to have me my own waterin' hole. We'll stick around until Dunn and Hijino have stirred up a hornet's nest. Then we'll crush the hornets just like this." Saber slammed his fist down on the fly that had landed next to his plate.

Chapter 6

It didn't happen often, but it did happen. The tracks were plain. A cow and her calf had strayed across the Rio Largo. In the summer the river was at its lowest and narrowest ebb, and there were spots where cattle could wade to the other side without getting their bellies wet.

Julio Pierce sat astride his grulla on the DP side of the river and stared across at the sprawling range of the Circle T.

"Why do you hesitate, *patrón*?" Hijino asked. "Are we not permitted to go on the gringos' side of the river?"

"Don't call them that," Julio said. It was only natural that he go after the errant cow and her offspring, but his father had certain rules, and one of them was that no one crossed onto the Circle T without first letting his father know. It had always seemed a silly rule to Julio. His father and Kent Tovey were good friends. The DP vaqueros got along well with the Circle T punchers. There was no reason not to go after the cow and her calf while their tracks were fresh and they could be quickly overtaken.

"I am sorry, *patrón*," Hijino said, the silver on his clothes and his saddle gleaming bright in the sun. "Old habits are hard to break. I am used to norte-americanos looking down their noses at our kind and calling us greasers."

"It is not like that here," Julio informed him, although there had been a few times when Julio thought the Circle T hands put on airs.

"Of course it isn't," Hijino said, and lifted the reins of his fine white horse. "Do we forget the cow and go?"

Something in his tone spawned resentment in Julio. He had grown to like the new vaquero. Unlike most of them, Hijino loved to talk, and Julio could listen for hours to his tales of life south of the border. Julio had always been partial to his mother's side of the Pierce family tree, but he was careful to keep it to himself in order not to hurt his father's feelings.

"*Patrón?*"

On an impulse, Julio spurred the grulla into the river. "They crossed only a few hours ago. We might as well go after them."

Halfway across, Hijino looked down at the sluggish current and commented, "Strange, is it not, how we let this river divide a valley that by rights should belong to one rancho?"

"We have been all through that," Julio said. Hijino had brought it up just the other day. "My father is content with the half he has."

"A good man, your *padre*," Hijino said. "A better man than me. Had I been the owner of the DP, I would not have let Kent Tovey or any gringo take what was rightfully mine."

Julio would put up with a lot, but not implied criticism of his father. "My *padre* always does what is best for everyone. You would do well to keep that in mind."

"I meant no disrespect," Hijino said mildly.

They rode in silence for a while. Julio was upset with himself for going against his father's wishes, but gradually the feeling faded. He had every right to reclaim DP stock.

The sea of rippling grass lent the illusion that they were alone in the world, just them and their horses and the sun and grass unending. Moments like these were special to Julio. They filled him with a feeling of closeness to the earth, and to life itself.

Presently, specks appeared to the northwest. Julio angled toward them. The cow was bound to join her kind, and where she went, the calf would go.

"May I ask a question, *patrón*?"

Absorbed in his musing, Julio said absently, "Of course. You may ask anything. You do not need to get my permission."

"I was just wondering," Hijino said, "whether you will let me work for you when the rancho is divided up."

"What are you talking about?"

"The DP, *patrón*. Your *hermano*, Steve, told me that when your *padre* dies and the rancho is divided between the brothers and sisters, he will still run things."

This was news to Julio. "Why is it Steve has never mentioned this to me? Do Armando and my sisters know?"

"Steve did not say if they do," Hijino said. "Perhaps it is an idea he came up with on his own."

"My brother would never do a thing like that without talking it over with the rest of us," Julio said. But in truth he was not so sure. Steve was the oldest, and at times seemed to think that gave him the right to tell the rest of them what to do.

The specks grew larger. Julio estimated fifty head, spread over five to ten acres, grazing contentedly. The cow should be easy to spot, since she would be one of the few with a calf.

"We are not alone," Hijino announced.

Four riders were approaching at a trot. Julio drew rein to await them, saying, "Let me do the talking."

"Sí, patrón."

Julio had met many of the Circle T hands at the annual rodeo and in San Pedro. He knew a dozen or so by name. But none of the four were familiar. As they came to a stop, he smiled and said, "Hola. I am Julio Pierce."

"I recognize you," said one who was bronzed from all his time outdoors. "I'm Jeb Wheeler. What can we do for you, Mr. Pierce?"

The name was not one Julio knew, but encouraged by the man's friendliness, he explained about the missing cow and her calf.

"I haven't seen any with the DP brand, but you're welcome to look for them," Wheeler offered. "We'll help."

"Muchas gracias, Señor Wheeler," Julio said. He swung the grulla toward the cattle, and Hijino made to follow.

"Land sakes!" a lanky cowboy exclaimed. "That there saddle is liable to blind me! Where did you find all that silver, bean-eater?"

"Do not call me that," Hijino said.

"What? A bean-eater? Why not? You sure as hell ain't no Chinaman." The cowboy chuckled. "I meant no insult."

"It is the way you say it," Hijino said. "You do not think highly of those of us with Mexican blood."

"Where in hell did you get a foolish notion like that?" the cowboy demanded. "I've been to Mexico and liked it there. The people were friendly as could be."

"My mistake, señor," Hijino responded, but he said it in such a way that he gave the impression it was not a mistake at all.

"You're an uppity cuss," the cowboy said.

Wheeler twisted in his saddle. "Let it drop, Demp. All of you spread out and look for the DP cow."

Julio held his tongue until the cowboys were out of earshot. Then he turned to Hijino. "Our rancho and the Circle T are on good terms and my father wants to keep it that way."

"As you wish, *patrón*."

"When you have been here longer, you will see that those who work for Señor Tovey are not like gringos elsewhere. They treat us with respect."

"Or do they only pretend to?" Hijino motioned at Demp. "But you are right. I will apologize if you want me to."

Julio thought it a great idea. "I want you to." It would please his father, should he learn of the incident. Julio concentrated on the cows and had examined six or seven when he heard a sharp oath, and then harsh words he could not quite catch.

Demp was glaring and gesturing angrily at Hijino. Hijino smiled that ever-present smile of his, which evidently made Demp angrier, for he grew red in the face and dropped his hand to his pistol.

Wheeler reached them a few seconds before Julio, and slapped the cowboy's arm from the revolver. "Leave that hogleg right where it is! What in hell do you think you're doin'?"

"It's him you should be hittin'!" Demp protested.

Julio was aware of the other punchers trotting up. "What happened?" he asked the vaquero. "What did you do?"

"Me, *patrón*?" Hijino rejoined. "All I did was ask him if other DP cows ever stray across the river."

Demp rose in his stirrups and pointed an accusing finger. "That's not all you said, you scalawag." He glanced at Wheeler. "The Mex claimed we help ourselves to DP stock!"

Wheeler's weather-seamed countenance became as hard as flint. He faced Hijino. "You accused us of bein' *rustlers*?"

Julio was appalled. There was no worse insult. In cow country, rustling was the worst thing a man could do, a crime considered more heinous than murder. "Is this true?"

Hijino spread his hands in innocence. "Before God and the Virgin, I swear to you it is not."

"Now you just called *me* a liar!" Demp was shaking with fury. "Name the time and place, and we'll settle this. Or better yet, let's settle it now." He poised his hand above his six-gun.

"I told you to leave it be!" Wheeler reined his mount between them. "There will be no gunplay, you hear me? Keep this up and I'll report you to Clayburn."

Demp deflated, but he was still mad. "No man can abide what this greaser did and still look himself in the mirror."

Wheeler glanced at Julio. "Maybe it's best if you go, Mr. Pierce. When we find your cow and calf, we'll return them."

Julio deemed it best, as well. The countenances of the other two cowboys left no doubt how they felt. It would not take much to provoke them. "Come along," he directed Hijino, and applied his spurs. He refused to look at the vaquero until they came to the Rio Largo. "When my father hears of this, you will be fired."

"Must you tell him? It was not me, *patrón*. The gringo bent my words."

Julio shook his head in disgust. Nothing like this had ever happened in the long history of the two ranches.

"You do not believe me?" Hijino sounded hurt.

"Whether he bent them or not, you should not have said whatever you did." Julio gigged the grulla into the water. "Now there will be hard feelings. We do not need that with the rodeo coming up."

"If the two ranchos are as friendly as everyone says, surely the gringos will not hold a grudge."

"I hope for your sake they do not." Julio debated whether to go to Berto. The DP foreman might be able to smooth things over without involving his father.

"Did you hear what that one called me?"

"*Sí,*" Julio said, the memory smarting like the sting of a bee. "But he did not mean anything by it."

"If you say so, *patrón.*"

Julio did not accept the explanation himself. It was obvious that some of the Circle T punchers regarded the DP vaqueros the same way many whites regarded all Mexicans. All these years, Julio had accepted his father's word that Kent Tovey would not hire such men, yet his own ears had heard the proof that it was otherwise.

"When we get back, I will pack my things and go, *patrón,*" Hijino said. "I do not want to cause trouble for the DP."

The offer took Julio by surprise. It might be for the best if Hijino left, but Julio found himself saying, "You are not going anywhere. Have we fired you? Until we do, you are still one of us. And we stand by our own."

"You are most kind, *patrón.*"

Julio shrugged the compliment away. He was not doing it so much for Hijino as for the DP. The more he thought about it, the more convinced he became that the Circle T cowboys were as much at fault, if not more so. Especially that hothead, Demp. *Why should Hijino be punished for Demp's fit of temper?*

As if Hijino were entertaining similar thoughts, he remarked, "Life is most unfair. I suppose now I will not be able to take part in the rodeo."

"Do you want to?" Julio came to the south bank and clucked to the grulla.

"*Sí.* Very much so."

"Which contest? The steer roping? The bronc riding? The calf throwing?" Julio always entered the latter. Last year he had claimed top honors.

"The pistol match."

Julio slowed so the white horse could come alongside. "Didn't you hear Paco the day we met? Jesco always wins the pistol match. Roman is always second. You would be lucky to finish third."

"I would still like to try to win for the DP," Hijino said. "To repay you for hiring me."

Nodding at the pearl-handled Colt, Julio asked, "Are you any good?"

Hijino's hand was a blur. The Colt leaped up and out and boomed, and twenty feet away a clod of dirt exploded. Almost in the same motion, Hijino twirled the Colt into his holster.

"*Madre de Dios!*" Julio breathed.

"Do you still think I do not have a chance?"

"You are better than most," Julio said in praise. "But Roman and Jesco are the best I have ever seen."

"Do all the vaqueros attend the rodeo?"

"We always leave a handful to watch over the house and the cattle," Julio disclosed. "The men draw straws to see who stays."

Hijino took out his Colt. For a few seconds, the barrel pointed at Julio. Then he tilted it and began replacing the spent cartridge. "Will you want me to draw a straw, too?"

Just once, Julio would love to win the pistol shoot. "No. I will inform Berto that you are to accompany us."

"The gringos might not be happy to see me."

"Who cares?" Julio said, and laughed.

Chapter 7

It was rare for John Jesco to have an hour to himself in the middle of the day. When he did, he always spent his spare time the same way. No sooner did Clayburn tell him that he was on his own than Jesco bent his boots toward the bunkhouse and took a box of ammunition from his war bag. His next stop was the corral. He was saddling a bay when hurried footsteps sounded behind him. Without turning, he asked, "A little bird tell you?"

"A big bird named Walt," Timmy Loring replied excitedly. "Please, can I? You know how much I like to watch you practice."

"Don't you have work to do?"

"Walt gave me a little time off," Timmy said. "Wasn't that nice of him?"

Jesco frowned. No, he did not think it particularly fine. Clayburn did not understand that he was dangling a dangerous carrot in front of someone who did not recognize the carrot for what it was. He gave the cinch a last tug and turned. "I'd rather be by myself."

"*Please*," Timmy Loring pleaded. The youngest hand

at the Circle T, he had turned seventeen a week ago. Curly blond hair poked from under the high-peaked hat that crowned his round, earnest face. He had blue eyes and big teeth. Peach fuzz dappled his chin. "I won't get on your nerves. I promise. All I want to do is watch."

Jesco sighed, and came close to saying no. But the kid was so sincere, so like a puppy in his anxiousness to please, that he reluctantly relented. "Saddle up, but be quick about it."

"Yippee!" Timmy dashed to the gate. "I'll have it done in three shakes of a calf's tail!"

Jesco happened to be next to the watering trough, and as he went to mount, he caught sight of his reflection on the still surface. It gave no indication of his height, but it showed nearly everything else: his Texas hat, his vest, the shirt Mary had made for him, his Levi's, his gun belt. His wolfish features, bare of mustache or beard, stared back at him, his dark eyes—smoldering pools, as Mary once described them. He imagined her bustling about the general store, and wished he was in San Pedro. It had been two weeks since he saw her last, and he missed her dearly. He had never felt for a woman the way he felt for Mary Turner. Maybe Walt was right. Maybe he had stepped into her loop, and now it was too late. If so, he didn't care. He wanted her, plain and simple. Wanted to spend the rest of his nights with her warm body at his side, and the rest of his days savoring her companionship as he used to savor the best whiskey in his wild and reckless days.

"I'm ready."

Jesco snapped out of his reverie. "Took you long

enough," he grumbled, and swung onto the bay's hurricane deck.

"Shucks, if there was a saddlin' contest at the rodeo, I'd win hands down," Timmy retorted.

Jesco rode northeast. The sun was high in a bright sky, and a vagrant breeze stirred his long hair.

"The arroyo again?" Timmy asked.

"Where else?" It was where Jesco usually went. Close to the ranch buildings, but not so close that Mrs. Tovey would hear. She was a good woman, but she had an unreasonable dislike for firearms. More than once she had commented on how if it were up to her, she would make the world a better place by causing all the guns to disappear. Which had to be the silliest notion Jesco ever heard. Nance liked to say that guns had no useful purpose, but tell that to a man cornered by Apaches, or to the poor soul a grizzly wanted to dine on.

"The rest will be jealous," Timmy said. "Only Walt has ever seen you do it. Everyone else would love to watch you practice."

"Would they, now?" Jesco said sourly.

It was lost on the stripling. "You can't blame them for bein' curious. Folks are still talkin' about that no-account you bucked out in gore a couple of years ago. Demp says he saw it, and he says you pulled your hogleg so fast, he never saw you draw."

"If the truth was coal, Demp would never need to wash his hands," Jesco remarked. "He wasn't in the saloon that night." Nor any other puncher that Jesco could recollect. It was just as well. They would only talk about it more, otherwise.

"Dunn was askin' about it the other night in the bunkhouse," Timmy offhandedly mentioned.

"Oh?"

"That, and your other shootin' affrays. He's naturally curious, as most any gent would be."

Jesco did not respond. But Lafe Dunn was part of the reason he was practicing today. He had seen the look in Dunn's eyes, that look that always warned him. Dunn tried to hide it, but it was plain to Jesco.

"I like him," Timmy chattered on. "He never pokes fun at me like some of the others. And he sure can work cows. Clayburn says Dunn is one of the best cutters he's ever seen."

"That's nice," Jesco said.

"He won't talk about his past much, though. He's like you, I reckon, in that regard," Timmy complained. "I swear that pryin' details out of you is like pryin' out a tooth."

"The words you don't say can't come back to haunt you."

"What in tarnation does that mean? I say a lot of words, and they never do me any harm. How can it hurt to talk about the lead-chuckin' you've done?"

Jesco sought to enlighten him. "Brags always lead to more bullets, and I've no hankerin' after an early grave."

"Don't even pretend you're scared of dyin'," Timmy said. "You've got more sand than everyone in the outfit put together."

"You're layin' it on a mite thick," Jesco scolded. "Every puncher at the Circle T would do to ride the river with."

"Maybe so. But you're the only one who's put windows in the skulls of half a dozen hombres." Timmy sighed wistfully. "That sure would be somethin' to see."

Jesco did not mince his reaction. "You're a damned fool, boy. Killin' is no cause for crowin'. It leaves a bitter taste deep down. You can't shake it, and you can't ever forget."

"Do you think Dunn has ever made wolf meat of anyone?"

"Why do you ask?" Jesco was willing to bet a year's wages that Dunn had killed. He had run into Dunn's type before.

Timmy shrugged. "Just a feelin' I have. Ever notice his Colt has black pearl grips? They're expensive, aren't they?"

"Very."

"How come you never fancy yours up like that? Pearl or ivory grips, maybe some etching on the barrel or the cylinder?"

Jesco tried yet again. "A pretty pistol doesn't make takin' a life any prettier." He had to get through to the boy, had to make him see that throwing lead was an invitation to Boot Hill. But the boy had the trigger itch, and had it bad.

"You say the strangest things," Timmy said. "I only hope to God I'm there to see it the next time you slap leather on someone."

Jesco came close to cuffing him. "I hope to God you're not. No more talk about killin' now, or back you go."

"No need to get mad."

Yes, there was. Jesco would not stand for having his past glorified. He took no delight in what he had done. On the contrary. "We chop our own wood, Tim. Just you remember that."

"There you go again. I swear, half the time you talk in riddles."

They rode the rest of the way in silence.

The valley floor was so flat, the grass so high, that unless someone knew exactly where the arroyo was, they could pass within fifty feet of it and not realize it was there. As was his custom, Jesco reined up on the south rim. He dismounted, rummaged in his saddlebags for a picket pin, and picketed the bay. "You would do well to do the same."

"I don't have a pin." Timmy let the sorrel's reins dangle. "Never much saw the need."

"You will the first time a horse runs off on you," Jesco predicted. Again he rummaged in his saddlebags until he found the box of ammunition. Then he ambled into the arroyo and hiked east several hundred feet to where it widened. Bits and shards of broken glass and a dozen or so rusted cans pockmarked with bullet holes littered the north bank. In a burlap bag lying at the bottom of the south slope were bottles and cans he brought out last time but had not used.

"Want me to set them up for you?" Timmy offered.

Jesco bent and gripped the bag. As he started to lift it, an ominous rattling turned him to stone. From under the bag slid a blunt, triangular head. A forked tongue darted out.

"A rattler!" Timmy cried.

Brownish splotches rippling, the rattlesnake slowly slithered from underneath. It was a large one, big and thick around as Jesco's forearm.

"Shoot it!"

Jesco admired the play of light on the scales. The snake moved with a sinuous grace that was marvelous to behold.

"Didn't you hear me? Shoot it before it bites you!" Timmy clawed for his revolver, and in his excitement nearly dropped it. His forearm shaking, he pointed the six-shooter at the serpent. "Hold still."

"No," Jesco said.

"What?"

"Let it be. It hasn't hurt us, and we won't hurt it unless it coils." Jesco firmed his hold on the burlap bag in order not to drop it. Two feet of rattler was visible, with more unwinding.

"It's just a snake!" Timmy squawked in disbelief. "I can make a necklace of the rattles, like I saw an Indian wear once."

"No. The snake has as much right to live as you or me."

Severely disappointed, Timmy jerked his arm down, and shoved his Colt into his holster. "If this don't beat all. Do you spare scorpions and wasps, too? I hope I'm not as squeamish when I'm your age."

"Nine years can make a lot of difference in a person's outlook," Jesco said. They had made a huge difference in his.

"I could live to be fifty, and I'd still shoot every damn rattler I came across," Timmy declared. "What if that one bites a cow or a horse? It will be on your shoulders."

"When was the last time we had a snakebit cow?" Timmy pondered a bit before he irritably responded. "Never, that I can recollect, but that doesn't mean it can't happen. Rattlers bite animals and people all the time."

Jesco could only think of two instances his whole life. The first had been a childhood friend who poked a stick into a snake den. The second had been a horse that stepped on a diamondback sunning itself. "Careless people and critters, mostly," he observed.

The snake had stopped rattling, and was crawling off into the grass.

Timmy pushed his hat back. "For your sake, I won't tell anyone about this. It's downright embarrassin'."

Jesco opened the burlap bag and carefully upended it. Bottles and cans tumbled and tinkled at his feet. He shook the bag to verify it was empty, then tossed it aside and began setting up targets. Timmy helped.

"How old were you when you shot your first man?"

"You know better," Jesco said. He had been the same age as Timmy. If he had that day to live over again, he would light a shuck for parts unknown rather than take that drunk's life.

"I can't help bein' curious. But if you still don't want to tell me, fine. It's not as if I plan to go to San Pedro and gun down the citizenry."

"That's nice to hear." Jesco stepped back and willed his body to relax. Tension slowed the reflexes and spoiled a man's aim.

Timmy had moved to one side, and was waiting in rigid expectancy.

Jesco focused on a tin can. He did not think about what he was going to do, he just did it. He drew and fired from the hip, and the can catapulted skyward. At the apex of its arc he fired again, and the can clattered down the slope and rolled to a stop.

"Woo-eee!," Timmy whooped. "That was some shootin'!" He scooted to the can and held it up. "Dead center, both shots! How do you do it?"

"Practice." Jesco commenced replacing the cartridges.

Timmy stuck the tip of a finger into one of the holes. "I could practice from now until forever and still not be as good as you."

"Why would you want to be? There are more important things to be good at. Look at the big sugar. His own ranch. A fine herd. A fine woman. Do somethin' worthwhile with your life. Be a rancher or a doctor or own a business. Don't live by the gun."

"You must rate me stupid," Timmy said. "I'm not Billy the Kid. I like bein' a cowboy. Sure, I wouldn't mind bein' slick with a hogleg, but not to kill folks. It'd just be so I could do as you're doin' now."

"Don't ever change," Jesco said. To some, the lure of the gun was irresistible. He had been fortunate in that his ma raised him to do to others as he would have them do to him. As a result, his conscience had plagued him terribly after that first shooting, and every shooting since.

"I'd be obliged for another lesson," Timmy said.

"You've had enough."

"Not when I miss more than I hit what I'm aiming at," Timmy protested. "Not when molasses moves faster."

Jesco had him stand facing a bottle with his arms limp at his sides. "Thumb back the hammer as you draw, so when you clear leather all you have to do is squeeze the trigger."

"You make it sound so simple," Timmy said. His gaze roved to where they had left their horses. "Say, looks like we've got company. Where did he come from?"

Jesco turned.

Strolling toward them was Lafe Dunn.

Chapter 8

John Jesco trusted his instincts. Bitter experience had taught him that to deny them was a surefire invitation to trouble. Now, as Lafe Dunn came strolling down the arroyo, his instincts flared, warning him as the day he first met Dunn that here was an extremely dangerous individual. A natural-born killer.

Timmy Loring did not have Jesco's experience. He did not have Jesco's instincts. Smiling warmly, he greeted the new puncher with, "Dunn! Come join us. You'll get to see Jesco shoot."

"Is that worth seein'?" was Dunn's dry reply.

"Haven't you heard?" Timmy indulged in the hero worship Jesco found so disquieting. "Jesco is the best gun hand on the spread. It's a treat to watch him practice."

"You don't say." Dunn stopped and regarded Jesco with what Jesco swore was a degree of disdain, then Dunn bestowed his attention on the slope littered with bits and pieces. "I was passin' by and heard shootin'."

Jesco's instincts flared again. The man was lying. He had followed them from the ranch.

"How are you with that hogleg of yours?" Timmy jerked a thumb at the black-handled Colt on Dunn's right hip.

"I've shot a few coyotes and such." Dunn's big hands were easy at his side. Suddenly he erupted into motion, and the black-handled Colt was out and level. A single crash, and a bottle dissolved into shards. He shoved the Colt into the holster and patted both. "That's about the best I can do."

It was better than most, Jesco noted. That in itself was revealing. The plain truth was that most men were no shakes at all with a six-gun. Back east many went their whole lives without touching one. West of the Mississippi was another story. Guns were essential, another tool in the taming of the land. But few practiced with any regularity. The punchers at the Circle T were typical; they all owned six-shooters, but hardly any could consistently hit a can at ten paces.

Like everything else in life, to be a skilled shootist took talent. Hours and hours of practice helped, but without talent, the best a man could rise to was average. Jesco's razor reflexes were a gift of birth. He was quick on the shoot, but he never bragged about it or gloried in it, as some were wont to do.

"Your turn," Dunn said to him.

Anger rippled through Jesco. He never liked being played for a fool. Ordinarily, he would not let himself be goaded, but now an urge came over him to show the new hand exactly what he was dealing with. His hand was lightning, the blast instantaneous, the Colt back in the holster in less than the blink of an eye.

"That was damn fine," Dunn said with genuine admiration. "So the stories they tell are true."

"I told you!" Timmy glowed.

"Well, I have work to do." Dunn looked at Jesco. "Thanks for showin' your fangs. I'll be sure not to get bit." Pivoting on his boot heels, he strode off.

Timmy scratched his head. "Strange, him mentionin' fangs after we just saw that rattler. What did he mean by that?"

"You'll have to ask him." Jesco was annoyed. Not with the boy or with Lafe Dunn, but with himself. He had shown a man he did not trust exactly what that man was up against. No wonder Dunn had thanked him.

"You're fixin' to practice some more, aren't you?" Timmy eagerly asked.

"I might as well."

"What's the matter? Why are you so down at the mouth?"

Jesco had to remember the boy was sensitive to his moods. Brightening, he fibbed, "I'm fine, mother hen."

Timmy laughed. "Quit teasin'. We're pards, aren't we?" He gazed along the arroyo. "There goes Dunn. Looks like he's headin' back. I like him. He doesn't say a lot, but he's nice enough."

"So was that rattlesnake until it coils," Jesco observed.

"Dunn is no snake. Your trouble is that you're too suspicious. You think everyone is out to shoot you in the back."

"It only takes one." Yet another reason Jesco hated the tales spread about his prowess. A reputation was a beacon. It drew every sidewinder hankering after fame from near and far.

The boy pulled his hat brim low to shield his eyes from the glare of the sun. "You don't need to worry about Dunn. I'd bet my bottom dollar on it."

Unknown to Timmy Loring, at that exact moment Lafe Dunn was thinking that when it came time to kill John Jesco, it would best be done by shooting Jesco in the back. From the front was certain suicide.

When Dunn had spied Jesco and the kid preparing to leave the ranch, he had guessed their purpose. Clayburn had mentioned that Jesco went off to practice now and then.

Thinking of the foreman reminded Dunn of *his* purpose for coming to the Circle T. So far all he had done was take stock of the opposition. Now it was time to start stirring the stew.

Dunn held to a canter. He was counting on most of the punchers being gone, and he was not disappointed. The buildings stood quiet under the hot sun. He rode straight to the bunkhouse and dismounted. Familiar odors assailed him as he entered, a mix of tobacco, sweat, rawhide, and smoke.

Most bunkhouses were a study in shambles, but not the bunkhouse at the Circle T. Kent Tovey insisted it be neat and tidy. The hands were required to make up their beds each morning, and must not leave clothes lying around.

Dunn stood just inside, letting his eyes adjust. No one was there. He shut the door and quickly moved down the aisle to the third from the last bunk on the right. It was Jack Demp's. Squatting, he groped about underneath the bed. He had watched the young cow-hand closely, and hoped the particular item he was after was still stashed in Demp's war bag.

Dunn's mouth curled in a rare smile. The folding knife lay amid an assortment of personal effects: a mirror, a tin cup, a plug of tobacco, a harmonica, a tin of boot wax, and more. He palmed the knife, slid it into his pocket, and replaced the war bag exactly where it had been. As he straightened, the door opened, spilling a rectangle of light along the floor.

"I thought I saw you come in here," Walt Clay-burn said. "When I give a man a job, I expect him to do it."

Dunn indulged in another smile. "I was just on my way to check for strays along the river, like you wanted."

The foreman scanned the bunks. "Some hands like to sneak naps when they can. Lazy is as lazy does."

"I'm not an infant." Dunn patted the pocket into which he had slid the folding knife. "I wanted a chaw and came back for a plug."

"Next time, go without. You've wasted an hour. At the Circle T we take our work seriously."

"Yes, sir." It grated on Dunn to be so civil when what he really wanted was to whip out his pistol and crack Clayburn over the skull. The foreman stepped aside, and Dunn went out and climbed on his buttermilk.

"Keep an eye peeled for DP stock. We don't want a repeat of what happened with Julio Pierce."

"I will." Dunn rode south. He was confident Clayburn had bought his lie, but to be safe, when he reached the Rio Largo, he pretended to search for cattle for a while, until he was confident no one had followed him. Then he set about his real business.

On a spur of land that jutted into the Rio Largo like an accusing finger, on the south side of the river, grew a stand of cottonwoods. Riders were in view of the trees from a long way off, and anyone hidden in the trees could spot them, which made it ideal. Dunn crossed from the north, and no sooner had the vegetation closed around him than the acrid odor of cigarette smoke tingled his nose. "Those Mex quirlies of yours stink to high heaven."

"To each his own, eh, amigo?" Marcario Hijino had one leg looped over his silver saddle horn and the other dangling down Blanco. "You are late, and I do not like to be kept waiting."

"It couldn't be helped." Dunn mentioned his chance brush with the Circle T foreman.

"But he does not suspect you, this Clayburn?"

"No. They're sheep, the whole passel." Dunn paused. "I take that back. There's one curly wolf. His name is Jesco."

Hijino sat straighter. "I have heard of him, usually in tones of awe. Is he really the *pistolero* they say he is?"

"I wouldn't try him except in the back," Dunn admitted.

"Really? You have seen him shoot with your own eyes?"

"Just today," Dunn said. "I wanted to see for myself. Glad I did. If anyone can give us trouble, it's him."

"I will get word to Saber. He should know." Hijino dragged on his cigarette and exhaled smoke out his nostrils. "Did you bring it?"

Dunn produced the folding knife. "It's not much. The blade is only about four inches long."

"So long as it is sharp." Hijino took the knife and opened it. He tested the blade by lightly running his thumb along the edge. A thin line of blood appeared. "*Sí*. It will do nicely."

"When?" Dunn asked.

"Tonight, I think," Hijino said. "It will stir them up. I will help without being obvious. As you say, they are witless sheep." He chortled merrily. "This is fun, is it not?"

"Any special problems that need to be dealt with on your end?"

"There is Berto. He trusts no one, and is fiercely loyal to the Pierces. But we expected that of him." Hijino dragged on his cigarette again. "The Pierces themselves are of no consequence. They handle ropes better than they do *pistolas*."

"Not one gun-shark in the whole outfit?"

"There is one. A small shark called Roman. I will deal with him when the time comes."

"Go easy," Dunn said, and lifted his reins to depart. He would continue his search for strays, and return to the Circle T by sunset. But Hijino's next comment stopped him.

"I talked with Twitch last night."

"You did? Why didn't you say so sooner? What did he have to say?"

"Only that Saber is pleased at how well you and I have done. Oh. And that if we need to get word to them, we must go to the Wolf Pass Saloon."

"What in hell are they doin' there?"

Hijino shook with silent mirth. "You will not believe it. But it seems Saber is the new owner."

Dunn was flabbergasted. The last thing they needed was to draw attention to themselves. Finding his voice, he growled, "Has he gone loco?"

"According to Twitch, Saber shot the hombre who was running it. Now he is telling everyone who stops that he bought the place. Serves them drinks and everything. Is that not just like him?"

"Damned idiot," Dunn fumed. "After all the trouble we've gone to, he pulls a stunt like this."

"It is a good thing he is not here to hear you say that," Hijino cautioned. "Or do you think you can fill his boots?"

"No one bucks Saber and lives," Dunn said, and was struck by a notion. "But you could take him, though. You're ten times quicker on the draw."

Hijino puffed a few times, then responded. "There is more to killing than being quick, amigo. A person must have other qualities. They must be willing. They must be tough. They must be like steel inside. No mercy, no feelings for others, ever. And that is why I am content to follow Saber's lead."

"You've lost me," Dunn confessed.

"I am faster than him, *sí*. But I am not as empty inside. Saber is more vicious than any of us, except maybe Creed, and we each know, deep inside, that if we go against him, we are done for. Even if we are faster, he will kill us. Even though we might be stronger, he will spit on our graves. Do you agree?"

Dunn had never heard it expressed quite so eloquently, but he felt exactly the same way. There was something about Saber, a deadliness that went beyond rhyme or reason. "I reckon so. But it's still damned stupid of him to take over that saloon. What if someone recognizes him?"

"He will kill them," Hijino predicted. "In the meantime, he acts the part of a respectable citizen. He is right under their noses, and they do not see it. You must admit he is clever."

"Too clever by half." Dunn did not care to talk about it anymore. He rode from the stand and crossed to the north side. Paralleling the river, he poked among the thickets and breaks, and flushed a few cows with the Circle T brand.

Dunn timed it so that he arrived at the cookhouse just as the hands were sitting down to supper.

Shonsey was in his usual irascible mood. "You're the new one, aren't you?" he said when it came Dunn's turn to be served.

The cook had asked the same question every day since Dunn was hired, and Dunn was tempted to tell the old fool that his mind was going, and he should be put out to pasture. But all Dunn did was nod.

A sly grin lit Shonsey's wrinkled features. "You're smart. You know when to keep your mouth shut."

"I like to eat."

Tittering, Shonsey added an extra slice of corn pone to Dunn's plate. "That's why I like bein' a cook. It's the next best thing to bein' God Almighty."

Dunn took a seat and gazed down the long table. Clayburn was there, and Jesco and his shadow, young Timmy Loring. So were Demp and Wheeler and Metz and many others, smiling and joking and laughing, enjoying what was the highlight of their day.

It amused Dunn to think that before another month was out, they would all be dead.

Chapter 9

Trella Pierce was excited. So excited, she tingled from head to toe as she examined herself in her mirror. She had chosen the dress with care. It was the best she owned. Best in that sense that it clung to her so snugly, it accented the slight swell of her hips and her small bosom. She thought she looked five years older.

Nervous, Trella fussed with her hair. It was almost time. She checked the clock on the wall. She had agreed to meet him at ten, and it was five minutes till. She went to the window. It creaked as she opened it. She froze in terror, fearing someone might pass by out in the hall and hear. But of course no one did. The sound had not been loud enough.

Trella chided herself for being childish. She was about to slide a leg over the sill when she remembered she must blow out the lamp. Sometimes her father and brothers were out and about late, and if they saw her window lit, they might wonder why she was staying up past her usual bedtime. The room plunged into darkness.

Trella moved confidently back to the window. She

knew her bedroom so well that she could navigate in total darkness if she had to, but she did not have to. Pale moon glow gave her more than enough light to see by. She slid over and out.

The cool night air caressed her. Trella paused to steady her breathing and smooth her dress. She was a bit in awe of her own audacity. Never, ever, had she done anything like this. It was bold, daring, reckless, with dire consequences if she was caught. But she could no more deny the feelings that compelled her than she could deny hunger or thirst. Feelings new and alien, yet at the same time, feelings women had been having since the dawn of time. They proved she truly *was* a woman, no matter what anyone else might think.

Her mother persisted in regarding Trella as her "sweet *niña*." Every time her mother called her that, Trella could just scream.

Her sister, Dolores, treated her as if she were ten years old. Once, when Trella mentioned that she was beginning to think of men in a different way, her sister laughed and remarked that Trella was much too young yet, and suggested that Trella should stick to playing with dolls and leave the men to Dolores.

Trella's brothers did not count. They treated her as special. To them, her age had never mattered. She was their *hermana*, their sister, and they saw it as their duty to protect her from the evils of the world. That included other men.

Trella thought of her father, and smiled. Of all of them, he treated her the best. She was his *princesa*. He adored her. He loved her with the depth and breadth of his being, and it showed. Her smile died as she realized how crushed he would be if she was caught. Unbidden, a talk they once had came to mind. She recalled every word as if it were but minutes ago.

The subject was a girl from San Pedro who had taken up with a drummer. Trella overheard two shocked women talking about it, and she had asked her father why the women spoke of the girl as if she were the vilest creature on the face of the earth when Trella well knew the girl was kind and pretty.

Her father had gotten a strange look, and drawn her to his knee. "You should ask your mother things like that, little one. But I reckon you're at that age where you're naturally curious." He had paused, apparently searching for the right thing to say. "Out here, a person's reputation is everything. How people think of you is how they treat you. If they think of you as good, they treat you with respect. If they think of you as bad, they don't."

His explanation satisfied him, but it had not satisfied Trella. "But what did Susan do that was so awful? She is eighteen. She is old enough to marry if she wants."

"That's just it," her father had replied. "She didn't marry the drummer. She let him trifle with her and go his merry way. Now her reputation has been tarnished. Everyone will think of her as a loose woman and treat her accordingly."

"That's terrible," Trella had said.

Her father had patted her head. "At your age, I'd have thought so, too. When you're twelve, the world is a simple place."

Trella had not quite understood. "Will you treat Susan like those ladies were doing?"

"Not if you don't want me to, no. I will treat her no differently than before. But she will find that churchgoing ladies won't want anything to do with her, and when she walks down the street, men will look at her differently." Her father had leaned down and said earnestly, "The important thing is that you never tarnish *your* reputation. Never do as Susan did, or you will live to regret it."

Trella's mouth went dry at the memory. Here she was, doing the exact thing her father warned against. She imagined the hurt he would feel if someone spotted her and reported it, and she almost climbed back in the window. Almost.

The path through the garden was a dim ribbon. Trella moved silently along it except for the rustle of her dress. Soon she came to the willow. Her father had planted it years ago, when the house was built, and the willow had grown to become the grandest tree on the rancho. Its overspreading boughs had shielded her from the hot sun on many a summer's day when she had played under it as a child.

Trella's heart was beating so hard, she thought it would burst. A thin line of sweat formed on her brow. It annoyed her. *Ladies should not sweat*, she told herself. *Especially at times like this*.

Something moved in the darkness, and Trella's breath caught in her throat. A figure materialized and came toward her, spurs jingling.

"You are exquisite in the moonlight, *señorita*," Hijino said.

Trella tried to think of something clever and bright to say, but all she could come up with was, "I came, as I promised I would."

"You honor me with your presence." Hijino took her hands in one of his and raised them to his lips.

Trella shivered at the kiss. He was so handsome, so dashing. She yearned to have his lips on hers, and flushed at the brazen thought. Clearing her throat, she whispered, "We must be careful. I do not want to get you into trouble."

"How sweet. You are more worried about me than about yourself." Hijino's other hand drifted close to a pants pocket.

"I do not extend my affections lightly, *señor*," Trella said.

"I am sure you do not." Hijino kissed her wrist, not once, but several times. "You are exquisite in every respect."

"Do you mean that?"

"Of course."

"Or do you say it merely to win my affection?" Trella had to ask. It was her secret fear.

"You doubt me? After I professed my love at the stable? After I brought you those flowers I picked?"

The flowers were in a vase in Trella's room, and if she had sniffed them once she had sniffed them a hundred times. "You must forgive me. This is all so new."

Hijino smiled, and slid his fingers into his pocket. "It is normal to be confused. Strong emotions do that, and love is the strongest emotion of all."

Some of Trella's fear evaporated. He said such fine things. He was wise and worldly, and that smile of his!

"Do you want to go for a stroll under the stars? I know a spot where we can be alone. It is not far."

"We are alone here," Trella said. She had agreed to meet him under the willow in part because it was close to the house and gave her a sense of security. She could always run inside if she had to, or cry out if he became more forward than she was willing to allow.

"Here it is, then, lovely one." Hijino gently cupped her chin and kissed her lightly on the mouth.

Trella's breath fluttered in her throat. *My first kiss! My first real kiss!* She bent her head to encourage him to do it again, and he did, several times, and would have kissed her more had she not pressed a hand to his chest and stepped back. Her head was swimming. "Wait," she said huskily.

"You are too beautiful to resist." Hijino kissed her neck, her ear.

"I said wait." Trella took another step back. Strange stirrings in her body filled her with turmoil. She craved him as she had never craved anyone, and that scared her more than anything. To give those cravings free rein invited consequences that would change her life forever, and she was not sure she wanted that to happen.

"What is it, little one? Tell me what troubles you, and I will make your troubles go away."

Trella simmered with resentment. He should not have called her "little one." It was what her father always called her. She almost changed her mind, almost went back inside. Then she saw his hand rise out of his pocket. He was holding something. A gift, she imagined, and stayed where she was.

"Is it me?" Hijino asked. "Do I go too fast for

you?'' He seemed about to say more, then suddenly grew rigid. "That is it, isn't it? I apologize."

"There is no need," Trella said.

"Would that were so. Go back inside, *señorita*. We can meet again if you want, when you are sure."

Trella did not know what to say. This was not how she expected their tryst to be.

"Please," Hijino said, touching her cheek. "I would never dishonor you. Think on us. Think on my love, and we will talk tomorrow."

"But—"

Hijino put a finger to her lips. "It is for the best. *Por favor*. Before I weaken. For both our sakes."

In a bewildered daze, Trella turned and walked woodenly along the path. She glanced back, and he raised a hand and motioned for her to keep going. Another step, and the rose bushes hid him. Confusion lent wings to her feet, and as she ran, she felt her eyes moisten.

For half a minute Hijino was motionless. Then he shifted and said quietly, "How long have you been listening?"

Out of the shadows came Berto, his hand on his revolver. "A while. I saw you leave the bunkhouse."

"Ah," Hijino said.

"How did you know I was there? I made no noise."

"Those cigars you smoke. Their smell clings to your clothes." Hijino turned the rest of the way, careful to hold his hands out from his sides. "What now?"

"Do you need to ask?" Berto gestured. "You are leaving the DP. Now, this moment. If you ever set foot on the Pierce rancho again, I will have you tied to a post and whipped."

"Be reasonable. Can't we talk about this?"

"You miserable bastard," Berto spat. "You deceive that poor girl. You betray our *patrón*'s trust. And you want me to be reasonable?" Berto started to pull his pistola. "I should shoot you where you stand."

"I have been sincere with her," Hijino said.

"I don't know which is worse. Your insult to her, your insult to Señor Pierce, or your insult to me."

"Will you permit me to collect my things?"

"I should take you to the *patrón*. But it would hurt him, his daughter behaving so badly." Berto gestured. "Head for the bunkhouse. I will be right behind you."

Hijino walked as one dejected by the developments, his shoulders slumped. "You misjudge me."

"Shut your mouth. I do not want to hear any more of your lies." Berto quietly swore. "I have myself to blame. From the beginning, there was something about you I did not like, something that warned me you bore watching. It was your eyes, I think. They hide the real you from the rest of the world."

"You make too much of this. All I did was kiss the *señorita* a few times. Is that truly so horrible?"

"I told you to be quiet," Berto growled. "I have not served this family for over twenty years to stand idly by while a snake insinuates itself among them."

"Now who is doing the insulting?"

"You deserve it. You have been up to no good the whole time you have been with us. I have heard about your talks with the vaqueros, and with Julio. Heard how you belittle gringos. Heard how you seek to have our vaqueros think badly of the Circle T." Berto paused. "Yes, a snake is what you are, and we will be well rid of you."

They were coming to a shed. The shortest route to the bunkhouse was to the right, but Hijino tucked his chin to his chest so it would appear he was not watching where he was going and bore to the left where the shadows were darker. He held his right hand close to his leg so Berto could not see what he held.

"I will have you escorted off the DP to be sure you leave. Paco and Roman can do it. I will tell Roman that if you turn back, he has my permission to shoot you."

"He is welcome to try," Hijino said. He was ready, but he took a couple more steps, then pretended to stumble. To catch himself, he braced his arm against the shed. Barely three seconds of delay, but it was enough. From under his hat brim, he saw that the caporal was within easy reach.

"What did you trip over? Your own feet?"

"Your grave," Hijino said, and exploded into motion. The folding knife's blade was only four inches long, but it was enough. He sliced all the way into Berto's belly, and ripped upward.

Berto tried to draw, but Hijino seized his wrist. In desperation, Berto sought to break free. He opened his mouth to shout. All that came out was a strangled gurgle, and blood. Then it was over.

Hijino eased the body to the ground and glanced about. The deed had gone unnoticed. He checked his clothes but found no stains. Dropping the knife, he circled wide to the stable, and from there casually strolled to the bunkhouse. A few vaqueros were up, talking. The rest were asleep. No one showed any undue interest as he walked to his bunk and stretched out on his back.

The vaqueros did not realize it yet, but the hounds of hell had just been unleashed in the Sweet Grass Valley.

Chapter 10

The ten riders came to the Rio Largo, and splashed across at a gallop. They did not slow when they came to a herd of Circle T cattle, but rode on through, scattering cows before them. Nor did they slow when Circle T punchers hailed them. The cowboys angled to intercept the ten, recognized the lead rider, and, bewildered by his cold, stern visage, fell in behind in puzzlement.

Walt Clayburn, John Jesco, and Timmy Loring were at the stable when the visitors appeared in the distance with their cowboy escort. Clayburn squinted into the sun and said, "What have we here? I do believe that's Dar Pierce headin' this way like his britches are on fire."

"What do you reckon he wants?" Timmy wondered.

"We'll find out soon enough," Jesco said.

"I'd best let the big sugar know." Clayburn hurried toward the house, and the other two tagged along.

Kent Tovey was in the parlor, listening to Nance discourse on the need to erect a pavilion to shade the women from the merciless sun when the rodeo was held.

A loud knock sounded on their front door. Kent excused himself and went to answer it. "Yes?" he said on beholding his foreman.

Clayburn pointed. "We've got visitors, Mr. Tovey. Unless my peepers are playin' tricks, it's Mr. Pierce."

Kent stepped to the edge of the porch and strained his eyes until they ached, but he still could not distinguish one rider from another. "I swear you have the eyes of a hawk."

"His sons are with him," John Jesco said. "All of them."

"I'll have my wife prepare refreshments." Kent went back in. He deemed it strange that Dar and all three boys were paying a visit. Normally, Dar left at least one son at the DP to oversee its operation when he was away, no matter how short the duration.

Nance beamed on hearing the news. "I'll have the cook put coffee on. I do so love it when Dar visits. He is always the perfect gentleman."

Kent went back out. The riders were near enough now that even he could see the sombreros most wore. The lone exception was Steve Pierce, who did not share his father's passion for everything Mexican.

"Want us to stay?" Clayburn inquired.

Kent was about to say they should go on about their work, but instead he said, "It might be best." Maybe it was the speed at which the DP bunch were approaching. He could not recall ever seeing Dar ride so fast. And, too, as a courtesy, Dar usually sent a rider on ahead to let them know he was coming. This time he hadn't.

"I'll round up some of the other hands if you want, Mr. Tovey," Jesco offered.

"What for?" Kent said. "Dar Pierce is one of my best friends."

At that moment, Nance joined them. She clasped her hands to her bosom in delight. "How wonderful! I only wish Juanita was with him."

The ten made a beeline for the house, sweeping past the outbuildings and the stable and surprised cowhands, without so much as a word or gesture of greeting.

Kent came down the steps. Raising a hand, he smiled warmly. Out of the corner of his eye, he observed Jesco take quick strides to one side, and stand with his right hand hooked in his gun belt inches from his Colt.

Amid the pounding of hooves and wisps of dust, the riders reined to a stop. Dar Pierce was foremost, flanked by Steve, Armando, and Julio. The rest were vaqueros.

Kent recognized Roman and Paco. They always took part in the annual rodeos. He noticed a new vaquero, one with a fondness for silver. "Well, this is a nice surprise, Dar," he declared, offering his hand. "What brings you here in such a rush?"

Dar Pierce leaned down to shake, but did not return the smile. He looked older than when Kent saw him last. A lot older. "I'm here on business. Damned serious business."

Nance came off the porch. "Surely it can wait until after you have some coffee? It is great to see you again. We want to hear all the latest. The cows can wait."

Dar swung down and doffed his sombrero. "My apologies, Mrs. Tovey, for my strong language."

"It's Nance, remember?" she said with a mild laugh. "My goodness, Dar. Why are you being so formal?"

It was Julio Pierce who answered her. "Didn't you hear my *padre*? This is not a social call."

Dar glanced sharply up at his youngest. "You will show respect when you talk to a lady. And never forget they are our friends."

"*Sí*," Julio said, scowling. "But you can't blame me. You know how highly I thought of him."

"We all did," Dar said sadly.

"What in heaven's name is all this about?" Nance asked.

"Berto is dead," Dar said softly.

"Your foreman?" Kent asked needlessly, since they all knew he was. "What happened? Was he thrown by a horse, or gored?" Kent assumed that an ordinary mishap was to blame. Fatal accidents were few, but they did happen.

Dar grew somber. "He was murdered."

"Murdered?" Nance repeated, shocked. "Who would do such a thing? How did it happen? Was he shot?"

Again it was Julio who answered her. "Berto was stabbed!" he snapped. "Gutted like a fish!"

"We found him lying in a pool of blood out behind a shed," Steve said, "and came here as soon as we pieced it together."

Kent Tovey was confused. He did not understand what the Circle T had to do with Berto's death, and said so.

"We're here because the killer is one of your punchers," Dar Pierce regretfully informed him.

Kent smothered a snort of disbelief. "Why, that's preposterous. What possible reason would one of my hands have for murdering your foreman? It makes no sense."

"Nevertheless, it's true," Dar responded, "and I can prove it." He turned to his sorrel, opened a saddlebag, and removed a folding knife with wood grips. "This was found next to Berto's body. Take a good look at the initials."

Kent had the knife in his hand before he realized it was smeared with scarlet. He had known Berto well, and liked him. To think that he was touching Berto's blood made him shiver with distaste. "J. D.," he read aloud.

"You have a puncher working for you by the name of Jack Demp, I believe," Dar said.

"We do," Kent admitted. "But again, what possible reason would Demp have?" He held the knife out. "It will take more than this to convince me."

"I have more." Dar turned to the vaquero whose clothes and tack glittered with silver. "This is Hijino. He was at the corral about the time Berto was killed, and saw a cowboy lead a horse away from our house. He did not think much of it at the time, since we often have guests." Dar motioned. "Describe the person you saw."

"*Sí, patrón*," Hijino said. "He was white. Maybe *veinte*, that is, twenty years old. No taller than I am, but thinner. He wore a hat with a high crown, a brown shirt, and black boots with small spurs. That is all I could tell."

"That description fits half the Circle T," Clayburn remarked. "Want me to fetch Demp anyway?"

Kent Tovey nodded. "Be quick about it. I want this settled right away. If it's true . . ." He could not bring himself to finish the statement. It was too disturbing, too horrifying.

"Demp is out on the range," Clayburn said. "It could take an hour or more to round him up."

"Take Jesco and Loring with you to help search," Kent directed. "And whoever else is handy."

"Timmy, you heard Mr. Tovey," Clayburn said. He exchanged glances with John Jesco. "But it's best if you stick around. To sort of keep an eye on things."

Nance was wringing her hands in anguish. "This is terrible, just terrible. Come inside while we wait, Dar, you and your boys. My husband will get to the bottom of this, I promise you."

"I am grateful," Dar said, and beckoned to his sons.

Steve and Armando alighted, but Julio did not. "I will wait out here, Father," he announced, betraying his reason by his tone and the look he cast at Kent and Nance.

"The Toveys are our friends, son," Dar reiterated with marked paternal patience. "You can't blame them for something one of their punchers might have done."

"*Did* do," Julio corrected him. "There's no doubt in my mind. We have a witness and the evidence."

"But why?" Kent fell back on the same issue. "What would Demp hope to gain? It's pointless."

"Who can say?" Julio challenged, without the courtesy of a "señor." "Perhaps he did it because he does not like Mexicans. With my own ears, I once heard him call Hijino a bean-eater."

Nance gasped. "We don't allow that sort of thing at the Circle T. Why wasn't I told?"

The question was addressed to Kent. "This is the first I've heard about it, dearest. Rest assured, I will discuss it with Demp and Clayburn when they get back." To Julio he said, "Please reconsider. You are always welcome in our house. Come in out of the hot sun."

"And this Demp?" Julio persisted. "What will you do to him?"

"If he's guilty, appropriate steps will be taken."

"If?"

"A person is innocent until proven otherwise," Kent said. "He must be given an opportunity to defend himself."

"As I thought," Julio said in contempt. "Already you take his side against us. Is this what you call justice?"

"What would you have us do? String him from a tree?" Kent meant it as a splash of cold logic to cool Julio down.

"That is exactly what we should do, *sí*. We must hang him as a warning to the rest of you gringos!"

"Julio!" Dar said sternly. "That is enough. If you can not be civil, you will go wait by the stable."

His jaw jutting defiantly, Julio wheeled his mount. The vaqueros fell in behind him.

"Please excuse my youngest," Dar said. "He and Berto were close. Julio has taken the death hard."

"I can't blame him," Nance sympathized. "Don't

worry. We won't hold his behavior against him." She placed a hand on Dar's arm. "Now how about that coffee? While we wait, you can tell us what your lovely wife and daughters have been up to since I saw them last."

Kent let Steve and Armando enter ahead of him. He indicated that Jesco should join them, but the tall cowboy shook his head and walked to a rocking chair.

"Out here will do, Mr. Tovey. Someone needs to keep an eye on those vaqueros." Jesco sat and hooked his left boot on the rail.

"Surely you are not suggesting they will cause trouble?" Kent was incredulous. "I grant you that Julio has been rude, but he has an excuse. We must forgive him."

"Turnin' the other cheek only works when the other gent turns his," Jesco remarked. "Otherwise you get yours blown off."

Deeply troubled, Kent hurried inside to catch up to the others.

Fortunately, Nance was her usual talkative self, and rambled on about the upcoming rodeo and the current price for beef and whether they would get any rain before the summer was out. Anything and everything except Berto's death.

The clock on the wall ticked off an hour. Then an hour and a half. Ten minutes more, and the front door opened and Jesco hollered, "They're comin', Mr. Tovey!"

Almost a dozen cowboys were with Clayburn, including Jack Demp. Apparently the foreman had not told Demp why he had been sent for, because the first thing out of his mouth was, "You wanted to see me, Mr. Tovey?"

Dar, Steve, and Armando were on the porch. Julio and the vaqueros had trotted up from the stable and were to one side, Julio with his hand on his revolver.

Kent took the incriminating evidence from his pocket. "Yes, I did. Is this folding knife yours?"

"Land sakes!" Demp grinned, and snatched it from Kent's grasp. "Where did you find it? I've been lookin' all over for this thing."

"Then it does belong to you?" Kent needed to be absolutely certain.

"Sure, it's—" Demp blinked and ran a finger along the grips. "Hold on. I never carved my initials in mine. And what's this red stuff? Good God. Is this blood?"

"But you do admit to owning a knife like that?"

Demp looked up and regarded the ring of intent faces. "Sure. I keep it in my war bag. Most every hand in the bunkhouse knows that. But it disappeared. Remember, Walt? I asked if you had seen it anywhere?"

"That's right," Clayburn said. "I plumb forgot."

Julio gigged his horse closer. "Of course he claims he lost it! Because he dropped it at our rancho when he fled!"

"What is he jabberin' about?" Demp asked no one in particular.

"They think you killed the DP's foreman," Kent Tovey revealed.

Demp's mouth dropped. "That's plain loco!" he blurted. "Why would I blow out Berto's wick when I hardly even knew him?"

"He was a greaser, as you like to call us," Julio said. "That is cause enough for a bigot like you."

"Mister, no one talks to me like that," Jack Demp said.

"I do," Julio declared. "You are a bastard and a murderer, but I am not afraid of you. I do not fear any gringo."

Demp looked down at Kent. "Do I have to take this, Mr. Tovey? Aren't you goin' to do somethin'?"

Kent hesitated. A wrong decision on his part could result in tragedy.

"You will continue to deny it," Julio was growling, "so if Berto is to be avenged, I must take the matter into my own hands." He paused. "Whenever you are ready to die, fill your hand. Killing you will give me great pleasure."

Chapter 11

For Dar Pierce, it was the moment when all he believed in, all he stood for, all he had tried to make of his life, hung in the balance.

Dar had been about his youngest son's age when he marched off to invade Mexico. The newspapers were full of editorials and rousing accounts designed to stir patriotic fervor to a fever pitch, and his was as stirred as anyone's.

Mexico was to blame, the government proclaimed. Mexican troops had attacked American troops on U.S. soil. The Mexicans countered that it was their soil, and the Americans were there illegally, but in the rush to arms, few north of the border gave the view of those south of the border any credence. Mexico was evil. Mexico was vile. Mexico must learn that it was the natural right of the United States, formally known as Manifest Destiny, for America to hold sway over the entire continent.

Dar bought the bill of goods. He had fallen for every half-truth, for every appeal to his devotion to his country, and done as thousands of other young men did: He enlisted. Initially, Dar fought with distinction. The newspapers and his superiors convinced him that if he did his part, the war would soon end. He had his first taste of combat at Monterrey. The frenzy, the blood, and the gore were not as glorious as he had been led to believe.

It was at Buena Vista that Dar's distaste for war became more than that. The senseless slaughter sickened him. He saw the Mexicans under Santa Anna charge again and again, only to be smashed by volleys of canister and grapeshot. The American artillery under a captain by the name of William Tecumseh Sherman felled the Mexican soldiers in droves, ripping their ranks to ribbons. After the battle, as the American troops cheered and whooped, Dar walked among the enemy fallen in a daze, appalled at the human capacity for butchering other humans.

By Veracruz, Dar was sick to his soul of the whole business. He had grown to despise war and all it stood for. He only wanted out, wanted an end to his part in the carnage.

Many American soldiers felt contempt for their Mexican counterparts. Insults were heaped on their adversaries. Mexicans were cowardly. Mexicans were runts. Mexicans were greasers, in every respect inferior to their conquerors.

Dar felt differently. He saw the Mexicans as brave. He saw them as dedicated. He admired their refusal to surrender after one crushing defeat after another. More, Dar saw that the common people, overlooked by both armies in the epic struggle, were possessed of a humility that endeared them to him.

Dar missed taking part in the battles of Contreras and Churubusco, thank God. He was detailed to guard prisoners. Not long afterward, Mexico City itself fell to the army from the north, and all that remained was the mopping up and the signing of a treaty that rewarded the conquerors with vast land holdings.

When Dar's enlistment was up, he did not return home. By then he was in what would become New Mexico Territory with a detachment about to be mustered out. He decided to stay in the West. He took up Mexican ways, adopted Mexican dress, and met the love of his life.

Juanita was an angel in mortal form. Elegant, graceful, and exceptionally lovely, she possessed the added quality of being at total peace with herself and those she came into contact with. She never got mad, never raised her voice. She was everything the war had not been, and Dar fell so deeply and completely for her that he asked her father for her hand after knowing her only three months.

Much to Dar's amazement, Juanita came to love him as much as he loved her. Her family had insisted they must wait a year before becoming man and wife, but neither of them minded. They knew, as surely as they lived and breathed, that they were meant for each other. One year or ten, they could be patient.

So it was that Dar found himself with the woman of his dreams, and no means to support her. He was working as a clerk at the time, and clerks barely made enough to feed a rabbit, let alone a family. So he had cast about for something else to do. Cattle interested him. Buyers in the States were eager for beef. Since Dar had been raised on a farm, he figured ranching would not be that much different, and took the plunge. He was wrong. Ranching imposed demands farmers never faced. It was hard, wearying work, that required him to be in the saddle from sunup to sundown, seven days a week, three hundred and sixty-five days a year. But it paid off handsomely.

Dar carved the DP out of the New Mexico wilderness. His rancho was one of the first established there by a white man. It prospered beyond his highest hopes. His family never wanted for anything. He saw to that. But he did not spoil them. He raised his sons to follow in his footsteps, working them as tirelessly as he had worked.

Life was good.

Then along came the Toveys. Kent Tovey established the Circle T north of the Rio Largo. Dar didn't mind. The land south of the river was extensive enough for him. He had all the cattle he needed.

Dar befriended Kent. Dar taught Kent the crucial aspects separating ranches that thrived from ranches that failed. He did all he could to help, and in the process, he and his wife became friends with Kent and Nance.

It was Dar who came up with the idea of the rodeo. For a week each year, the two ranches mixed and mingled. The vaqueros and cowboys took part in friendly competitions. Dances were held, and feasts for all. Ties that bind, Dar called them, and was pleased by the result of his cleverness.

Now this.

Berto had warned Dar that something was amiss.

Someone—Berto had a suspicion who but he would not say without more proof—was spreading unrest among the vaqueros, and even among Dar's own family.

Steady, dependable Berto. He had been more than a foreman. Berto had been Dar's dear and close friend. His murder was a shock. The violence of the outside world had crept into Dar's private sanctuary. Were it up to Dar, he might have buried Berto and left it at that. But his vaqueros, and his sons, demanded justice. They insisted he ride to the Circle T and hold the guilty to account.

Dar gave in, but he was troubled. The folding knife found by the body was too convenient. The initials on the grip were too freshly carved. He suspected a ruse, until Hijino stepped forward and said he saw a Circle T cowboy on the DP about the time Berto was slain.

A witness changed everything. Dar's vaqueros were for riding to the Circle T in force and demanding at gunpoint that the killer be handed over to them. Dar refused. The potential for bloodshed was too great. He'd had enough of conflict in the war. So he compromised. He brought his sons and six vaqueros. Enough that they could defend themselves if need be, but not so many that he could not control the flow of events. Or so he believed.

Now Dar was confronted by his worst nightmare. His own son was about to commit the ultimate folly. Julio and Jack Demp were a whisker's width away from drawing when Dar intervened. "Enough! There will be no shooting! Do you hear me, Julio?"

Kent Tovey sprang to Dar's aid. "The same goes for you, Demp! We must get to the bottom of this without violence."

The tableau froze. Tension crackled like invisible lightning. The vaqueros were ready to back up Julio. The cowboys were prepared to defend Demp. All it would take was a tiny spark, and the ground would run red.

That was when Nancy Tovey came calmly off the porch and joined her husband and Dar. She did not say anything. She did not need to. No man there would risk harming a woman. Any woman. As surely as if she had punctured them with a needle, their hatreds deflated, and Julio and Demp reluctantly restrained themselves.

Kent turned to Dar. "Feel free to question Demp as you see fit. I'm sure he won't mind."

"I have nothin' to hide," Demp said.

Dar got to the crux of the matter. "A vaquero saw Berto shortly before ten o'clock last night, so he was alive then. His body was found about midnight when one of the dogs caught the scent of blood, and took to howling its fool head off. It wouldn't stop, so Paco had some of my men look around. They found Berto."

Jack Demp brightened. "Between ten and midnight? Then it definitely wasn't me! I was in the bunkhouse playin' checkers with Shonsey. Everyone saw me." He glanced at Walt Clayburn. "Tell them."

The Circle T's foreman nodded. "It's God's own truth. I was there the whole time and so was he."

Julio refused to give up. "You lie to protect him!

All you gringos stick together. But he dropped his knife. It had to be him."

Bristling, Demp coiled as if to leap from his saddle. "I keep tellin' you. I never carved my initials in my knife. If you ask me, you did it."

"That is the most ridiculous thing I have ever heard," Julio declared. "I killed a man who was like an uncle to me, so I could blame you?"

Dar put a hand on his youngest's boot. "Don't start up again. If he was where they say he was, then we have made a terrible mistake."

"You take them at their word?" Julio was incredulous.

"They are our friends. They wouldn't lie." Dar wanted to believe that with every fiber of his being. He *needed* to believe it.

"Oh, Father," Julio said.

His tone seared Dar like a red-hot poker. His own son, the fruit of his loins, one of the six people he loved most in the world, had lost faith in him. It crushed him almost as much as Berto's death.

"Come inside," Nance was saying. "All of you. We can talk this over like civilized folk."

"My father can talk if he wants, but I will not be made a fool of." Julio reined his mount toward the stable. "I will wait, and go back with him."

The vaqueros went along.

"Please forgive my son," Dar said to Kent. "Julio has always been wilful. When he gets like this, only his mother can talk any sense into him."

"If only he knew how highly we value your friendship," Kent Tovey said.

Nance was ushering Steve and Armando into the house. Dar climbed the steps, and paused to gaze regretfully at his youngest. When they got back to the DP, Dar would sit Julio down. He had to make Julio see past his fury to a troubling possibility: If the Circle T cowboys were telling the truth and Jack Demp could not have murdered Berto, then clearly someone had plotted to put the blame on their shoulders. Who? And why? Dar could think of only one motive, namely, to cause trouble between the two ranches. To drive a wedge between the Toveys and himself. To what end, though? The ultimate goal eluded him.

"Are you all right?" Nance asked.

"I fear we have a sidewinder in our midst, and they've drawn first blood," Dar sought to enlighten her.

"If that's the case, working together we'll settle their hash for them," Nancy vowed. "As for your son, don't fret. He'll simmer down eventually."

Dar hoped so.

Over by the stable, Julio dismounted and paced back and forth. Clenching and unclenching his fists, he snarled, "My own *padre*, duped by these gringos! He is blinded by his own goodness."

"I warned you," Hijino mentioned. "I told you the gringos would deny it."

"And you were right," Julio said in disgust. He stopped and smacked his hand against his leg. "But I swear to you, to all of you, that Berto's death will not go unavenged."

"What can you do?" Paco asked. "What can any

of us do? To go against the Toveys is to go against your father."

"Perhaps . . ." Hijino said, and stopped without finishing his statement.

"Perhaps what?" Julio goaded.

"There is a saying the gringos have," Hijino said. "Fight fire with fire. We must do to the guilty one as he has done to Berto."

Paco recoiled at the suggestion. "Kill Jack Demp? The other cowboys would seek our blood."

"Let them!" Julio spat in disdain. "I am not afraid of the Circle T. I would welcome an excuse to crush them."

"You are talking about a range war," Paco pointed out.

"So? Maybe it is long overdue. My father should never have permitted the Toveys to settle here. He gave up half the valley without a fight. I hate to say it, but he has always been timid."

Roman, who had remained quiet until now, stirred. "How do you propose to go about it, *patrón*?"

"You will find a way to challenge Demp," Julio said. "He is no match for you with a *pistola*."

"I must be clear," Roman said. "You command me to kill him? To goad him into going for his gun?"

"I would never force you to do anything against your will," Julio said. "It must be your decision."

"Your father would fire me."

"Not if we do it right. Not if we arrange things so the gringo appears to be to blame," Julio proposed.

Paco whistled softly. "I say again, we risk a range war. Rancho against rancho. It is not to be taken lightly."

Hijino sleeved dust from his silver saddle horn. "I agree. But either that, or we swallow our pride and our manhood and let Berto's killer go unpunished. I, for one, can not stand for that."

"Nor I!" Julio declared. "But we will let the gringos think they have tricked us. We will bide our time until the rodeo, and then Roman will uphold the honor of the DP."

"I hope we know what we are doing," Paco said.

Julio glared at the white house. "The more I think about it, the more I realize there is room in this valley for only one rancho, and that rancho is the DP." He looked at each of them in turn. "Are you with me?"

"Need you ask?" Hijino smiled. "You can count on me to back you in anything you do."

"I wish all the vaqueros were like you," Julio said.

Chapter 12

Saber was having a grand old time. He'd always thought that running a saloon would be the perfect job if he ever decided to give up riding the high lines and become respectable. Not that he ever would. For as fond as he was of whiskey and cards, he was fonder of danger.

Straitlaced churchgoers would find it hard to comprehend, but Saber relished the outlaw life. Stealing, killing, mayhem, they were nectar to his jaded senses, intoxicating in their sweetness—addicting, too, in that once he had started down the bloody and violent path he craved, he couldn't stop. To always do as he pleased, to satisfy his every whim and craving, *that* was real living. To do as the common herd of humanity, to abide by laws and rules made by others, was to live in a prison bounded by invisible bars.

On this bright and sunny afternoon, with the surrounding peaks of the Nacimiento Mountains towering high in the sky, Saber stood behind the bar of the Wolf Pass Saloon sipping the best coffin varnish in the place, and gazed out the open door. Some of his men were asleep in the back. Others lounged at the tables, playing cards and drinking.

"Yes, sir, boys," Saber declared. "This here is the life."

The comment caused Creed and Twitch to stand and come over. Both were in sour moods, and Saber could guess why.

"What will it be, gents?"

"Enough of this playactin'," Twitch said. "How much longer do we have to sit around twiddlin' our thumbs?"

Saber bristled. The merest hint of disagreement always angered him. Only by force of will did he keep his wild bunch in line. They must never suspect weakness, or they would turn on him like a pack of starving wolves. That was how it was done. "How many times must we go over the same damn thing?" he snapped.

"I am bored," Creed said. "I don't like doin' nothin'."

"Is that what you call this?" Saber gestured. "A roof over our heads. All the booze we can drink. Enough food in the pantry to last us a good long while. And what do you two do? Complain."

"That's not fair," Twitch groused. "It's not you we're gripin' about. It's the waitin'."

"We can't move until the time is right," Saber said with rare patience, "and the time won't be right until Hijino and Dunn have the Circle T and the DP at each other's throats."

Twitch smirked. "I've got to hand it to you, cousin. This is your best brainstorm ever. We'll make more money than we ever dreamed, once we sell off all those cows and help ourselves to whatever else is worth havin'."

"I am still bored," Creed said.

Were it any other member of his gang, Saber would browbeat them into submission. But he had to handle the black with care. They were all killers, but Creed was the worst. He would kill anyone, anything, anywhere, anytime. Creed was the only one of them Saber secretly feared might turn on him if pushed too far.

"Why don't you go practice with your six-shooters? That always makes you happy."

"I did that yesterday."

"Well then—" Saber began, but stopped when Creed shifted and tilted his head as if listening to something in the distance. The black's senses were uncanny. Creed heard things long before any of them, saw objects too far off for anyone else to see. "What is it?"

"Someone comes."

Saber smiled in anticipation. Two days ago a rotund drummer had shown up on his way north. An old acquaintance of Mort's, he had been surprised when Saber told him the former owner sold the saloon and lit out for Denver.

"I thought Mort loved this place," the drummer had said. "He told me he would live out the rest of his days here."

Saber had shrugged. "I made him an offer he couldn't rightly say no to." He then changed the subject by offering the drummer a free drink, and listened to the fool babble about how hard it was to sell ladies' corsets for a living.

"Females are fussy creatures. They always want the best corset money can buy, but they always want it at half price."

"That's only natural," Saber commented. He had as much interest in corsets as he did in the mating habits of toads.

"Easy for you to say, my good man. You don't have to put up with their endless griping."

"If the work bothers you so much, do something else." Saber thought that a nice touch, since he had no intention of letting the idiot leave Wolf Pass alive.

"Ah. But there are compensations. I get to travel. I get to meet new people. And sometimes—not very often, but on occasion—a lady will let me help her try on a corset." The drummer's piglet eyes sparkled with lust. "Those are the moments I live for, as would any man with blood in his veins."

Saber was of the opinion that if you had seen one naked female, you had seen them all. Oh, some were short and some were tall, some were skinny and some were heavyset, but they all had the same body parts, and one breast was as good as another under the sheets.

Saber had taken as much of the drummer's prattle as he could stand, and when the drummer went to use the outhouse, he signaled to Creed. Shortly thereafter, Creed came back in with the forty-seven dollars the drummer had on him.

The coyotes feasted well that night.

Now Saber went to the door and gazed at the point where a rutted track merged into the clearing from the southeast. In under five minutes, a pair of riders appeared. Right away, Saber pegged them as prospectors. They were cut from the same coarse cloth: unkempt, weather-beaten clothes, bushy beards. Each man led a pack animal laden with the tools of their hardscrabble trade. Angling to the hitch rail, they stiffly climbed down.

Saber stepped outside, plastering a smile on his face. "How do, gents? Welcome to the Wolf Pass Saloon."

The pair had rifles crooked in their elbows, and each wore a brace of pistols. "How do, yourself," said the burliest. "I'm Zeb, and this here rascal is my pard, Roscoe."

Saber indicated the pack horses. "Off into the mountains after gold or silver, I take it?"

"Either will do," Zeb drawled. "We're not particular about how we get rich."

"Just so we do," Roscoe amended with a chuckle.

Prospecting was difficult work, the rewards never certain. Saber had a much more practical way of meeting his needs. He regarded nugget hounds as greed-blinded yaks, but he kept that to himself and said, "Care to wet your throats? I've got red-eye that will curl your toes."

"And put hair on our chests?" Zeb joked. He already had more hair than a bear. His wrists and the backs of his hands were covered.

"Heard about any strikes in these parts?" Roscoe asked.

"Afraid not," Saber answered. "Most folks don't go that far in, and those that do are more interested in keepin' their scalps than rootin' in the ground." Actually, he had no idea how many used the pass each year.

"That's fine by us," Zeb said. "It means the ore is still there, waitin' for us to find it."

"We're overdue for a strike," Roscoe remarked.

Saber never could understand ore hounds. They were dreamers, chasing elusive wisps. Their chances of striking it rich were about the same as that of a cow sprouting wings. His way was better. He simply took whatever he wanted, whenever he wanted it.

"Never expected to find a saloon so far up in these mountains," Zeb commented as he strolled in.

"I don't suppose you have a dove or two workin' for you?" Roscoe asked hopefully. "It's been a spell since I fondled me a female."

"The only doves hereabouts are squaws," Saber said, "and they don't cotton much to white folks."

"I lived with an Injun gal once," Zeb said. "Bought her from her pa for a couple of horses and a blanket. She wasn't much of a talker, but she could cook. At night she was a regular wonderment." He winked at Saber.

Roscoe snickered. "That's about all women are good for, anyway. Unless you count complainin'."

Saber went behind the bar, while the two prospectors idly surveyed the room, showing little interest in anyone else. "What will it be?"

Zeb placed his Sharps rifle on the counter with a loud thump and noisily smacked his lips. "Bug juice. I'm not finicky, so long as it burns goin' down."

Roscoe stared at Creed as if he had never beheld a black before. "Same here," he parroted.

As Saber set out glasses and chose a bottle, he debated what to do with them. Other than their guns and their horses, they had nothing of value. He was inclined to let them ride away. Then Roscoe leaned toward him so as not to be overheard.

"How come you let him in here?"

"Him who?"

"The nigger. Where I come from, their kind ain't allowed to mix with our kind. It's not decent."

Saber savored the icy chill that washed over him. He opened the bottle and slid it toward them. "Help yourselves. The first drink is on the house."

Roscoe resumed digging his own grave. "So what if we can't keep 'em as slaves anymore. Niggers ought to know their place."

"Did you hear him?" Saber hollered to Creed. "This gent says blacks have no business minglin' with whites."

Everyone in the saloon froze. All sound ceased. Roscoe's mouth opened and closed a few times until, coughing, he sputtered, "What in hell did you do that for?"

"We don't want no trouble," Zeb said.

Creed slowly set down his glass. He slowly turned and just as slowly came toward them. His features might as well have been carved from marble.

Twitch shadowed him, giggling in anticipation.

"We don't want no trouble," Zeb said again, to Creed this time. "My partner didn't mean anything."

"That's right," Roscoe nervously bleated, his eyes on Creed's Remingtons. "I was makin' small talk."

"Pitiful," Saber said. "Downright pitiful. They have no more gumption than a couple of chipmunks."

Creed stopped about six feet from the prospectors. "I'll let you jerk your hardware first."

"Now hold on," Roscoe said. "I meant no disrespect. I was just tellin' this fella how things are in some parts of the country."

"You should be worried about how things are here," Creed said. "A minute from now, you'll be in the hereafter."

Zeb surveyed the saloon as if hoping someone would side with his partner and him, and when no one did, he appealed to Saber. "What kind of place are you runnin' here, anyhow? Invite us in for drinks, then stand by and do nothin' when this darkie threatens to blow out our wicks?"

"Some days it just doesn't pay to get up, does it?" Saber asked.

"I don't get this," Roscoe declared. "Somethin' ain't right."

A human statue, Creed was waiting for them to claw at their hardware. From experience, Saber knew that the black could stand still for hours. Creed was like an Apache in that respect. It was spooky.

"Well?" Zeb prodded. "Say somethin'!"

Saber took a swig from the bottle. Wiping his mouth with his sleeve, he responded, "You brought this on yourselves, boys. The only thing to do now is take your medicine."

"Damn it." Zeb was fingering his Sharps. "We're goin' to back on out, nice and peaceful like."

"All we want is to be left be," Roscoe said.

"You'll never reach the door."

Ignoring Saber, moving as if they were stepping on eggshells, the prospectors sidled toward the entrance. "That's it," Zeb said, covering the rest. "Don't anyone be hasty, and we'll all live to see the sun set."

Roscoe had not taken his eyes off Creed. He

seemed mesmerized, like a bird unable to look away from the snake about to devour it.

"I will give you to three," the black said.

Zeb grew ashen. "Please. We don't want to spill blood. How about if we say we're sorry? Would that satisfy you?"

"One," Creed counted.

"God Almighty, this can't be happenin'!" Roscoe exclaimed. "What sort of man are you that you would gun us down over a trifle?"

"Two," Creed said.

"Please," Zeb pleaded. "We apologize. We're as sorry as sorry can be." He had the Sharps in front of him, the muzzle angled at the tables.

"Three." Creed's hands swooped and rose. In unison, the nickel-plated Remingtons gleamed and boomed.

Zeb and Roscoe both cried out as their right knees were shot out from under them. Zeb pitched onto his other knee and tried to level his Sharps, but took a second slug in the shoulder that smashed him to the floor. Roscoe clutched at the bar to stay upright, grimacing in agony, and screeched when the lead bored through his vitals.

Creed methodically emptied his pistols into the pair, shot after shot after shot, until the hammers clicked on spent cartridges. He did not check the bodies for signs of life. There was no need. They were shot to pieces.

Saber rose onto his toes to peer over the bar at the spreading pools of scarlet. "You know, you're right," he said. "I'm startin' to get bored, too. That wasn't half the fun I figured it would be."

Twitch hunkered and dipped a finger in the blood. Tittering, he drew red circles on the cheeks of both prospectors, then wiped his fingers clean on Zeb's shirt. "I hope we hear from Dunn and Hijino soon."

"Makes two of us," Saber said. "I have a powerful hankerin' to kill a heap of cowboys."

Chapter 13

Dunn had to hurry. He had to reach the spot he wanted well ahead of the Pierce party. He had intended to sneak away from the Circle T sooner, but Clayburn had gathered together the punchers who happened to be there at the time, to inform them that they must be on their best behavior.

"Mr. Tovey has persuaded Mr. Pierce that Demp was not to blame for murderin' the DP foreman. But some of Pierce's vaqueros refuse to believe he's innocent. They're spoilin' for a fight. All they need is an excuse—any excuse—to squeeze the trigger, and Mr. Tovey wants me to make sure that none of us give them that excuse." Clayburn paused, and raked those present with a hard stare. "This is deadly serious, gents. If we're not careful, we'll find ourselves breathin' gun smoke."

No one said anything. They all appreciated the gravity of the situation.

"Timmy, I want you to take a horse from the corral. Ride north over the range, and warn every hand you come across. Wheeler, you do the same to the south."

"What do we tell them, exactly?" young Timmy Loring asked.

"That until Mr. Tovey gives his permission, under no circumstances is a Circle T puncher to cross the Rio Largo onto the DP spread. We are to fight shy of them until tempers cool. That means no one will be going to San Pedro for a spell."

A few of the cowboys muttered resentfully. San Pedro was their one diversion. The only place within a hundred miles, other than remote Wolf Pass, high in the mountains, where the hands could go for a glass of red-eye, a game of cards, and, in San Pedro's case, the warm glance of a friendly dove.

"I know, I know," Clayburn said. "But it's only for a short while. Only until Mr. and Mrs. Tovey have smoothed things over. They plan to visit the DP in a week and speak to the vaqueros personally."

"What?" This from John Jesco, who had been leaning against a twin bunk. "Is that wise?"

"Maybe not," Clayburn responded. "But the boss has his mind made up. I suggested he take fifteen or twenty of us along as protection, and he said he would settle for two or three."

"I'm one of them." Jesco was not volunteering. He was stating a fact.

Clayburn grinned. "Took the words right out of my mouth."

The meeting ended. Dunn was near the door, and turned to slip away unnoticed, but Clayburn hollered his name and told him to keep an eye out for any punchers who might stray in off the range before the Pierces left, and fill them in.

Dunn chafed at the delay. But he could not leave without arousing suspicion, so he bided his time, and when the Pierces came out of the house and prepared to depart, he hurried to Clayburn and offered to go out and help spread the word among the hands on the range. "I know you sent Loring and Wheeler, but it's a lot of ground for two men to cover."

Clayburn seemed a bit surprised. But he thought a moment, and nodded. "You're right. I should have sent a few more. Off you go. Be back by nightfall."

Now here Dunn was, riding like the wind for the Rio Largo, cutting across country rather than use the trail to the river that Dar Pierce would shortly take.

Things were about to come to a head. Dunn imagined how pleased Saber would be when he heard the news. Soon the entire valley would run red. The range war to end all range wars, Saber had called it. Open feuding between ranches was rare, but there had been a few instances. Never a situation like this, though. Never a range war created for a specific purpose.

Dunn had to hand it to Saber. The scheme was brilliant. The Circle T and the DP would never know they had been tricked. They would kill one another off, and once there were too few of them left to offer much resistance, Saber would swoop in and finish off the rest, and that would be that. Saber would lay claim to the entire valley. The cattle would be rounded up, herded to Mexico, and sold.

Dunn couldn't wait. The last he had heard, cows were going for up to thirty dollars a head, bulls for as much as seventy-five. Both herds, combined, would fetch hundreds of thousands of dollars. Each member of the gang stood to pocket over fifty thousand.

Fifty thousand! Dunn never had more than a thousand to his name his entire life. Fifty thousand was a fortune. He could do whatever he pleased. Maybe go back to Texas, where he had been born and raised, and buy a nice place of his own. Live out the rest of his days high on the hog.

Fifty thousand! Most people were lucky to earn a hundred dollars a month. Cowboys made forty or so. Clayburn earned twice that amount, but he was foreman. Lawmen averaged a hundred and fifty.

Fifty thousand! When good land in Texas could be had for five dollars an acre. When a house as big and grand as the Tovey's cost no more than five thousand.

Dunn could have it all. The house, the land, and all the trimmings. He would treat himself to an endless stream of doves. A different gal every night. Or maybe, just maybe, he would find a pretty young thing and marry her. He always had been partial to the young ones. Hell, once word got out how rich he was, pretty young things would fall over themselves for the privilege of becoming his missus.

Dunn laughed. The possibilities made him giddy. He had to remind himself not to put the cart ahead of the horse. Nothing was certain. The plan might fall apart. But he would do all he could to ensure his part was carried out exactly as Saber required.

Dunn wanted that fifty thousand. He wanted it more than he had ever wanted anything. He wanted it so much, he lay awake at night thinking of all the things he could buy, all the things he would do. Life would be fine. Life would be glorious.

Money. That was the key to happiness. Lots and lots of money. The more money a man had, the happier he was. Dunn has always been envious of those who had it, always wished he was just like them. Unbelievably, incredibly, soon his wish stood an excellent chance of coming true.

That a lot of people had to die in order for that to happen did not bother Dunn one bit. He had killed his first man when he was fourteen, a drunk who became forward with Dunn's sister. They had been walking down the street, minding their own business, talking and laughing as kids will do, when the drunk lurched out of a saloon and took to pawing Cynthia and making lewd comments. Dunn had warned the man to back off, but the drunk cursed him and threatened to take him over a knee and spank him. So Dunn had pulled his knife and buried it to the hilt in the man's chest, and the man had died squealing in terror.

Dunn fled. He hugged his folks and kissed his sis, and lit a shuck. He'd never been back. He always intended to, but one lawless deed led to another, then to having a price on his head. He'd drifted west, into New Mexico, with the notion of starting over. But he hadn't been in New Mexico two months when he hooked up with Saber. That was a year ago.

Now here he was. Still living outside the law. A regular curly wolf, with no desire to change.

Dunn shook himself. He was almost to the Rio

Largo. Time to concentrate on what he had to do. He could not afford a mistake. Not with fifty thousand dollars at stake.

Dunn smelled the water before he came to it. So did his horse. It wanted to drink, but he reined west and paralleled the meandering waterway, until he came to a cluster of cottonwoods about a hundred yards from the crossing the Pierces would likely use.

Dismounting, Dunn wrapped the reins around a sapling, shucked his Winchester from the saddle scabbard, and glided to within a few yards of the tree line. Sinking flat, he parted the waist-high brush. Yes, it was perfect.

Dunn took off his hat and placed it beside him. He levered a round into the Winchester, and set the rifle in front of him. Then he folded his forearms and rested his chin on his wrist to wait.

Dunn thought of what he was about to do, and the slaughter that would result. Men would die because of him, a lot of men, but he didn't care. He was used to killing. He had accounted for eleven so far. What was another two or three dozen?

He remembered every one. The clerk who had tried to stop him from robbing a bank. The farmer who objected to having a horse stolen. The old fool he had beaten and robbed after the man insulted Texas and Texans. Then there were all the others, each easier than the last. Now he felt no qualms whatsoever about pulling the trigger or plunging a knife into someone's hide.

Dunn never saw himself as a hardened killer, though. He wasn't like Hijino, who killed out of perverse delight. Or like Saber, who killed because he had no regard for human life, or any other kind. He certainly wasn't like Creed, either, who had killed women and children as well as grown men. Creed was different.

About six months ago, they had stumbled on a family of emigrants in a prairie schooner and massacred them. Creed shot the three kids himself, since no one else wanted to do it. That night, after a few glasses of whiskey, Dunn asked Creed how he could look a child in the eyes and blow its brains out. "I couldn't do that," Dunn freely confessed. "I'd feel guilt for the rest of my life."

Creed had been in a rare talkative mood. "I've never felt any. I've never felt anything."

"Nothing at all?" Dunn had said skeptically.

Draining the bottle in a gulp, Creed had wagged it back and forth. "I'm as empty as this is. Always have been. Always will be. When I kill, I don't feel a thing. It's no different whether I kill a lizard or a person. I feel nothin' at all."

Dunn had repressed a shudder. "What about friendship? Saber and you are close pards."

"He thinks we are," Creed said. "But I only stick with him and his bunch because he needs a lot of killin' done."

Dunn refused to give up. "What about love? Haven't you ever met a female you were fond of?"

"I don't cotton to women. They're abominations."

Stupefied, Dunn had half expected Creed to grin to show it was a joke, but Creed was serious. "Isn't that a mite harsh?"

"The way they think, the way they move, their bodies, everything about them sickens me."

"You've never wanted to kiss one? To crawl under the sheets and partake of her charms?"

To Dunn's amazement, Creed had shuddered. "I would rather lie with a goat. Or an ewe. I had a pet sheep once. Pretty little thing. I called her Wendy."

Dunn had absorbed the implications, and then *he* had shuddered. "Good God."

"What?"

"This rotgut has gone right through me," Dunn had said to get out of there. "I'll be right back." But when he did come back, he sat next to Twitch instead of Creed.

A slight vibration snapped Dunn out of the past and into the present. There was the faint drum of hooves in the distance. He raised his head. To the north, a cloud of dust heralded his victim. It would be a while yet.

Dunn thought of Nancy Tovey. Now there was a fine figure of a woman. A little on the lean side, but she had an ample bosom and lips ripe for sucking on. He wouldn't mind indulging, if the opportunity arose. Unlike Creed, he liked women better than sheep.

Riders became visible. Dunn counted them. Ten in all, as there should be. Pierce, his three sons, Hijino, and the five vaqueros. He imagined that Hijino had enjoyed killing Berto; Hijino liked to snuff out lives almost as much as Saber did.

Dunn once asked Saber how many people he had killed. Saber couldn't remember. "I've lost count. Somewhere between fifty and a hundred, I reckon."

Dunn never asked Creed how many he had killed. It was not healthy to pry into Creed's past. The last man who did, or so Saber told him, Creed had knifed, then shot, then poured kerosene on the body and burned it.

Creed was one nasty son of a bitch.

Now the riders were close enough for Dunn to tell who was who. Dar Pierce was in the front, Steve and Armando next, Julio between Paco and Roman. Hijino brought up the rear behind the vaqueros.

Dunn flattened. He had it all worked out in his head. He would fire twice—the extra shot to be sure—then he would race for his horse and ride like hell. By the time they worked out where the shot came from and found his tracks, he would be halfway to the Circle T. They might give chase, but Dunn's horse was as fleet as an antelope. With enough of a lead, they had a snowball's chance in Hades of catching him.

The Pierces came to the river, and drew rein to let their mounts drink. Steve Pierce climbed down and inspected one of his animal's front hooves.

Roman shifted and scanned the grassland behind them, his one hand under his jacket. "No one follows us, *patrón*."

"I didn't think anyone would," Dar Pierce responded. "Kent Tovey trusts me not to go after Demp."

"I do not trust Tovey. We are not safe here," Julio grumbled. "We will not be safe until we are across the Rio Largo."

"I believe them," Steve said. "I believe Jack Demp had nothing to do with Berto's death."

"You would."

"That is enough out of you, Julio," Dar said. "Your

mother and I will have a long talk with you after we get back. You were unforgivably rude to Kent and Nance, and it must not happen again."

"They are not our friends, Father. They never were."

"You are young yet. You do not see what is right in front of your face." Dar gigged his mount into the water. "Let's go."

The others were quick to follow suit. Water sprayed and frothed.

Hijino glanced at the trees, at the exact spot where Dunn lay. His perpetual grin widened a trifle. No one else noticed.

Dunn wedged the Winchester's smooth wooden stock to his shoulder. He centered the sights on his target's back. But he did not shoot. Do it too soon, and the vaqueros might catch him.

Dar Pierce was almost to the middle. Rising in the stirrups, he looked back. Why, Dunn couldn't say. Maybe fate was making it easy for him. Dar opened his mouth to say something just as Dunn steadied the barrel, took a deep breath, and fired. In a twinkling, he fed in another round and squeezed off his second shot.

Dar Pierce's face dissolved in a shower of scarlet.

Chapter 14

Trella was napping when a commotion woke her. She lay on her side, staring at the sunlit window, puzzled by loud voices and the patter of running feet. She should rise up and see what was going on, but she did not want to get out of bed. It was cool and comfortable, and she was perfectly content.

Trella's parents would deal with it. Or her brothers and sister, who were bound to criticize her for meddling in matters that did not concern her. They always treated her the same. To them, she was the youngest and the least experienced, and needed to be protected—or, worse, treated as if she did not have a brain between her ears and certainly could not think for her own.

Trella hated it. She wished she had been born first so she could boss them around as they bossed her. She closed her eyes, intending to fall back asleep, but the insistent clamor would not let her. Annoyed, she stared at the window and said aloud, "Some people have no consideration."

Suddenly her bedroom door was flung wide, framing her sister. Dolores had a strange look on her face, and seemed to sway slightly. "Get up," she said urgently. "It's father."

"What do you mean?" Trella asked, but Dolores had already turned and run off.

Trella remembered that her father had gone to the Circle T to talk to the Toveys about Berto. She had been as stunned as everyone else by his murder. He always treated her nicely, much nicer than her siblings. When she was small, he would bring her presents. Now he was dead, and one of the cowboys was to blame. She tended to agree with Julio that their father should never have permitted the Toveys to settle there. By rights the DP should own the entire valley.

A loud cry filled the house. A shriek such as Trella had never heard. Startled, she sat bolt upright, her fingers squeezing her pillow until her knuckles were white. *It sounded like her mother!* But what could tear such a wail of anguish from her mother's throat? Her mother was always so calm, always so composed.

Trella slid off the bed. A sob punctuated the shriek—a great, racking sob such as only the crushing of a heart could produce. For once Trella did not check her hair and her dress in the mirror. She ran toward the front of the house. Outside, someone shouted, barking commands.

The front door was open. Trella paused in the doorway, absorbing the scene before her; her brothers staring aghast at a prone form on the porch; her sister clutching a post for support, tears streaking her cheeks; her mother on her knees, hands clasped to her bosom; and her father on his back with his arms folded across his chest, hatless, part of his face blown away.

The world around Trella swirled. She reached for the jamb, about to faint. Hands took hold of her, bracing her. Numbly, she realized it was one of the maids. Normally she resented such familiarity from the servants, but now she did not object. She was too dazed. Too bewildered. *"Padre?"* she breathed.

Her mother gently placed a hand on her father's chest, and said softly, "Tell me again how it happened."

Steve answered her. "We were on our way back, crossing the river. Someone shot at us from the trees. Two shots. Both hit father. I caught him before he could fall in the water, but there was nothing I could do. Nothing any of us could do."

"The bastards!" Julio roared. He shook from the intensity of his emotion. "It was a gringo from the Circle T. It had to be."

"We don't know that," Steve said.

Julio whirled on him. "You were there! You saw the tracks! The direction they went! Back to the Circle T. Kent Tovey sent a cowboy to murder our father just as Berto was murdered."

"Tovey had no reason to want our father dead," Steve said. "They had talked things out. They parted as friends."

"Listen to you!" Scorn dripped from Julio's voice. "Defending them! Taking their side when our father lies here as proof of their treachery!"

"Julio," Juanita said, still in that quiet way. "You will show proper respect for your brother."

"I will not!" Julio cried. "He has always been a gringo at heart. Always preferred their ways. Look at how he dresses! You would not know he had a drop of your blood if you had not given birth to him."

"*Enough*," Junita said in a rare display of sternness. "I gave birth to you, too, and as your mother I require you to show the same love for your family as I do for you."

Her rebuke caused Julio to flinch in remorse. "I am sorry," he said contritely. "But the gringos are to blame. I feel it in my soul."

Juanita touched what was left of Dar's blood-flecked cheek. She closed her eyes and groaned. Armando started toward her, but she opened her eyes and waved him off. "I can not bear to see the man I love disfigured like this. Dolores, fetch a blanket. Steve, send riders to round up the vaqueros. All of them."

"But the cattle—" Steve began, and promptly stopped. "Yes, Mother. It will be as you wish."

"Yes!" Julio savagely exclaimed. "We will ride to the Circle T and wipe them out! Every last gringo!"

"I am calling in the vaqueros to attend the funeral," Juanita said. "Or would you rather we dig a hole in the ground right this moment and throw your father in?"

"No, of course not," Julio responded, chastised. "But after the funeral, we will have our revenge, will we not?"

"You worry me, son," Juanita said lovingly. "You truly do." She went to stand, and Steve was there, supporting her. "Now, listen to me. All of you." Juanita paused and gazed searchingly at each of them. "I have lost the man I adored more than life itself. You have lost your father. But we are still a family. We stand by one another." She waited for a reaction, but no one said anything. "We will lay Dar to rest in the family plot, with the dignity he deserves. Only after that is done will we find out who shot him, and see that justice is done."

Julio scowled and shifted his weight from one foot to the other, but he did not dispute her.

"Armando, have a casket built, the best our carpenter can make," Juanita directed. "Julio, ride to San Pedro and bring back the undertaker. He can do things with the body that we can not."

"Why me?" Julio objected. "Why not a vaquero?"

Juanita walked over to him and gently cupped his chin. "Because Dar is your father, not theirs. Leave immediately. Bring the undertaker whether he wants to come or not."

"I will tie him and throw him over a horse if I have to," Julio vowed. He turned toward the steps, but stopped when their mother said his name.

"One more thing. Ask around while you are there. Find out if any strangers have passed through San Pedro recently."

"Strangers, mother?"

"Just do as I say." Her dress rustling, Juanita came toward the doorway, but stopped on seeing Trella. "Are you all right, young one?"

"How can you ask that at a time like this?" Trella could not keep her voice from breaking. She was close to breaking herself, and barely able to hold her tears in check.

"I am going to my room to cry myself out," Juanita said. "You would be advised to do the same."

A lump formed in Trella's throat.

"It is not fitting to weep in front of everyone," Juanita continued. "We should indulge our misery in private."

"I will do as I please," Trella said. But she returned to her room, flying on wings of sorrow. Throwing herself onto her bed, she buried her face in the pillows and cried and cried, a torrent of tears that drained her physically and emotionally. Later, spent, she stared at the same sunlit window she had stared at so sleepily earlier, her world turned topsy-turvy.

My father is dead. Trella let the truth of it seep through her. One of the two people who loved her most in the world was gone. He had been a fine father, always treating her kindly, even when she misbehaved. She remembered many a winter's evening when she climbed into his lap and he rocked her to sleep in front of the fireplace, and many a summer's night when they had sat out on the porch contemplating the stars.

Trella would miss him. She had not realized until that instant exactly how much. His had been the strong hand that guided their family. He had been the rock on which they all depended.

More tears came. Trella gave them full release. Afterward, she wiped her nose with her sleeve, not caring if she was a mess. These were special circumstances. She would clean up later.

Trella wondered if Julio was right, if the Circle T was to blame. If so, they must die. All of them. A mental image of Nancy Tovey being shot or hung jarred her. She had always liked Nancy. But if the Toveys were involved, then they had to pay.

Next, Trella considered who would run the DP now that Dar was gone. Steve was the oldest. It would fall on his shoulders. *Or would it?* Trella asked herself. Her mother had never shown much interest in overseeing the day-to-day operations, but that might change. It was not unheard of, a woman running a ranch.

Trella wished Hijino was there. She had not spoken to him since the other night, but she thought about him often, about how handsome he was, and the sound of his voice, how it stirred her. Most vividly of all, she remembered the feel of his lips on hers. She would very much like to feel those lips again.

A soft sound caused Trella to rise on her elbows. She gave a start when her sister unexpectedly sat beside her and put a hand on her shoulder.

"Are you all right, little one?"

"A stupid question," Trella flared. Even at a time like this, Dolores treated her like an infant.

"I ask because I care. We need to talk."

Trella rolled onto her back. Her sister's face was a wreck, streaked by drying tears. Trella almost giggled at how silly Dolores looked. "What about?"

"We must be strong for Mother's sake. She will take this hardest of all of us. You and I must tend to matters she normally would, until she is recovered enough to do them herself."

"Such as?" Trella thought she had some idea, but she wanted to be sure.

"The cooking, the cleaning, the thousand and one things mother oversees. We must take charge of the servants, and not let them disturb her."

"They'd better not," Trella said.

"There will not be time to contact our relatives and friends south of the border and have them attend the funeral. It would take weeks for them to get here. We will be the only support mother has."

"I know that," Trella peevishly responded.

"You must keep Julio under rein. Have him control that temper of his, and not argue with mother so much."

"Why me?"

"You have always been closest to him. He will listen to you where he will not listen to me or his older brothers. Talk to him. Make him promise not to do anything rash. We do not want more blood spilled."

Trella disagreed. "We do if it is the blood of Father's killer. I am with Julio in that."

"Do you truly think the rest of us do not want whoever is responsible to be punished? But we must proceed with care. We must be sure before we act." Dolores bit her lower lip, then said, "Father talked to me before he left. He told me how sad he was over Berto, but that he would not let himself be blinded by anger. He was going to the Circle T to uncover the facts, and he would only act once all the facts were known. We must do the same with his own death. We must not let anger sweep us away."

"I suppose you are right."

Dolores smiled and squeezed Trella's arm. "We have not always gotten along, you and I. We scratch at each other, as sisters will do. But I love you, little one. I love all our brothers, too."

"And I love you," Trella said, although it bothered her that once again her sister had referred to her as "little."

"It is our love that binds us. Our love that will see us through this." Dolores stood. "I go to see if Mother needs me. Make yourself presentable, and instruct the cook to prepare a light meal. No one will have much of an appetite, but our brothers must be hungry after their long ride."

"I will take care of it."

Dolores whisked out. Trella slid her legs off the bed, and moved to the mirror. She recoiled at her reflection. She looked hideous, her face as much a mess as her sister's. Quickly, she tidied herself, and was about to go to the kitchen when light tapping sounded on her windowpane.

Trella brightened like the sun. She dashed over and opened it, and did not resist when Hijino enfolded her in his strong arms.

"Have you missed me, my love?"

"Perhaps," Trella said. Then, more sincerely, "If my brothers catch you, they will shoot you."

"I will only stay a minute. I came to say I am here for you if you need me. You can depend on me for anything. Your slightest wish is mine to carry out."

"I thank you for your concern."

Hijino stroked her hair. "I am sorry about your father. It is most terrible."

The lump returned to Trella's throat.

"Whoever did it must pay with their life. I will kill them for you, sweet one. I will kill them gladly."

Trella coughed, and whispered, "Can I see you to-night? After all the others have gone to bed?"

"Under the willow?"

"No. Here. My bedroom."

Hijino's smile was brighter than ever. "Need you ask? Have I not made it clear? I am yours to command. I will do anything for you, anything at all." He tilted her face up to his. "You can always count on me."

Chapter 15

"Dar Pierce is the best friend we ever had," Nancy Tovey declared.

"No argument there," Kent responded, and refilled his glass. When he thought about how close the two ranches had come to spilling blood, it scared him.

"Isn't that your third Scotch?" Nance asked, with a hint of disapproval. "You're being awfully generous to yourself."

"It's only my second." Kent set her straight. "And for your information, I am celebrating. Our head was in the lion's mouth today, and the lion didn't bite." He sank back into his easy chair and raised the glass in a toast. "To the DP and the Circle T. May they last a thousand years."

"Oh, my," Nancy said. "That will definitely be your last. When you start waxing poetic, I know you have had more than enough."

Kent sighed and took a sip. When it came to liquor, he always bought the most expensive brands. He savored his indulgence, wishing he could do it every night. But Nance had her rules.

"Are you sober enough to focus?"

"Oh, please." Kent disliked it when she nagged, and she nagged often. Little nags and big nags. He supposed there were middling nags, but the distinction was too fine to matter. Nagging was nagging and that was that, and as natural to women as breathing. The thought made him grin.

"What is so humorous?"

"Nothing, dear," Kent said. "Please continue." The subdued light from the parlor lamp cast her features in a softly romantic glow. Or maybe it was the Scotch.

"The question still remains. If Jack Demp did not murder poor Berto, then who did? And why? More to the point, why was a knife exactly like Demp's found near Berto's body?"

"I don't have the answers," Kent admitted. But another possibility occurred to him, one he had not considered until this moment. "What if," he began, and had another sip, "what if someone is out to pit the two ranches against one another?"

"How's that?"

"Put the pieces together. Demp's knife disappears. Berto is killed by a knife exactly like it, with Demp's initials carved into the grips. But Demp swears he didn't carve his initials in his. Where does that lead us?"

Nancy had always been quick-witted. "Whoever killed Berto stole Demp's knife and added the initials as extra insurance that the blame would fall on Demp's shoulders."

"So it appears."

"Oh, my," Nance said, her forehead furrowing.

"That's quite ominous, indeed. It means someone is out to destroy us."

"Us and the Pierces, both," Kent said. "They want us at each other's throats."

"To what end? And who could be so unspeakably vile?"

Kent lowered his glass to his knee, and absently ran a finger around the rim. "As to the purpose, I can only speculate. With us and the Pierces dead, the valley would be ripe for taking. As to who, your guess is as good as mine."

"We have no enemies," Nance noted. "And Dar is one of the most well-respected men in the territory."

"That's true," Kent conceded. To one and all, Dar Pierce was the consummate cattleman. Everyone in San Pedro admired him highly, which was understandable, given that Dar helped build the town. "But someone sure as blazes is out to cause us misery."

"I have faith that Dar will figure it out. He promised to get to the bottom of it, and he's a man of his word."

There were times, Kent mused, when his wife seemed to regard Dar Pierce almost as highly as she did, say, Moses. "I am not without resources of my own. I have already instructed someone to find answers, and I have complete confidence he will."

"Who?"

"John Jesco."

Nance did not exactly frown, but her reaction was close to it. "Why him? Why not Clayburn? Walt is our foreman, after all."

"He's also indispensable to the running of our

ranch. What's wrong with Jesco? It was Walt who
suggested I use him."

"I don't care for Jesco much. He's a killer as much
as a cowboy. The stories they tell cast doubt on his
reliability."

"To the contrary, my dear," Kent said. "Walt says
that Jesco is the most valuable hand we have. All our
men are loyal to the brand, but Jesco has extra worth
precisely because of his reputation."

"Your logic eludes me."

"Every outfit needs someone like Jesco. Someone
with the bark on, as the cowboys like to put it. Someone who will give those who might do the Circle T
harm second thoughts."

"That's hardly worth the lives he has taken," Nance
stated flatly.

Kent resented her attitude. She regarded the taking
of human life, *any* human life, as evil. He could never
make her understand that there existed the human
equivalent of rabid wolves, and those wolves must
be dealt with as any rabid animal would be, with the
finality of death. "Whoever murdered Berto won't
hesitate to kill again. Would you have me give the
job to Timmy? Or Shonsey?"

"Set a killer to catch a killer, is that it?" Nance
gazed out the window. "Do as you want. But don't
expect my approval. Were it up to me, we would not
have someone like Jesco in our employ."

"Dar Pierce has Roman," Kent said, taking pleasure in pricking her conceit.

"Implying that if Dar has a *pistolero* on his payroll,
it's all right for us to do the same? Two wrongs don't
make a right."

"Right and wrong don't enter into it. Survival is the issue. The stronger the Circle T is, the fewer coyotes will nip at our flanks."

"I hear Walt in that remark. Be that as it may, shooting a man dead is heinous, whether done in self-defense or not. Were it up to me, all the guns in the world would be melted down and used to make railroad ties."

Kent could not contain himself. "That has to be the silliest thing you have ever said. Were it not for guns, we wouldn't be here. The Navajos and Apaches would have driven all the whites out. Hell, the Comanches would still own Texas."

"Don't swear. And don't patronize me. We have discussed this before, and nothing you say will change my mind."

That was the devil of it, Kent sourly reflected. Once his wife made up her mind, neither reason nor the Almighty could persuade her to change it. To say she was pigheaded was an understatement. To say it to her face was marital suicide. He prudently changed the subject. "I've asked Walt to call in all our hands from the range. I will inform them what has happened, and require that they be on their best behavior around the men from the DP. With the rodeo coming up, we must take every precaution not to inflame hotheads like Julio."

"That boy has a temper," Nance agreed. "Thank goodness Dar keeps him in line."

"There's more," Kent said. "I've instructed Clayburn to post men at the crossings. Julio might take it into his head to sneak across the river some night and do God knows what." He paused. "I've also given instructions that the men are to go every-where armed."

"Is that really necessary?" Nance asked, in a tone that implied it was not.

"The murderer is still on the loose. I would be remiss if I did not urge the men to be on their guard."

"I suppose," Nance said.

"They must be able to protect themselves if need be. There are times, whether you will admit it or not, when guns serve a purpose."

"Don't be petty. It ill becomes you."

Kent Tovey reached for the bottle.

Judging by the Big Dipper, it was well past mid-night. John Jesco was in a stand of trees at one of the four river crossings Clayburn wanted watched. Wheeler would relieve him at dawn. His back to a cottonwood, a blanket over his shoulders to keep him warm, Jesco sat with his Winchester in his lap, fight-ing drowsiness. Again and again, he snapped his head up and shook himself to stay awake, only to have his eyelids grow leaden and his chin dip to his chest.

Jesco had jerked upright for the umpteenth time, when a sound to the east pricked his ears. The faint drum of hooves, of someone riding toward the Rio Largo from the south. From the DP. Instantly, Jesco was on his feet. There was no earthly reason for someone to be abroad at that time of night. He moved to a grassy bank, where he could hear better. Whoever it was reached the south side to the left of Jesco's position, and the hoofbeats stopped.

Without being aware he was doing it, Jesco held his breath, waiting for the rider to ford. But the night stayed quiet. He peered intently into the darkness, but could not spot anyone. So long as the rider stayed on the other side, there was nothing Jesco could do. Clayburn had been quite specific. Under no circumstances was he to cross over onto the DP.

"Those orders come straight from Mr. Tovey," Clayburn had stressed. "We're not to do anything that might incite them."

Jesco debated whether to cross anyway. He had about decided it was best to do as his boss wanted, when hooves once again thudded. Only this time they were behind him, not in front.

A second rider was coming from the north, from the Circle T. Whoever it was, they were not making for the crossing. They were heading for a spot directly across from where the rider on the south side had stopped.

Jesco threw off his blanket, hastily rolled it up, and tied the roll on his saddle. Quickly forking leather, he reined in the same direction. He held to a walk. They would hear him otherwise.

In his mind's eye, Jesco imagined the two riders meeting secretly. To what end was impossible to say, but simple common sense told him they had to be up to no good.

To Jesco's recollection, the Rio Largo ran fairly straight for the next half mile or so. Up ahead a ways, a spur jutted into the river from the south. The water was shallow, but the spot was not used as a regular crossing because the spur was too narrow and too thickly wooded to funnel cattle through. It was perfect, though, for anyone who wanted to meet secretly.

Jesco had his hand on his Colt. Landmarks were difficult to judge, but presently he was near enough. Drawing rein, he dismounted and cautiously advanced along the water's edge.

Jesco was abreast of the spur, when something moved in the vegetation. Crouching, he braced for the blast of a shot but none came. The source of the movement stepped into view: a riderless horse, its reins dangling, cropping the grass. Whoever had ridden him was in among the trees.

Jesco tried to remember exactly how deep the river was at that point. In the winter and early spring, fed by runoff from the mountains, the depth averaged five feet. The rest of the year, it was barely three.

Sitting, Jesco removed his boots. He left them on the shore and eased into the river. A chill, clammy sensation spread from his feet to his knees as the water level rose. He was halfway across, when the horse raised its head, spotted him, and whinnied.

Jesco drew his revolver. He thought for sure the rider would come running, but no one appeared. He moved faster. Unexpectedly, his left foot came down on a jagged rock lodged in the bottom. Pain seared the sole. Reflexively, he jerked his leg up, and nearly fell. Gritting his teeth, he pressed on.

The horse had turned, and was disappearing into the cottonwoods.

Jesco was careful not to splash. Gradually, the water dropped to his knees, and then his ankles. His socks and the bottoms of his Levi's were soaked. His first step on dry land resulted in a *squish* that was much too loud for his liking. But once again, whoever was in the trees failed to hear him.

Gliding from cover to cover, Jesco had not gone far when muted voices fell on his ears. He did not recognize them, nor could he tell what they were saying. One of the men, though, had the distinct accent of someone born south of the border.

Jesco crept toward them. A pair of silhouettes materialized, darker than the night. One wore a sombrero. That much was obvious. The other was a big man with broad shoulders. A few more yards and Jesco would be close enough to demand they throw down their hardware. It would be easier to shoot them, to say nothing of safer, but Jesco wanted them alive.

Then the one in the sombrero cried out, "Look there, amigo! We have been discovered!"

Muzzle flashes stabbed the dark. Jesco answered, but there were so many trees, the brush so thick, he undoubtedly missed.

A second pistol boomed.

Jesco dived flat. Dirt kicked up by slugs sprayed his face. Hs arm straight, he took deliberate aim. He had the man in the sombrero in his sights when both silhouettes abruptly melted into the undergrowth. They had split up, the one in the sombrero going right, the other left.

Jesco hesitated for a split second, then went right. *Damn, but the man is fast!* he thought, gaining speed. But he forgot he was in his stockinged feet. Down came his foot, and up coursed agony. Whether he had stepped on another rock or something else was irrelevant; it slowed him down. Limping, he snapped off a shot more out of frustration than anything else.

The man in the sombrero did not respond in kind.

The next moment, Jesco lost sight of him. Hooves pounded, and Jesco glimpsed a pale horse, racing south. He snapped the Colt up, but too many trees intervened.

From the vicinity of the river came a loud nicker. Whirling, Jesco ran flat out. He stepped on a downed branch, but he didn't care. He had lost one, and he would be boiled in tar if he would lose the other. But when he burst into the open, the second rider had reached the north bank. Again Jesco went to shoot, only to have his quarry vanish into the night.

"Damn," Jesco said. By the time he crossed and put on his boots and reached his horse, the man would be long gone. But he had learned something important. Someone at the Circle T was in cahoots with someone at the DP. Now all he had to do was figure out who.

Chapter 16

In the lonely hours between midnight and dawn, Juanita Pierce buried her face in her pillow and gave vent to more tears. She missed Dar, missed him so much. A great ache tore at her core, threatening to topple her into the pit of despair.

Juanita could not believe he was dead. They were together thirty years. He had become as much a part of her as her arms or legs. His was the first face she saw every morning; his was the warm body she held close every night. For three decades, she had loved him with a deep and abiding passion. He was more than her husband; he was friend, lover, confidant. Their souls were mutual mirrors. "Kindred spirits," Dar had called it, and she could think of no better way to describe the entwining of their hearts.

Now Dar was gone. Tomorrow, his mortal remains were to be lowered into the ground, and the most vital man she ever met would be gone from her life for good and forever.

Juanita told herself she must be strong. She must not show weakness in front of the children. But it was hard, so unbearably hard, to act as if all was right with the world, when in truth her world had crumbled in emotional ruin and would never be the same.

Lying there, her cheeks slick with tears, Juanita remembered the day Dar came into her life, so tall and handsome and courteous. From the start, she was smitten. Some women from south of the border would never think to take a man from north of the border for a husband. In fact, some in her own family tried to talk her out of it. Scandalous, an aunt informed her, for her to succumb to one of *them*. Her cousin, until then the dearest of friends, flatly stated she was appalled that Juanita would stoop to living with a gringo.

The color of Dar's skin never mattered to Juanita. When she gazed at him, she did not see a *white* man; she saw only *a* man, the man she loved. His race was not a factor. To all the naysayers she had replied, "I do what I have to." She could no more deny her heart than she could stop breathing.

Dar was a devoted husband. His sole purpose in life, he once told her, was to make her happy, and to that end, he laid claim to the fertile grassland to the south of the Rio Largo and built the DP into a prosperous ranch.

"My sweet beloved," Juanita breathed into her pillow. She yearned to have him beside her, to take him in her arms and smother him with kisses. If only it were all a bad dream. If only Dar and Berto were still alive.

Sniffling, Juanita rolled onto her side. She would unravel the mystery of their deaths if it was the last thing she did. She did not believe for a minute that the Circle T was responsible. The Toveys were too decent, too honorable. *To what end?* was the question she always brought up when they were accused. The notion that the Toveys wanted to take over the entire valley was laughable.

But if not them, then who? Juanita had asked herself that a thousand times. Clearly, someone was out to inflame not only her family, but the vaqueros, as well. Seeds of hatred had been planted, and unless something was done, those seeds would result in more violence and more bloodshed.

Juanita suspected an outside influence. Someone was trying to set the two ranches against one another. It was the only possible explanation for the knife found near Berto's body. She saw through the deception, even if some of her own children did not.

Her children. Juanita feared for their safety. Her sons in particular. Logically, they were next on the killer's list. She had asked them to be careful and not go anywhere alone, and although they assured her they would not take unnecessary risks, they had their pride, and would not be coddled.

A sudden gust of wind on Juanita's damp cheek brought her up onto her elbows. The door to the small patio outside her bedroom was open. Many a night, she and Dar had sat out there, she with her head on his chest, sharing their dreams and their love.

Juanita was fairly sure she had closed the door before retiring. Then again, caught up in her grief, she might well have forgotten, and only imagined she had. She slid off the bed, gathered her nightgown about her, and crossed the room to remedy her oversight. One of the heavy curtains rustled.

Juanita wondered if a storm was brewing. She opened the door wider, and peered skyward. Not a cloud to be seen. She started to draw back, and pull the door closed after her.

Belatedly, Juanita saw an arm reach from behind the curtain. She twisted away, but she was too slow. A calloused hand clamped onto her mouth, and she was dragged roughly to the floor. Before she could cry out, metal glinted. Pain exploded in her head. The world faded to gray, and then black.

It was like falling into a bottomless well.

Motion roused her.

Juanita was aware of a swaying movement. She was on her belly, over a horse. Her head hurt abominably, so much so, she could barely think. She was still in her nightclothes, and she was cold. Her wrists pained her. When she tried to move her arms, she discovered they were bound. So were her ankles.

"Do not struggle, *por favor*."

The voice pricked her. Juanita knew that voice, but she had to think before she had a face to go with it. "Hijino," she said.

"*Sí*, Señora Pierce," came the reply. "Your humble servant."

"A humble pig," Juanita rejoined. She turned her head. He was on his white horse, leading the animal that bore her.

Hijino laughed gaily. "Your tongue is as sharp as my knife. But I never take offense at a lady's insults

as I would a man's. Women deserve special consideration."

"Is that what you call this? Special consideration?
What do you think you are doing? Kidnaping me?"

Again Hijino laughed. "You will figure it out soon
enough. When you do, do not blame me. Blame
yourself."

"You talk in riddles. Was it you who killed my
Dar?"

"No. Berto, yes. But not your husband."

Juanita believed him. She tested her wrists and
ankles again. The rope was so tight it dug into her
flesh.

"I told you not to struggle," Hijino reminded her.
"No one has ever slipped a knot of mine."

"You said I was to blame?"

"*Sì*, señora. When you told your son to ask around
in San Pedro about strangers, I knew you suspected
the truth. You had to be dealt with, I am afraid."

Fear stirred within her, but Juanita smothered it
by force of will. "You would not dare. Murdering
men is one thing. Murdering a woman is another."

"Not to the murderer. Killing a woman is no different than killing a man. But you have a point. Others see it differently. To them, killing a woman is the
worst offense of all."

"Second worst. The worst is killing a child."

"I have done that, too, señora. But I always make
it quick. They do not suffer. Nor will you suffer.
Much."

Juanita's mouth went dry.

"Out of respect for your daughter, I will grant you
that boon."

"My daughter? Dolores?"

"Oh, please. She would not permit a vaquero to touch her. No, it is sweet, young Trella. Last night she gave herself to me. Completely. Of her own free will." Hijino smacked his lips. "She is a delight. So innocent, yet so wild. Does she take after you in that regard?"

Juanita cursed him. She used words she had heard, but never used. When she paused for breath, he fed her anger by laughing.

"You sound like my mother. She had a mouth. She could swear better than anyone in our village. Outdrink anyone, too."

Clutching at a straw, Juanita asked, "What would she say if she knew what you plan to do with me?"

"She can not say anything. I killed her long ago."

Juanita had heard of men like him. They plagued the frontier. South of the border they were called bandidos. North of the border they were called outlaws. Whatever they were called, they had certain traits in common: no respect whatsoever for human life, or for another's property. They lived as they pleased, accountable to no one. Most lived short, violent lives that ended at the end of the rope, or by a bullet through a vital organ. The wild ones. The reckless ones. The ones Dar has shielded her from. She missed him now more than ever.

"Nothing to say, señora? Did I shock you?"

"Don't flatter yourself," Juanita said. "I am not a child like Trella. I am not swayed by swagger and deceit." She arched her back to raise her head as far as she could. In vain, she searched for the lights of the ranch, or a campfire.

Hijino divined her purpose. "We are alone. You can scream if you want. No one will hear you."

"How did you spirit me away without anyone noticing?"

"It was easy," Hijino said. "All the vaqueros were asleep. Your house was dark. I had the horses waiting nearby."

"What do you hope to accomplish?"

"Need you ask? You are not stupid. With my share, I will live like a prince. Or maybe go to Spain. I have always wanted to visit Madrid."

The absurdity of her plight impressed itself on Juanita. Here she was, calmly talking to a man who in a very short while was going to murder her. "What if I pay you to let me go?"

"Do not insult me."

"I am serious. How much would it take? Five thousand dollars? Ten thousand dollars? I give you my word you will be permitted to leave in peace."

Hijino slowed, and tugged on the lead rope so the spare horse came up alongside his white one. "Ten times that amount would not be enough. The men I am with, they would do things to me that would sicken you if I betrayed them."

Juanita was desperate. "What if I offer to protect you?"

"You are too kind. And silly to think your vaqueros are a match for those I ride with." Hijino shook his head. "No. We must see this through, you and I. Try to be brave. We will be at the river soon." He gigged his horse.

Juanita realized she must have been unconscious longer than she thought. She began twisting her wrists as much as the rope allowed. For minutes on end she kept at it, not caring how much it hurt, or how much she bled. Her life was at stake. She must not give up.

Hijino began whistling. He glanced back only once to say, "I will take care of Trella myself when the time comes. She will not suffer. This I promise."

"Bastard," Juanita said. Her wrists throbbed with torment. She twisted and twisted and twisted some more, and now she could move her wrists half an inch. But it was not enough.

"They will wonder what became of you," Hijino said. "Julio will blame the gringos from the Circle T. He will have no proof, but he will blame them anyway. With you gone, Steve and Armando will not be able to stop Julio from doing as he has wanted to do since Berto died. Julio will attack the Circle T. They will attack the DP. On and on it will go until there are few left on either side."

"You have it all worked out."

"Not me, señora. A man named Saber. Perhaps you have heard the stories they tell of him? Compared to Saber, I am a saint."

The rope bit so deep into Juanita's right wrist, she grit her teeth to keep from crying out. Her forearms were slick with blood. She wrenched her right wrist to one side, then back again, and was elated when the rope slackened enough for her to slide her hands out. Fearing he had noticed, she glanced at Hijino. He was gazing to the north, whistling again.

Now came the hard part. Juanita could not straddle the horse with her ankles tied. But she had ridden sidesaddle often enough. Could her horse outrun the white one? She was about to find out. Shifting, she slowly slid onto his hips and gripped her mount's mane. Balancing carefully, she swung her legs over one side. The horse's head came up, but thankfully he did not nicker.

Hijino was holding the reins loosely in his hand, his sombrero pushed back on his head.

Juanita tensed. She would have one chance and one chance only. Easing forward, she reached for the reins.

"I think I smell water, señora. It will not be long."

Now! Juanita yanked with all her might. Simultaneously, she slapped her legs against her mount. The animal performed superbly. It bounded past the white horse, its momentum enough to tear the reins from Hijino's grasp. Another second, and she raced away into the night.

"Stop!" Hijino cried.

Juanita bent low, in case he shot at her. She realized she was heading north, and immediately reined to the east to loop back toward the rancho. The horse was a swift one. Hijino's doing, no doubt, in order to elude possible pursuit. She glanced over her shoulder. He was after her, lashing the white madly.

· Juanita lashed her animal. Her hair was whipped by the wind, her nightclothes, too. The thunder of her mount's hooves was music to her ears. The seconds became minutes. When next she looked back, the white had not gained.

I can do it! Juanita inwardly bubbled with glee. She covered fifty more yards. A hundred. Then, without warning, her mount stumbled and pitched toward the earth. She heard the *crack* of a leg bone as she went sailing over its neck. Too late, she flung out her arms. The ground rushed to meet her head. There was another *crack*, only louder. She came to rest on her back, the breath knocked out of her. Panic-stricken, she tried to jump up and run, but her body would not obey. The stars dimmed. A blurred moon hovered above her, and spoke.

"Can you hear me, señora? You have broken your neck. I was going to drown you, but this works out better, I think. Yes, much better."

Juanita wished she could scratch out his eyes. Once again, the world faded to blackness, and her last thought, before the void swallowed her, was that soon she would see Dar again.

Chapter 17

Nancy Tovey could not sleep. She tossed and turned and turned and tossed, and finally, afraid she would wake Kent, she got up, donned her robe, and padded to the kitchen in her bare feet to make coffee.

Nance was troubled. Dar had assured them he did not hold the Circle T responsible for Berto's death. But after her talk with Kent earlier, she was not certain that was enough. Someone had tried to point the finger of blame at their ranch by leaving that knife near the body. The question she could not answer, the question that caused her to toss and turn, was simply: *Who?*

To Nance's knowledge, they did not have any enemies. Kent was always fair in his business dealings. He never cheated anyone, never inflated a tally when he sold cattle. He had never clashed with other ranchers over water or land. Dar and he got along wonderfully.

Nance put a coffeepot on to brew. On the counter was a sheet of paper on which she listed items they needed the next time she visited San Pedro. Now she took the sheet and a pencil to the kitchen table, and sat in her usual chair. Tapping the pencil against her chin, she mulled the question that burned in her brain. As she saw it, there were two possibilities. The culprit was someone they knew, or an outsider. Since she could not think of anything an outsider stood to gain, she concentrated on the former.

Is there anyone, Nance asked herself, *who has ever shown the least little hostility toward Kent and me, or the Circle T in general?* She thought and thought and tapped and tapped, and was stumped. Years ago, Kent had fired a cowboy for being lazy, but that was hardly an excuse for the cowboy to come back and kill Berto. There was no one else.

Could it be someone with a grudge against one of their hands? Nance had not considered that before, and it intrigued her. The men went into San Pedro regularly to drink and carouse. But they were never in any fights of which she was aware, and with one exception, they had not been in any shooting affrays.

That exception was Jesco.

Nance's dislike of the man brought a flush of anger. Were it up to her, she would boot him off the Circle T. But Kent would never stand for it. He was too fond of the man. That nonsense about Jesco's reputation somehow helping to safeguard the Circle T was preposterous. It hadn't scared off whoever slew Berto.

Nance was about to write Jesco's name on the paper, but hesitated. Surely, anyone out for revenge on him would not slay the foreman of the DP instead. And why frame Jack Demp and not Jesco himself?

Nance shook her head in exasperation. All this thinking was getting her nowhere. She was stumped. She had never heard a single soul speak ill of the Circle T, never witnessed anyone express the least little resentment toward—

Suddenly Nance sat straighter, her entire body pulsing. There *was* someone! Someone she had overlooked because she always considered him a friend. But now she recalled the savage spite on his face when he spat out, "All you gringos stick together!"

Julio. Nancy wrote his name at the top of the sheet. Yes, now that she thought about it, Julio had always been the least friendly of the Pierces. At the rodeo last year, he got into a heated argument with two Circle T punchers over a trifle—something to do with a dispute over who should have won the calf-roping event.

Going back further, Nance remembered comments Julio had dropped. There was the time Dar and Juanita invited Kent and her to spend a weekend at their rancho. During supper, after Dar asked Kent how things were going at the Circle T, Julio remarked how fortunate it was that his father had allowed Kent to lay claim to the north half of the valley. "Had it been me," Julio said, "I would want the whole valley for myself."

Nance had not thought much of it at the time. Julio was young and brash, and those his age did not always keep a lid on their tongues. Now, in hindsight, his resentment of the Circle T was much more apparent.

Nance circled the name, and after it wrote, *Why did I not see it sooner?* Pleased to be making some progress, she underlined the question three times. Then her bubble burst. Julio would never kill Berto.

They were the best of friends. With her own eyes, she had seen that Berto was more like an affectionate uncle than a foreman.

About to cross off Julio's name, Nance smelled the coffee, and put the pencil down and stood. Cups and saucers were in a cupboard next to the pantry. She was reaching for one when something scratched lightly at the kitchen door.

Nance turned. It had to be Crackers, her cat. With all that had happened, she had forgotten about him. Crackers was a yellow tabby she raised from a kitten, pampering it so much, Kent liked to joke that Crackers was the child they never had. It amused him more than it amused her. She had always wanted children. They'd tried and tried, and ultimately went to a doctor. But the doctor could find nothing wrong with either of them. "Sometimes it's not meant to be," was his less-than-encouraging opinion.

The scratching came again.

Smiling, Nancy went to the door and opened it. "Crackers, you scamp. Where have you been?" She blinked in surprise. The cat was not there. "Crackers?" She looked right, then left, then took several steps, the chill night air on her feet bringing goosebumps to her skin. "Crackers? Where are you?"

The cat had an independent streak, and would sometimes stay away for days at a time, haunting the stable and other buildings in search of mice. The punchers treated it to milk, and even grumpy old Shonsey was always feeding it scraps.

"Crackers?" Nance took another step. She sensed rather than heard swift movement behind her, and was startled out of her wits when an iron arm encircled her waist, and a firm hand clamped over her mouth. The next instant, she was being carried away from the house.

I'm being abducted! Nance began to struggle, but whoever had hold of her shook her, hard, and hissed in her ear.

"Be still, or I'll slit your throat!"

Raw fright froze the blood in Nancy's veins. The man who murdered Berto now had her. It had to be him.

Every instinct Nance possessed screamed at her to resist, to claw and bite and kick until the hand came loose and she could scream. A couple of screams would do it. Kent was bound to hear. Their bedroom window was cracked open. The punchers would hear, too, and come on the run. They liked her. They would not let anything happen to her. But as if the man were privy to her thoughts, he shook her again.

"I mean it! Let out a peep and you're dead!"

Nance believed him. She did not resist. He was practically running now, her weight no more hindrance than an empty flour sack. Large shapes hove out of the dark. Two horses were waiting.

The man roughly lowered her to the ground, and growled, "Put your hands behind you."

Nance did as he instructed. Within seconds, he'd bound her. He pulled on her hair, lifting her face. Something brushed her nose, then wrapped around her mouth. His bandana, she guessed. He tied it at the back. Gripping her shoulders, he rolled her over. She recognized him: It was the new hand, Dunn. He seemed gigantic looming above her. "Try to escape, and you die."

Nance winced as he hauled her erect. His fingers were spikes in her arms. He heaved her onto one of the horses, and she straddled it. He took the reins, and climbed on the other horse.

They started off. Nance glanced toward the house. If only Kent would wake up! If only he would wonder where she got to, and look for her. She glanced toward the bunkhouse. Maybe one of the cowboys would wake up and need to use the outhouse. But no one did, and soon the house and the bunkhouse and the rest of the buildings were swallowed by the murk.

Nance wrestled with fear. She must not lose control. Her hands were bound, but her legs were free. That was something.

She considered working the bandana loose and screaming. But they were already far enough from the house that no one would hear her, and Dunn would be furious. No, she would rely on her legs, not her lungs.

Dunn brought the animals to a canter. He was in a hurry to get away, but not in so much of one that he would risk exhausting the horses. He had not looked back since they started out.

The tall grass swished to their passage. Nance was glad for the grass. It would cushion her. She might break an arm or a shoulder, but that hardly mattered compared to what Dunn had in store.

Nance leaned to the right, as low as she could go without losing her balance. The grass was so close she could smell it. *Please, God!* she prayed, and pushing clear, she dropped. The horse cantered on. She hit, but not as hard as she expected. Her shoulder absorbed the brunt, the pain fleeting. Then she was up in a crouch.

Her unwitting captor had not slowed.

Whirling, Nance ran back the way they came. She was not young anymore, but she was in good shape for her age. Several times a week, she took long walks. Walking wasn't as strenuous as running, but she could move swiftly when she needed to. She fairly flew, her long legs flashing.

Nance would start shouting the instant she saw the buildings. The punchers always left the bunkhouse windows open. They would rush to her rescue. As for Dunn, she would have Kent send men to track him down and bring him back. Alive if they could. He had the answers they needed. Dunn might refuse to talk, but there were ways. Jesco would make him. Nance grinned at her hypocrisy.

The thud of hooves rekindled her fear.

Angling left, Nance sprinted a short way, and dived prone. She was none too soon. The hoofbeats grew louder. Out of the night swept Dunn, the spare horse in tow, but he was thirty or forty feet away, and did not spot her.

Nance was thankful for the moonless vault of sky. The dark and the grass were her allies. They hid her. She waited until the hoofbeats faded, then she was up and running. She remembered that rattlesnakes did most of their hunting at night. Or she might step into a hole or a rut. Each stride became an exercise in anxiety. She kept her gaze on the ground. Because of that, she did not see the horses blocking her way until she nearly collided with them.

"Bitch."

A boot caught Nance across the temple. She staggered, but would have stayed on her feet had Dunn not kicked her again. She fell hard, dazed and distraught.

"I should kill you here and now," Dunn snarled. "But Saber wants it done a certain way."

Nance barely heard him over the roaring in her head. She pushed to her knees, but was overcome by weakness, and her forehead sank to the ground.

"Get up, damn you," Dunn commanded.

Nance stayed where she was.

"I won't tell you again, Mrs. Tovey. Rile me and you'll regret it. Do as I say, and it will be a little easier."

"If you intend to kill me, shoot me and be done with it." Nance was praying her head would clear.

"Don't think I wouldn't," Dunn said. "But gunshots carry a long way at night. And as I just told you, Saber is particular about how I'm to do it."

That name again. "Who?" Nance asked, buying precious seconds. The pain was still too much to cope with.

"Never mind. On your feet."

"I feel sick. You about kicked my head in."

"You'll feel a lot worse if you don't do exactly the hell what I tell you to do. Now get up, damn you."

Nance rose partway. She wanted to cradle her head in her hands, but couldn't. "I tell you, I'm going to be sick."

"You're still breathin'," Dunn said. He jabbed a thumb at the spare horse. "Climb on."

"With my hands tied?" Nance snapped. "Be sensible, will you?" She had an idea. "Give me a boost."

Dunn swore. His saddle creaked as he dismounted

and let the reins drop. "Women are next to worthless." He placed a hand on her shoulder.

Nance deliberately sagged against him so she could mentally mark the spot on his pants. She must not make a mistake.

"Stand up," Dunn commanded, and hauled on her arm. "I don't have all night for this."

"That's too bad," Nance said, and drove her knee into his groin. He doubled over, gurgling and grunting, and Nance once again sought the sanctuary of the encompassing darkness. Dunn clutched at her nightclothes, but could not hold on. She forgot about the rattlers and the holes and sped like an antelope for her life.

Nance figured she had a minute, maybe two, before he was after her. Since he expected her to make straight for the ranch buildings, she veered to the west. She listened for hoofbeats but did not hear any.

Nance smiled. She had done it.

Then the staccato smack of churning boots burst her bubble of hope.

Incredulous, Nance glanced back.

Dunn was ten yards behind her. His high-heeled boots were not made for running, and he looked for all the world like a drunk weaving from too much alcohol. But he was gaining, and he had his Colt in his hand.

"No!" The cry was torn unbidden from Nance's throat. She tried to go faster, but her body was at its limit. She changed direction, toward the house and her husband. In doing so, she inadvertently enabled Dunn to overtake her. All he had to do was cut off the angle.

Nance cried out as fingers locked in her hair. She was wrenched into the air and slammed onto her back. "All right!" she breathlessly declared. "I give up."

Dunn reared over her. He arced the Colt on high. "Too late," he snarled. "You had two chances. You don't get a third."

The Colt descended. Nancy Tovey attempted to twist aside, but the hand in her hair held her fast. He struck again and again and again. The *crunch crunch crunch* of metal on bone rang in her ears. But it was not the last sound she heard. The last was her whimper.

Chapter 18

Steve Pierce had lived what he liked to think of as an ordinary life. He had been born and raised on a ranch, so it was only natural that he lived, breathed, and ate ranching. He loved everything about being a rancher. The work agreed with him. Up at the crack of dawn, a hearty breakfast with his family, then busy, busy, busy all day, until sunset or beyond, when he would ride wearily home to supper. Then an hour or two of talk with his parents and siblings, and then early to bed in order to be early to rise. That had been his routine for as long as he could remember.

Then everything was shot to hell. Berto, dead. His father, dead. By rights, as the oldest, the running of the ranch should fall on his shoulders. He had been groomed for it since childhood, and should have no qualms about taking over. But he did. Secretly, he worried he was not up to handling the crisis they faced. So he was tremendously happy when his mother assumed the mantle. Her calm self-possession was reassuring to the rest of them, but especially to him.

But now the worst that could happen, had happened. Steve could still not quite believe it, hours after they discovered his mother was missing. His sisters were frantic. Armando was so upset he had withdrawn into a shell, like a turtle, and would not speak unless spoken to. As for Julio, he was nearly rabid, a boiling cauldron of seething emotions he made no attempt to hold in check.

It was close to noon.

Steve stood on the porch in the shade of the overhang, anxiously scouring the range from end to end. He had sent everyone who could ride a horse out to search. The vaqueros, most of the servants, his brothers and Dolores, had all been out since early morning. He wanted to go, too, but someone had to stay.

Steve squinted at the sun, then balled his hands into fists, the nails biting into his palms. They had to find her. They *had* to. She would be alive and unhurt, with a perfectly logical reason for why she had disappeared. She would continue to oversee the ranch, continue to make the important decisions he was glad not to have to make. Not decisions involving the everyday operation of the ranch. Steve could handle those. He knew cows better than anyone. Everything about them. From calving to branding, from roundups to driving herds to market, he was an expert.

No, the decisions Steve wanted nothing to do with, the decisions he feared, had to do with what to do about the murders. Julio and many of the vaqueros thirsted for revenge. They blamed the Toveys, and wanted to ride to the Circle T. What they would do when they got there was not entirely clear. They could not very well gun the Toveys down without proof the Toveys were involved. They still believed Jack Demp was to blame for Berto, and there had been dark muttering about treating Demp to a strangulation jig.

Steve was as upset as anyone about the deaths. But he had sided with his father, then his mother, in advocating that they proceed with care and caution. The last thing Steve wanted was to spill innocent blood. Julio was almost at the point of not caring so long as he had his vengeance, and once Julio reached that point, Steve wondered if anyone could hold him back.

Just then, the door opened and closed. Steve did not look around. "It is better if you stay in your room. I told you I would send for you when I have news."

Trella came over, her arms clasped to her bosom, the dry tracks of tears on her cheeks. "I will go loco if I stay in there by myself any longer. I need someone to talk to."

"You can talk to me, but I don't know what good I will be." Steve always felt uncomfortable around women, even his sisters. They did not think or act like men. He could never predict what they would say or do. He preferred cows, predictable creatures if ever there were any.

"This is a nightmare," Trella said. "A nightmare that gets worse each day."

Steve could not agree more.

"Who will be next? You? Me? Armando? Dolores? Someone is out to kill us. Each and every one of us."

"We don't know that," Steve said.

Trella spun on him. "What will it take to convince you? How many of us must die before you face the truth?"

"I wish we knew what the truth really was."

"It is obvious. Someone wants our rancho, and they will stop at nothing to get their hands on it."

"Who?"

"Who else but the Toveys? They are not content with half the valley. They want all of it. Unless they are stopped, by the end of the month there will not be any of our family left."

"You sound like Julio." Steve had hoped she would be more sensible.

"What is wrong with that? He is willing to stand up to them. To stop the killing, and protect what is ours."

"He would paint the valley red with blood." A prospect that horrified Steve. His father had taught him that the taking of a life was not something done lightly, and his father should know.

"Again, what is wrong with that, if it is not our blood?" Trella countered. "Are you going to twiddle your thumbs and do nothing while the Circle T takes us over? Have you forgotten they outnumber us? Hijino says we must strike before they do."

"Who?" Steve was distracted by tendrils of dust to the south.

"One of our vaqueros. You know him. The one who rides the fine white horse, and is fond of silver."

Something in her voice drew Steve's gaze from the dust. She was smiling sweetly, and it occurred to him that it was the first time all morning she had smiled like that. Her eyes were aglow, too, with a peculiar inner light. It puzzled him. His mother had often had the same look when she held his father's hand and strolled with him in the garden. The realization jolted him. *My little sister and a vaquero?* What would their mother say? What should *he* say?

Fortunately, Steve was spared from having to say anything by the approaching dust cloud. Trella had noticed, too.

"Someone returns in a hurry. I pray they have found her, and she is safe."

"That makes two of us." Steve dreaded the alternative. He would become the true head of the family, with all the responsibilities it entailed.

"If anything has happened to her . . ." Trella did not finish. Tears moistened her eyes, and she dabbed at them with a sleeve.

"No one would harm a woman," Steve said. It was the straw at which he clutched. Even on the frontier, there were things men just did not do. Steal, yes. Swindle, yes. Rustle, yes. Kill, yes. But never, ever hurt a woman. It was considered so vile, widespread outrage inevitably resulted in swift punishment.

"Apaches and Comanches do it all the time."

"That's different," Steve said. He counted seven riders. They must have found something. He had given orders that no one was to return before nightfall otherwise.

"You must be strong, Steve," Trella said. "Do what must be done for the good of the rancho."

"What makes you think I will not?" Steve responded, a trifle defensively.

"I know you. I know how you think. You will not act until you have all the facts. But sometimes that is not possible. Sometimes we must act on our feelings."

"You would have me be like Julio, and think only of getting revenge?" Steve shook his head. "I will do as our father would do. He always said to think before we act. To be reasonable in all we do."

"And where did his thinking and his reason get him? I loved him as much as you, so when I say he was not as strong as he should be, I say it out of my affection for him."

Steve had never struck his sisters, but he came close to slapping Trella. "You call that affection? Insulting the memory of him?"

"You know yourself that he was much too considerate of others, at our expense. Look at the Circle T. Those gringos had no right to that land. Father should have driven them off before they built their house. By any means necessary."

"I have never heard you use that word before."

"Which word? Gringo? Just because I have not spoken it does not mean I have not thought it. Besides, they call us greasers, don't they?"

Steve was shocked by her expression. It was a mask of hate. "Kent and Nancy Tovey have never called us that. They have always treated our family with the utmost respect."

"Hijino says all gringos do that. They smile and extend one hand in friendship while with their other hand they stab you in the back."

"I must have a talk with this Hijino."

Concern replaced her hate. "What for? He is my friend. Don't you dare say anything to him. I do not meddle in your personal life, do I?"

"With father gone, I have an obligation to look after you. To protect you. To see you are not taken advantage of."

Trella put her hands on her hips. "I am perfectly able to take care of myself. Just because I am the youngest does not make me a fool. I am offended. You will apologize this instant."

"I am sorry you are upset," Steve said, "but I will still talk to him. He must not get any ideas about you."

"What does *that* mean? I can spend time with whomever I want, whenever I want, and if I chose to spend some of it with him, there is nothing you can do about it."

"We shall see."

The seven riders were near the outbuildings. Dolores was at the forefront, distinct by her dress and her quirt. At her side rode Armando. The rest were vaqueros, Roman and Paco among them. They were so closely bunched that they had passed the stable before Steve realized his brother was leading an eighth animal, and that draped over it was a slender form wrapped in a blanket. The size and the shape left no doubt.

"Dear God," Steve breathed.

Trella dashed to meet them, crying, "No! No! No! No! No!" As Armando brought the horse to a stop, she flung herself at the blanket and began sobbing.

"We found her," Dolores said sorrowfully. "Or Roman did, and fired three shots into the air."

Armando slid his sombrero off his head and onto his back, so that it hung by its chinstrap. "The rest are still out searching. I sent Paco to find Julio."

Steve stopped a few feet from the body. He could not bring himself to touch it. Not yet. "How did she die?"

"In a fall would be my guess. I am no doctor, but I think her neck is broken," Armando revealed. "We also found a dead horse. Its leg was broken, and its throat had been cut."

"Was the horse one of ours?"

"*Sí.* The sorrel we bought from the Circle T a year ago."

Sniffling, Trella raised her grief-stricken face. "The Circle T again! What more proof do we need?"

It had to be a coincidence, Steve told himself. "You are being silly."

"No more so than you! You are blind to what is happening, and your blindness will get the rest of us killed." Trella burst into more tears, her face pressed to the still form.

Steve opened his mouth to dispute her, but closed it again at a gesture from Dolores. He helped Dolores down. Together with Armando, he carried the body into the parlor and gently laid it on the settee. Trella trailed after, weeping. No sooner did they step back than Trella threw herself on their mother again, bawling uncontrollably.

At a gesture from Dolores, the three of them quietly moved into the hall.

"She is hysterical," Dolores whispered so their sister would not hear. "I do not blame her. I cried the whole way here. For the moment I am out of tears."

"Who did it?" Steve was struggling to contain his own grief until later, when he could be alone. Men did not weep in front of others. It simply was not done.

Armando sagged against the wall, his shoulders sagging. "Would that I could tell you, *mi hermano*. We know there was another horse and rider. I instructed Carlos to backtrack them. He is one of our best trackers. If they lead to the Circle T, there will be no holding Julio back."

"There will be no holding him back anyway," Dolores said. "He is beside himself. I have never seen him so mad. Once he hears we have found her body, he will go berserk."

"Maybe I should not have sent Paco to tell him," Armando said.

"What's done is done." Steve's own emotions were in a whirl, and it was all he could do to concentrate. *My father and mother, both gone.* The weight of the ranch bore down on his shoulders with crushing effect.

"The important thing now," Dolores said, "is to keep our heads, and not do anything rash. We must find out who has done this terrible thing, and punish them, and we must do it quickly."

"I agree," Armando said.

Dolores stared at the settee. "First we bury mother and father. Next to each other, as they would have wanted."

Steve nodded. "Out of respect, everyone on the rancho will attend. I will call in every last vaquero."

"What about outsiders?" Armando asked. "Friends from San Pedro?" He paused. "And the Toveys?"

"Under the circumstances," Dolores said, "inviting

Kent and Nancy would be like waving a red cape in front of a bull's nose. Julio would shoot them the moment he set eyes on them."

"I reckon they will understand," Steve remarked. "Once we have it all sorted out—" He broke off as boots thudded on the porch, and someone knocked loudly and urgently on the front door.

"What now?" Dolores wondered aloud.

Paco had his sombrero in hand, and was wringing the brim. "It is terrible, *patrón*. Most terrible," he said the moment Steve opened the door. "I found Julio and told him about Señora Pierce, as Armando told me to."

"And?" Steve feared the answer.

"I regret to report, *patrón*, that Julio and five vaqueros have gone to kill the Toveys."

Chapter 19

Timmy Loring was keeping watch at the middle crossing when he heard riders in the distance. He sat with his back to a tree, a blade of grass between his teeth, daydreaming about a certain dove in San Pedro who had caught his fancy. Her name was Betsy. She had been at the saloon eight months now, and he still had not mustered the courage to speak to her.

Betsy was short, not much over five feet, but exquisitely shaped. Timmy particularly liked how her legs swished against her dress. He could sit and stare at those legs for hours, and usually did, from a corner table where no one would notice.

Jesco had noticed, though. Jesco noticed everything. He had not teased Timmy about it, as some of the other punchers would. He had merely asked if Timmy was in love with the girl.

That gave Timmy pause. He was not quite sure if he was in love or in lust. Lust he savvied. It was a powerful hankering to have a female under the sheets. Something Timmy had never done, although he'd had the hankering many a time. As for love, now there was a mystery. Maybe Timmy was in love and didn't know it, having never known what it was to actually be in love. Love or lust, either way, Timmy could not stop daydreaming about sweet little Betsy and those wonderful legs of hers that swished so exquisitely.

At the rumble of hooves, Timmy sprang to his feet, his hand dropping to his revolver. It took a few seconds for him to realize the riders were not approaching the Rio Largo from the DP side, but were coming from the Circle T.

Timmy stepped from the trees to see who it was, and promptly stepped back under cover again. Jesco had warned him not to take chances. "Never take anything for granted," were Jesco's exact words. So Timmy figured he better stay hidden until he was sure it was safe.

Timmy would never admit it, but the business with the DP had him spooked. He had never killed anyone. Hell, he had never even shot anyone. Nor, he was surprised to discover, did he really want to. All this time, he had been dogging Jesco like Jesco's shadow, thinking that he wanted to be just like him, thinking it would be the greatest thing in the world to have a reputation like his. But now, with the talk in the bunkhouse of more violence on the horizon, Timmy found that he was not as keen on killing as he thought. It was one thing to imagine gunning down hordes of outlaws, it was another to squeeze the trigger and slay another human being.

Timmy hoped it would not come to that. The latest word, though, was that Dar Pierce had been shot, and that the DP's vaqueros were blaming the Circle

T. Dunn had heard the news from a friendly vaquero, and told everyone. Timmy had been there, and happened to be looking at Jesco when Dunn broke the news. Jesco had the strangest expression. Only for a few seconds, and only Timmy noticed. He had intended to ask Jesco about it, but forgot.

The riders appeared. Two, hell-bent for the crossing. Timmy could not tell who they were yet; they were too far off.

The smooth grips of his six-gun reassured Timmy. He glanced down. He had been practicing for months now. Jesco had taught him to how draw, taught him how he should empty his mind and let his body take over, and cock the hammer as he cleared leather. Jesco warned him not to try to be fancy and shoot from the hip like Jesco did, because he did not have Jesco's years of practice.

"Bring your arm straight up, take quick aim, and shoot. It will take you an extra split second," Jesco had said, "but that split second can mean the difference between breathin' air and breathin' dirt."

Jesco sure had a pretty way of putting things.

Timmy looked up, and relaxed. The two riders were Jeb Wheeler and Ray Ornley. Older, dependable hands. Ray occasionally teased Timmy about his age, but the teasing was generally harmless. Wheeler never teased anyone. Wheeler was always serious about everything. They drew rein in a flurry of dust motes.

Timmy walked into the open again, and grinned. "Where are you gents off to? San Pedro?"

"No, you infant," Ray said. "We're here to fetch you."

"But I'm supposed to keep watch until tonight," Timmy said. "Clayburn himself told me."

"The big sugar is callin' everyone in," Wheeler said, and grew even more somber than was usual. "Brace yourself, boy. We bring bad news."

Timmy tried to think of what could be worse than Dar Pierce being shot. He had always liked Mr. Pierce. "How bad can it be?"

"Nancy Tovey is dead."

Stunned, Timmy could only gape.

"She was beat to death," Wheeler related. "Had her face caved in. The son of a bitch took her right out of the house in the middle of the night."

Timmy found his voice. "God in heaven!" It simply could not be. No one ever killed a woman. Ever.

"The boss cried for hours," Ray said. "We all heard him, clear over to the bunkhouse. But we don't blame him. We'd have done the same, I reckon."

Wheeler took up the account. "Then he came out and hollered for Clayburn, and damn, Mr. Tovey was mad. He knows who did it. He found a clue in the kitchen."

"A clue?" Timmy bleated.

Wheeler nodded. "Mrs. Tovey had time to write the name of her killer on a sheet of paper. Maybe she saw him through a window. Or maybe she was at the table when he came in through the door."

"However it was," Ray said, "we know who to string up."

"Who?"

Wheeler and Ray looked at one another, and Wheeler said through clenched teeth, "Julio Pierce."

Timmy's blood chilled. That cut it. There would be

hell to pay. Gallons and gallons of hell, and all the gallons were red.

"The boss is gatherin' everyone up," Wheeler said. "Every last puncher. They should all be in by tonight."

"Tomorrow we ride for the DP," Ray said. "Heaven help them if they try to stop us."

Wheeler nodded. "He'll demand they turn Julio over. If they don't, well, that's just too bad. There are more of us than there are of them, and Mr. Tovey isn't about to take no for an answer."

"Fetch your horse," Ray said.

Timmy hurried into the trees. He had the reins in hand and was about to lead his mount from the shadows when Jeb Wheeler hissed, "Stay under cover, boy! Don't say or do anything, you hear me?"

More riders were approaching. Only this time they were coming from across the river.

Timmy's mouth went dry. He counted six. They came to the crossing and splashed across the Rio Largo. He did not understand why Wheeler and Ray just sat there. The three of them should ride to the ranch for help.

Jeb Wheeler held up a hand and announced, "That's far enough."

Shock spiked through Timmy. One of the six was Julio Pierce. He almost drew and squeezed off a shot, but Wheeler had instructed him not to do anything. He did not know any of the vaqueros. One gleamed with silver everywhere.

"Let us pass," Julio said. He and the others had spread out, the one with the silver on the right, nearest the trees.

"Like hell," Ray Ornley spat.

"You have your nerve, comin' here like this," Jeb Wheeler said. "She was as fine a woman as ever lived."

Julio acted perplexed. "If you are talking about my mother, *sí*, she was. She is the reason I am here."

Now it was Wheeler who was confused. "Your mother? What does she have to do with anything? We're talkin' about Nancy Tovey."

"You murderin' bastard," Ray snarled.

"What?" Julio's surprise seemed genuine. "Are you saying Nancy Tovey has been killed?"

Timmy was as confounded as everyone else. He was amazed none of the vaqueros had spotted him but they were focused on Jeb and Ray.

"Out of our way, gringos." The man with all the silver was leaning on his saddle horn. A pearl-handled Colt glistened in his holster. "We are after those responsible for the death of Juanita Pierce."

"She's dead, too?" Wheeler exclaimed.

Ray Ornley pointed at Julio. "First things first. We know you beat Mrs. Tovey to death, you son of a bitch."

"Me?" Julio blurted.

"Don't listen to them, *patrón*," the one with the silver said. "They seek to confuse you. Think only of your mother and your father. Kent Tovey and the Circle T have much to answer for."

Wheeler's hand was on his revolver. "Are you accusin' Mr. Tovey of murderin' Juanita Pierce? Why, that's plumb crazy."

Julio snapped out of his befuddlement. "That is exactly what I am doing. First Berto, then my father, now my mother. Your intent is plain."

"Mister, we don't know what in hell you're jab-berin' about," Ray Ornley said. "We had nothin' to do with your ma and pa dyin'."

The vaquero wearing the silver smiled. "You lie."

"We'll let Mr. Tovey get to the bottom of this," Jeb Wheeler said. "Shed your hardware. We're takin' you to the Circle T."

Again it was the one with the silver who re-sponded. "You expect us to hand over our *pistolas*? Now who is crazy?"

"We're not talkin' to you, whoever you are," Wheeler said.

"I am called Hijino," the fancy vaquero revealed. "Remember that name when you are both in hell."

Julio Pierce motioned. "No, Hijino. Something is not right here. How can both my mother and Nancy Tovey be dead?"

For a few seconds Timmy thought bloodshed would be averted. Julio was not angry anymore; he was baffled more than anything.

"Hand over your artillery," Wheeler insisted.

Hijino uttered that mocking laugh of his. "*Sí*. We will hand over our *pistolas* so you can shoot us in the back. We are not stupid, gringos."

"We will not hand them over," Julio said. "But we will go with you peacefully. I very much want to talk to Kent Tovey."

"Not wearin' your pistols, you're not," Ray in-formed him. "For the last time, you're on the Circle T, and you don't go a step further unless you hand over your revolvers and rifles."

"I promise no harm will come to you," Wheeler said.

"Oh, no," Hijino scoffed. "Not until they get us to their rancho, *patrón*. You heard them. The Tovey woman is dead, and they blame you. You will not leave their ranch alive."

"I did not kill Nancy Tovey," Julio insisted.

"Then why did she write your name right before she had her head bashed in?" Wheeler demanded.

Julio jerked as if pricked with a knife. "She did what?"

"See, *patrón*?" Hijino said. "They make up lies so they can hang you. Gringos are fond of hanging. With your permission, I will dispose of these two, then you can have your revenge on Kent Tovey."

Fury turned Ray Ornley red. "I'd like to see you try to dispose of us, you stinkin' greaser." And with that, he drew.

So did Hijino. Timmy saw it, and marveled. The pearl-handled Colt was out so fast, it was almost like magic. It boomed, and Ray Ornley twisted and went limp and oozed from his saddle.

Jeb Wheeler sat frozen a few seconds. Then, growling deep in his throat, he clawed at his six-gun.

Hijino shot him. Once, through the chest, smack through the heart. Hijino laughed as Wheeler fell. Wheeler's mount bolted.

"You should not have done that," Julio Pierce said.

"It was them or us, *patrón*." Hijino casually began to replace the spent cartridges. "I was only protecting you."

"What do we do now?" another vaquero asked.

"Do we push on to their rancho?" a third wanted to know.

"I must think." Julio ran a hand across his brow.

He was staring at the bodies, at the spreading pools of blood. "Can it be true? What they said about Nancy Tovey?"

Timmy stared at the bodies, too. Jeb and Ray were friends of his. Part of him boiled with rage, with the desire to draw and start shooting. But another part warned that he was outnumbered six to one, and if he gave in to his rage, he would surely end up like Jeb and Ray.

"Does it matter?" Hijino had asked.

"Of course it matters!" Julio declared. "Don't you see? Both my mother and Nancy Tovey. I must talk to Steve and Armando. There is more to this than we thought."

Hijino finished reloading. He gigged his white horse closer to the bodies, then reined around so he faced his companions. Wagging his Colt, he said, "This holds six shots."

Julio's eyebrows pinched together. "Most *pistolas* do. What is your point? We must get back."

"My point," Hijino said, "is that there are only five of you." With blinding speed, he straightened and fired, five shots one after the other. Julio and the other vaqueros were taken completely off guard. Julio's forehead exploded, and he toppled. The faces of the next two vaqueros erupted in scarlet. Only the last two had split seconds in which to smother their astonishment and stab for their revolvers, but neither cleared leather. All of them were dead and on the ground before the sound of the shots faded.

Timmy was rooted with horror and fear. He had never seen anyone draw and shoot so fast. Not even Jesco.

Hijino reloaded again. He spun the pearl-handled Colt into his holster, then clucked to his white horse. As he went past Julio Pierce, he grinned and said, "They make it too easy."

Timmy had a clear shot at the killer's back. He did not draw. His fingers curled and his hand twitched, but he did not move until Hijino was across the Rio Largo and a speck in the haze. Then, and only then, did he swing onto his horse and race like a madman for the Circle T.

Chapter 20

Trella was in her bedroom, facedown on her pillow, when there came a light knock at her door. She sat up stiffly, too devastated by the loss of her mother to care how she looked. "Come in."

It was Dolores. She came to the bed, but did not sit. Her complexion was ghastly, as pale as the sheets under the bedspread on which Trella lay.

"If it is more bad news, I do not want to hear it." Trella did not think she could take any more. She wanted to curl into a ball and weep for a week.

"Brace yourself."

"Dear God. There *is* more?"

Dolores spoke as one in a daze. "Hijino has just brought word. Julio is dead. Circle T cowboys killed him."

Numb with horror, Trella nearly fainted. She had loved him most of all her siblings, in part because they were the youngest, in part because they were so much alike. More tears gushed from eyes she would have sworn were cried out, and she choked for breath.

"Steve is waiting for the last of the men to come

in from the range," Dolores continued in her bizarrely calm manner.

Trella sought to blink back the new deluge, and failed.

"Armando is mad at him. Armando wanted to leave sooner with the men already here, but Steve refused. Now Armando blames Steve for Julio's death."

"Can it get any worse?" Trella mewed.

"The last of our vaqueros will arrive within the hour," Dolores said, still in that strange manner. "Then they are heading across the river. There will be more killing. A lot more." She paused and licked her lips. "I thought you should know."

"Thank you."

Dolores turned to go. She took a step, but staggered and had to reach for the wall table for support.

Between sobs, Trella asked, "Do you need help?"

"No," Dolores replied. But she did not move. She leaned there, her head bowed, her disheveled hair hiding her face.

"Maybe you should sit down," Trella suggested. She moved back from the edge of the bed to make room.

Nodding, Dolores slowly eased down. She was misery incarnate, broken in spirt and body.

"Are you sure you are all right?" The smell of wine crinkled Trella's nose. "You have been drinking." She knew her sister was fond of the juice of the grape, and enjoyed a glass or two every night before retiring. "How much have you had?"

"A bottle or two," Dolores said without looking

up. "I started and couldn't stop. Now I have none left. Do you have any?"

"I think you have had enough." Trella gently rested her hand on Dolores's shoulder. "Lie down and I will have a servant bring coffee to clear your head."

Dolores's hair moved from side to side. "I do not want coffee. I do not want a clear head. I want to take a *pistola* and put it to my temple and squeeze the trigger, that is what I want."

"Don't talk like that."

"Hasn't it sunk in yet? Mother is gone. Forever. She was everything to me. I loved her with all my heart and all my soul."

"And I did not?" Trella asked defensively.

"You were always closer to father. But what does it matter? We have lost both of them, and now Julio. There are just the four of us left, and if Steve and Armando go to the Circle T, we might lose them, too. The Circle T has more cowboys than we have vaqueros."

"What if"—Trella was jarred by a possibility that had not occurred to her—"what if the cowboys attack our rancho while our brothers are off attacking the Circle T? Who will protect us?"

"They would not stoop so low as to slay unarmed women."

"They killed Mother," Trella bitterly reminded her. Until this moment, she had not been afraid for her own life. Now the fear was like a lance thrust deep into her chest. "They will stop at nothing. They are out to destroy the DP."

Dolores was quiet for a bit. Then she slid off the bed, saying, "Come with me." Without waiting, she walked unsteadily into the hall.

Trella hurried after her, patting her hair and wiping her cheeks with her sleeve. "Where are we going?"

Dolores did not answer. Presently they came to the kitchen. Steve and Armando were there, seated across from one another.

Paco and Roman and a pair of nervous vaqueros were waiting by the door. They all took off their sombreros.

"So it is settled," Steve was saying. "We hit them hard and fast. Strike and run, again and again, until we have whittled their numbers."

"It is cowardly," Armando said.

Steve disagreed. "It is smart. There aren't enough of us. Our only hope is to wear them down without losing a lot of our own men." Steve's jaw muscles twitched. "They have an advantage, but we have justice on our side."

"I am glad you have come to your senses, and I do agree we must strike quickly," Armando said. "There can be no doubt they mean to wipe us out. They are not content with half the valley. They want it all."

Dolores stopped at the kitchen table. "Trella and I are coming with you," she announced.

"Be serious, sister," Armando said.

"Think, *hermano, think,*" Dolores snapped. "They have killed Mother. As Trella points out, what is to stop them from killing the two of us while you are away? With all the vaqueros gone, we would not stand a chance."

"Surely they would not," Armando said, and then scowled and rumbled deep in his throat like a bear at bay. "No. I must stop deceiving myself. The rules of civilized society are nothing to them. You are right. If they caught you two unprotected, your lives would be forfeit."

"They murdered Mother," Trella brought up again as confirmation. She gazed out the window, imagining how it must have been for Juanita: abducted from her home, forced to ride north, dying of a broken neck. A thought struck her, and she gasped. "How did they know?"

"I beg your pardon?" Armando said.

"How did they know it was safe to take Mother? That everyone else was asleep? Did they take it for granted? Or were they watching our casa? Are they watching our casa now?"

"We would see them if they were out there," Steve remarked.

"Not if they were a long way off," Trella said. "Not if they are using a spyglass like the one Señor Tovey has."

Armando came out of his chair. "She is right! Remember when he showed it to us? A cowboy could be out there right this minute."

"What about his horse?" Steve was skeptical. "We can spot horses and cows from a long way off."

"Not if they are lying down," Armando noted, "and horses can be taught to do that. Remember the cowboy at the last rodeo? The one who taught his horse all those tricks?"

"If so, there is nothing we can do about it," Steve said. He glanced at Trella and Dolores. "But getting back to these two. I do not think we should take them along. There will be shooting. A lot of it."

"You talk about us as if we are not standing right here," Dolores said. "But you can not leave us here unprotected."

"I agree," Armando said.

"Four vaqueros will stay," Steve proposed. "If the cowboys attack, Dolores and Trella and the servants can hide in the root cellar."

Dolores shook her head. "What if the cowboys burn our casa down around us? No. You can not spare the four vaqueros. We are going, whether you want us to or not, and this is final."

"I do not like putting you at risk" Steve said.

Dolores refused to be denied. "We are safer with you than by ourselves. Or would you rather Trella and I end up like Mother?"

All eyes were on Steve. He smacked the table, and looked fit to strangle someone, but he said, "Get ready to go."

Timmy Loring rode like the wind. He had to get word to Kent Tovey and Clayburn. They must learn about Hijino. Everything was not at all as it appeared. He was not quite sure what was going on, but Mr. Tovey and the foreman would figure it out.

Timmy wondered what they would do. Maybe send a rider to the Pierces with word of the slaughter he had witnessed. They must grab Hijino and question him, find out why he did what he did.

The Circle T's buildings were a lot farther from the river than the DP's. Timmy still had a couple of miles to go when he spied a rider galloping west. The man spotted him, and immediately changed direction to intercept him.

Reining up, Timmy waited. His horse nickered and stamped. "You won't believe it!" he declared when he recognized who it was. "You just won't believe it!"

"Believe what?" Lafe Dunn asked.

Excitedly, Timmy told him about the shooting, ending with, "Then Hijino up and trotted off as casually as you please! What do you make of it? Him blowin' the wicks out of his boss and those other vaqueros?"

"There's more to this than anyone suspects," Dunn responded. "A lot more folks will die before it's over."

"Maybe not." Timmy arched his spine to relieve a slight cramp in the small of his back. In doing so, he placed his right hand on his revolver. "Once Mr. Tovey hears about this, he might offer to meet with the Pierces. To sit down and talk."

"They will refuse. By now they don't trust him."

"Knowin' Mr. Tovey, he'll persuade them to listen to reason." Timmy had dallied long enough. "Well, I have to go." He gigged his mount.

Within a dozen yards, Dunn was alongside him. "I'll ride with you, if you don't mind. I'd like to hear what Mr. Tovey has to say."

"Be my guest." Timmy rose in the stirrups, but he could not see the house or stable yet, and they were the highest structures. "What were you doin' out this way, anyhow? It looked as if you were lightin' a shuck for the high country."

Dunn gave a start. "What makes you say a thing like that?"

Timmy shrugged. "Call it a hunch. I wouldn't blame anyone for stayin' shy of this mess. Look at all the people who have died."

"Quite a few," Dunn said. He turned from side to side, surveying the valley far and wide. "And you're next."

Dunn's revolver swept at Timmy's head. Timmy tried to duck, but the barrel slammed into him above his ear. He felt himself start to fall. Unconsciousness claimed him, but not for long, because when he opened his eyes, he was being hoisted onto his saddle, his wrists bound in front of him. His hat had been jammed on his head.

"There. Anyone spots us, they won't suspect anything unless they get close, and I won't let anyone get that close."

"What's the big idea?" Timmy's head hammered with pain, and drops of blood trickled down his neck.

"It will come to you, boy." Dunn gripped the reins, climbed on his mount, and headed west toward the distant peaks.

Timmy absorbed that while marshaling his strength. "You're the one behind all this!" Another insight jolted him. "It was you who murdered Mrs. Tovey!"

"That I did, boy. But it's not my brainstorm. I'm followin' orders, just like Hijino."

"The two of you are workin' together? Why? What do you hope to get out of it?"

"Don't strain your brain, boy," Dunn said.

"Quit callin' me that! I'm not no boy!" Timmy bristled. "I do a man's work. I'm entitled to some respect."

"All any of us are entitled to, *boy*," Dunn replied, "is a hole in the ground and maggots eatin' our innards." He brought their mounts to a gallop, ending conversation for a while.

Timmy considered wrenching the reins from the big man's grasp and racing to the ranch, but Dunn could easily shoot him before he went a hundred yards. Nor did jumping Dunn and trying to wrest a weapon from him promise much success. Dunn outweighed him by more than a hundred pounds, and was built like a stone wall.

Hours rolled by. Once, to the northeast, Timmy thought he spied riders, but they vanished moments after he set eyes on them, and might have only been cattle.

By late afternoon, the foothills were near enough that Timmy was seized by a sense of imminent danger. Something told him that Dunn would stop soon, and when Dunn did, Timmy wouldn't like it. If he was going to do something, he must act soon, but for the life of him, Timmy could not choose the best course. He wished Jesco was there. Jesco would know what to do.

The foothills rose in arid contrast to the lush, irrigated grassland. Largely barren except for a few isolated springs, they were shunned by cattle and most everything else. Dunn climbed the first one, and rode over its crest to the other side. "Here will do." He drew reins. "It's where I'm to meet the others."

"Who?" Timmy asked, not really caring. Staying

alive was all he could think about. He must not give up, not so long as breath remained.

Dunn did not answer. Dismounting, he palmed Timmy's Colt, which he had wedged under his belt, and pointed it at Timmy. "Get down. Nice and slow, if you don't mind, and even if you do."

Awkward because of his bound wrists, Timmy did as he was instructed. He tried to swallow, but had no spit. "What do you aim to do to me?"

"Need you ask?" Bending down, Dunn slid his other hand into his left boot and produced a knife. "If you're wonderin' how, don't worry, I'm not goin' to shoot you. Not right away, anyhow." Smirking, he hefted the knife. "I like to whittle some first."

Chapter 21

Saber watched Twitch splash kerosene on the front wall of the Wolf Pass Saloon. "Hurry it up, slowpoke. We have a lot of ground to cover before nightfall." The long, hard ride would do them good, he reflected, after the easy spell they had enjoyed.

Careful not to get any on his boots, Twitch upended the last of the kerosene. "Dunn won't mind if we're late, cousin."

"I will," Saber said. "By now, the cowboys and the vaqueros will be at each other's throats, and we need to be there to pick up the pieces."

Creed came out of the saloon holding a full bottle of whiskey. "I'm takin' this along."

Saber's lips pinched together. He had given explicit orders. No liquor from here on out. Everyone else had heeded. If he let Creed go unchallenged, the others might brand him as weak. "You can't survive a few days without coffin varnish?"

"Killin' always gives me a powerful thirst," the black said, "and we have a heap of killin' to do."

"How much of a heap depends on how many of that cow crowd are still breathin' after the gun smoke settles," Saber said. "With any luck, there won't be but a few."

"You call that luck?" Creed opened his saddlebags, and shoved the bottle in. "There better be more than a measly few. I have the itch."

Saber looked away. That was what Creed called it when the need to kill came over him. "The itch." Like it was a rash, and blood the only salve.

Twitch was set to light the kerosene. "Seems an awful waste to me, burnin' all the tarantula juice we haven't drunk yet."

No one else grumbled. They knew better. Saber climbed on his chestnut, saying, "Everyone will reckon it was an Injun raid. They killed the owner and burned the place down."

"You always were clever," Twitch tittered.

"More clever than most. It's why I ain't never been caught, and why I never will be," Saber boasted. He patted his hogleg. "Lead has its uses, but savvy is what keeps us from havin' our necks stretched, or rottin' behind bars."

Flames flared to vivid red and orange. Snickering, Twitch stepped back as they licked at the porch and climbed to the overhang. "Fire is almost as pretty as a naked dove."

"Almost," Saber said. As a boy, he had delighted in setting toads and lizards and frogs ablaze, after cutting their legs off so they could not get away. A few years ago, for the thrill, he had burned a drummer alive. To this day, he fondly recalled the shrieks and screams.

"Fire does nothin' for me," Creed said.

Some of the others, though, were as fascinated as

Saber and Twitch. The flames reached the roof and spread rapidly, spawning thick columns of smoke that spiraled skyward.

"What if they see it down in the valley?" one of the men asked.

"So?" Saber rejoined. "They have too much on their minds. No one will come."

The heat was terrific. Saber reined a safe distance from the crackling inferno, as much for his skittish mount as for himself. Inside, bottles were bursting. Something went up with a loud *whump*. It galvanized Saber into asking, "Was that keg of black powder still in there?" Blank expressions greeted his query. With an oath, he hauled on the reins, bellowing, "Ride like hell, you jackasses!"

Saber was almost to the trees when the saloon exploded. A man-made volcano of flame and wood spewed fiery pieces and bits in a trillion trajectories. The slowest of the gang, a burly hardcase named Caleb, howled when burning bits seared his neck and cheek. Fritz's mare pranced in fright.

Cackling merrily, Saber came to a stop. He half hoped the mare would throw Fritz, but no such luck. Everyone reached the woods, singed but alive. "We should burn more places down. It beats playin' poker all hollow."

"If you say so," Creed said.

"I say so." Saber grew suspicious. This made twice in the past few minutes that the black man had stepped on his toes. Had it finally come? Was Creed about to make a bid to become the new leader?

"I like playin' poker when I win," Twitch remarked.

"Who doesn't?" Saber sometimes wondered if they truly were kin. No relative of his could be so dumb. He tore his gaze from the conflagration, and used his spurs.

That high up, they were afforded a spectacular vista. Lower slopes, dappled with color, merged into the foothills, which in turn merged into the green of the valley floor. Saber was not much for admiring scenery, but he had to admit New Mexico Territory could hold its own with the likes of Colorado and Utah. He was trying to recollect where he had come across acre after acre of the most amazing rock formations, when he acquired a shadow. Instantly he lowered his right hand to his revolver. "What do you want?"

"To talk," Creed said, so quietly that Saber barely heard him.

"About what?" Saber asked, and tensed to draw. *This is it.* Creed was faster, but Saber would get off a shot or two and make each count.

"Cows."

Saber let some of the tension drain out of him. "Since when are you interested in the critters?"

"Since you told us that we could sell the two herds for hundreds of thousands of dollars split eight ways."

"Seven ways. I shot Hank, remember?"

"Why so many?"

"I don't follow you," Saber said, although he understood perfectly.

"Split only two or three ways, it would be more money for those of us who live to split it."

"You, me, and Twitch, you mean?" Saber studied

the black with renewed interest. "What about Fritz, Caleb, Lutt, and Harvey? We need them to help drive the herd to market." As it was, even with Hijino and Dunn helping, they might need a few more men.

"We won't need them after."

It always fascinated Saber how changeable people were. "True. But Fritz and Lutt have ridden with me for a coon's age. It wouldn't hardly be right."

"Something for you to think about," Creed said. "You don't need to make up your mind right away."

Saber had more than that to ponder over the next couple of hours. Until the Circle T and the DP killed each other off, he and his men must stay clear of them. He counted on the Pierce family getting the worst of it—helped along by Hijino—if only because of their fewer numbers. Dunn would do what he could at the Circle T, and by now should have taken care of Tovey's wife. That was bound to incense the Circle T's punchers into a feverish frenzy. They would finish off the last of the Pierce outfit, losing some of their own in the fight. That was when he and his men would swoop down and wipe out the survivors, leaving him in control of both ranches and a fortune in prime beef.

The sun was well on its westward arc. They came to a sparsely timbered ridge. Below were the foothills, brown footstools to the ramparts they were descending. Saber kneed his animal lower, and once again acquired a shadow.

"Have you thought about it?"

"Yes."

"And?"

"As I said, Fritz and Lutt have been with me almost as long as Twitch. I'd need a damn good reason."

"All that money isn't reason enough?"

Saber chuckled and winked. "It damn sure is." He started to laugh, but abruptly fell silent at the crack of a shot from lower down, from about the spot where he was supposed to meet Lafe Dunn.

The parlor was dark. The curtains had been drawn, but that was not enough. Kent also hung a blanket over the window. Another blanket had been spread over the body on the settee, but now lay on the floor where he had thrown it.

Kent was on his knees, his hands on Nance's arm, staring at the ruin that had once been, to him, the loveliest face in all existence. Now it was destroyed. A horrible, grotesque travesty. A pulped, distorted image of the woman he had adored.

She's gone. Kent could not bring himself to accept the truth. It was why he had spent every waking moment, since the punchers brought her body to the house, here in the parlor. He could not bring himself to leave her.

Long since, Kent had run out of tears. He had cried and cried until he had cried himself dry. He doubted he would ever cry again. No loss could match this. No loss could rip his heart and soul to shreds as this loss had done.

Clayburn had been in an hour ago. Again. To suggest, ever so kindly, that they bury her. Kent knew Clayburn was right, that it was unnatural of him to keep her there, that the men were whispering, but Kent refused. "Not yet. I'm not quite ready."

They understood. They had seen the depth of his love for her. They had witnessed the breadth of his devotion. They would not begrudge him until the body became rank, and he would not let it go that far.

"I miss you so much." Kent stroked the arm, once so warm and soft and vital, now cold and unyielding. He took her hand in his, and squeezed. Once, those slender fingers would have squeezed back. Now they were lifeless sticks.

"Oh, Nance." Kent bowed his head. Outside, a horse nickered. He had not looked out the window in a while, but he imagined they were still out there, every puncher on the spread, called in by Clayburn, ready to ride to the DP. Ready to wage war.

They would not leave without Kent. He must lead them. But he could not tear himself away. They were ready to do what must be done, but he was not. He had never killed, never given the command to kill, never seen a shooting, even. But that was not the real reason he kept them waiting.

"Oh, my sweet Nance." Kent bent over her. Her nose had been beaten flat, her mouth was mangled, one eye terribly swollen, the other amazingly untouched and open. Clayburn had offered to shut it, but Kent had motioned him away. That eye was the one part of Nance's face that still reminded him of her. He gazed into it. In life, her eyes had mirrored her love for him, and he had never tired of gazing into them. Now they were as empty as the awful emptiness inside him.

"I shouldn't do this, I know. It's childish. But I can't help myself. I can't cut the string."

Kent slowly reached out and touched his fingertip to what was left of her lips. A crushed tooth protruded through the rent skin. Whoever did this had not been content with beating her to death. They had continued to beat her well after she was dead. The sheer viciousness of it sickened him. To do something like *this* to someone as sweet and kind as Nance was hideous.

"It's my fault," Kent whispered.

Clayburn had told him not to blame himself, but Kent could not help it. She was spirited away right under his nose. The torment she had undergone, the fear, and all the while, he was sound asleep in their bed, dreaming God knew what dreams, oblivious to her peril. He should have heard something. He should have sensed something. He had failed her, failed her utterly when she needed him most.

"It's my fault," Kent repeated, the constriction in his throat making it hard to breathe. He tenderly caressed her elbow, and noticed a dark droplet he had missed when he cleaned up the blood. Clayburn had offered to do it, but Kent did not want anyone else to touch her.

"Who could do this?" Kent asked the question he must have asked a hundred times. His punchers blamed the DP. They believed Nance had been murdered to get back at the Circle T for Juanita. One of his men had been in San Pedro, and heard about her death from the bartender. That serene, wonderful woman, Nance's best friend. The vaquero who told the bartender made it plain the Pierce family held the Circle T responsible. As if Kent or any of his hands could ever do something like that.

"They're idiots," Kent said. But was he any better? He had no proof the DP had slain Nance in revenge.

That was not entirely true. The new puncher, Dunn, had seen a lone vaquero galloping south at first light the morning Kent woke up to find Nance missing.

Two and two still made four.

"They will turn over whoever did this to you, or I will burn the DP to the ground," Kent vowed to the corpse. He entertained the hope, however slight, that the Pierces would not put up a fight.

A new thought left Kent breathless. *What if*, he asked himself, *it had not been a vaquero? What if it had been one of the Pierces themselves?* Both Armando and Julio wore sombreros, and could be mistaken for vaqueros in the tricky glow of predawn.

"If it was, they die," Kent said, staring into the lifeless eye. He placed his forehead on her shoulder, and that close, smelled the odor. He shuddered, his stomach churning. Bile rose in his throat, but he swallowed it and drew back. "Sorry," he whispered.

Once, after hearing about a woman they knew who died of consumption, Nance had told him that if anything ever happened to her, he was to remarry. "Don't spend your life alone," she had said. "Nothing is worse than loneliness."

Kent swallowed. She had been right. But it would be a snowy day in Hades before he took another woman for his wife. Nance had been everything to him. No woman could replace her, ever.

Reluctantly, Kent rose. He had put it off long enough. Time to bury her. Time to ride to the DP and settle accounts, one way or the other. He strode to the front door and opened it, recoiling as bright sunlight seared his eyes like twin daggers. Blinking, he shielded his face and called out, "Walt?"

In seconds, Clayburn was there. He did not say anything. He did not have to.

"Fetch the shovels and pick three men to help me dig. Advise the rest we leave in an hour. I won't hold it against any man who refuses. This isn't a roundup we're going on. Some of us might not come back."

"We've already talked it over," Clayburn said. "We'll paint the valley red if we have to. It's more than bein' loyal to the brand. It's for Mrs. Tovey."

"I loved her so much," Kent said.

Chapter 22

The last hundred feet taxed John Jesco's self-control. He wanted to run. To charge up the slope. Any moment, he dreaded the crack of a pistol shot or the rattle of a death scream. But neither occurred. Jesco reached the top of the hill and hunkered down.

Timmy Loring stood with his hands tied, defiantly glaring at Lafe Dunn, who had a revolver in one hand and a knife in the other, and was wagging the blade in front of Timmy's face.

Jesco had only seconds to act. He glided to the left, circling around and coming up on Dunn from behind. Neither Dunn nor Timmy saw him when he unfurled. His Colt leaped into his hand.

Dunn chuckled and jabbed Timmy in the chest with the point of the knife. Not hard enough to draw blood, but hard enough to make Timmy wince. "Any last words before I start carvin' on you, boy?"

"Go to hell."

"That's it? Hell, boy. Curse me to high heaven if you want. It's what some would do. I've had others cry and blubber like babies. A few have passed out.

Since it's no fun when they can't feel it, I always wait until they come around."

"I have a question," Timmy said.

Dunn lowered the knife a few inches. "Do you now? Well, this is new, I'll grant you that. What is it? Maybe I'll answer it, maybe I won't. But you can ask."

"What's this all about? I don't want to die not knowin' why."

"You're a disappointment, cub," Dunn said. "Nancy Tovey fought harder than you, and she was a woman."

"As God is my witness, you'll pay for what you did to her."

"Hell, boy," Dunn scoffed. "If there's a God, why'd He let me do it? Heaven and hell is bull."

By then, Jesco was where he wanted to be. He had been careful to keep Dunn between him and Timmy so Timmy did not see him and give him away. At arm's length he extended the Colt and touched the muzzle to the back of Dunn's neck. Simultaneously, he thumbed back the hammer.

At the click, Dunn froze.

"I know what you're thinkin'," Jesco said. "Can you turn and shoot me before I shoot you. You're welcome to try if you'd like."

"Jesco?"

"Drop the six-gun and cut Tim loose. If the knife slips, your brains decorate the grass. Savvy?"

"You must be part Apache to sneak up on me like this."

"I'll count to three. If you haven't let go of the

revolver, I squeeze the trigger." Jesco paused. "One. Two . . ."

The Colt landed with a thud. Dunn carefully applied the edge of the knife to the rope around Timmy's wrists, and slowly sawed back and forth. "How is it you were able to follow us without me spottin' you?"

Jesco extended his other arm past Dunn's shoulder so Dunn could see the object he held. "With this. I was in the hayloft in the stable, keepin' watch like Clayburn wanted. I saw you wallop Tim."

"A stinkin' spyglass," Dunn growled.

Timmy was gawking in amazement. Now he beamed, and exclaimed, "I thought I was a goner! I've never been so happy to see anyone in all my born days!" He glowered at Dunn. "Hurry it up! I can't wait for you to be the guest of honor at a hemp social."

"I won't die at the end of a rope, boy. Any way but that."

Jesco gouged the barrel into Dunn. "You're takin' too long. I won't warn you again."

Dunn sliced faster. "Came alone, did you?"

"Less dust raised," Jesco said, which was explanation in itself.

The instant the rope parted, Timmy stooped and snatched up his revolver. "I've got him covered, John," he said, stepping quickly back.

Lowering his arm, Jesco moved around in front of Lafe Dunn. "So you're the one who murdered Mrs. Tovey." He did not wait for an answer. He kicked Dunn in the right knee, and when Dunn cried out and staggered, he kicked Dunn between the legs.

Dunn cupped himself and doubled over. Gurgling and hissing, he sank to the ground, spittle dribbling over his lower lip onto his chin. "B-B-Bastard!" he sputtered. "Miserable, rotten bastard."

Jesco pressed the muzzle to Dunn's forehead. He had never hankered to blow out another's wick as much as he hankered to blow out Dunn's.

"Don't!" Timmy said. "He's not alone. Others are in it with him, but he wouldn't say what they're up to."

"It's not hard to guess," Jesco said. "Mrs. Tovey dead. Mr. Pierce, Mrs. Pierce, and Berto—"

"Julio Pierce, too," Timmy broke in. "I saw it with my own eyes. An hombre named Hijino shot Julio and some vaqueros as slick as you please. Lordy, he was quick."

Dunn looked up at Jesco. "I hope Hijino and you tangle. You think you're fast? Mister, he'll put a window in your skull so fast, you'll be dead before you can blink. He's better than me. Better than anyone."

Jesco held the Colt's muzzle an inch from Dunn's left eye. "Unbuckle your gun belt. We're takin' you to the Circle T. Mr. Tovey will want to ask you some questions."

"He can ask until doomsday, but he won't get anything out of me," Dunn blustered. "Time is on my side."

"Is it?" Jesco responded, and pistol-whipped Dunn across the temple, knocking Dunn onto his side. Dunn thrashed and wheezed, his teeth bared. "Suppose I ask a few myself, then."

"Go to hell!" Dunn spat. His hat had fallen off, and a deep gash was bleeding profusely.

"You first," Jesco said, and drove the toe of his right boot into Dunn's ribs. He did not hold back. The *snap* that resulted was like the breaking of a tree limb.

Lurid oaths exploded from Dunn as he bucked and heaved, one hand to his chest, the other still over his groin. Beet red with rage and agony, he did not stop thrashing for a good long while.

"I can do that again if you want," Jesco said. "I forget how many ribs a person has, but you have plenty left. Toes, too." Hiking his leg, he stomped down with all his might on the tip of Dunn's left foot. This time there was a crunch, and Dunn thrashed even longer.

Timmy was smiling, but he appeared uneasy. "Is this necessary?"

"You saw Nancy Tovey."

"Yes. I did. And I agree he should be punished. But shouldn't we leave it up to Kent? He has the right, more than anyone."

Jesco glanced at his young friend. Not in resentment, but in relief. For he suddenly saw that for all Timmy's talk about how much Timmy wanted to be like him, Timmy never would. The youth lacked the one thing that set men like him apart from the common herd. "You're too kindhearted."

"I am not!" Timmy objected. "I'm only sayin' it's not ours to do."

In the brief moments Jesco allowed himself to be distracted, Dunn's hand drifted toward his holster. Jesco did not tell Dunn to hold still. He did not give Dunn any warning whatsoever. He simply shot Dunn in the arm.

Minutes elapsed before Dunn stopped rolling back and forth, and lay panting in anguish, a spreading stain high on his sleeve. His ear and cheek were smeared crimson, as well.

Jesco removed the gun belt himself and tossed it away. "On your horse," he directed. When Dunn did not rise fast enough to suit him, Jesco seized him by the wounded arm and hauled him to his feet.

Dunn's legs nearly buckled from under him. "Damn you!" he fumed. "Damn you to hell!"

Jesco shoved him toward the horses. "Save your breath for ridin'." His own mount was at the bottom of the hill.

Dunn had to try three times before he managed to climb on. Battered and weak, he clung to the saddle horn.

The whole way down, Timmy was silent. His expression was sufficient to reveal his sentiments.

On reaching his horse, Jesco stepped into the stirrups and swung east, leading Dunn's. He did not think to look back, so he was more than mildly surprised when, five minutes later, Timmy hollered and pointed at the foothills they had so recently vacated. Silhouetted atop the last of the receding hills were seven riders. "Who can they be?"

"Dunn mentioned he was meetin' friends of his," Timmy revealed. "You don't suppose—?"

"Light a shuck," Jesco said, and suited his own horse to the command by jabbing his spurs.

"They're comin' after us."

Indeed, strung out in a row, the seven were rapidly descending.

Jesco wasn't worried. They had a sufficient enough lead that he was confident they would reach the ranch before the seven overtook them. He stayed at a gallop until the horses grew tired, then slowed, and tugged on the reins to Dunn's animal so it came alongside his. "Tell me about your pards."

For once, Dunn did not argue. "Why not? It won't do you any damn good. They'll catch you and make you wish you had never been born. I only hope I see it. Better yet, I hope I'm the one who kicks your teeth in."

"Names," Jesco said.

"Sure. Ever hear of Saber?"

Jesco had to think. Snatches of bunkhouse gossip came back to him, as did a few accounts from elsewhere. "He's the one who killed that judge up in Colorado, and the one wanted in Mexico for terrorizing whole villages."

"That's him," Dunn confirmed. "He does as he pleases, the governments of both countries be damned. He's made worm food of more people than you can count, and he has his sights set on this valley, and the cattle."

"So that's it," Jesco said.

"You've got to hand it to him. He had this all thought out before he made a move. Pittin' the two ranches against each other. Some of us figured we were bitin' off more than we could chew, that it would never work, but you know what?" Dunn did not give Jesco time to reply. "It's been easier than I reckoned it would be. For all the highfalutin' talk about the Toveys and the Pierces bein' the best of friends, and the two ranches gettin' along so well, all it took was a little push, and now they hate one another.''

Timmy overheard. ''Killin' poor Nancy and the Pierces is your notion of a little push?''

''Whatever it takes, boy. Saber had it all worked out from the beginnin'.''

''Did that include you being caught?''

''Poke fun, but it's not over. If you're still alive tomorrow mornin', then you can crow.''

The afternoon waned. Jesco alternated between hard riding and walking the animals. Every time he looked back the seven riders were there, on the horizon.

At one point, Timmy commented, ''They're not tryin' very hard to catch us.''

''Why should they?'' Dunn said.

Jesco wondered about that. The three of them would reach the ranch shortly after nightfall. Saber did not have enough gun sharks to go up against all the Circle T hands, so what did he have in mind? Picking off the punchers from out of the dark?

In due course, a flaming red disk hovered on the western brink of the world. Jesco glanced over his shoulder yet again and saw only cattle. He scanned the valley to the north and to the south, but the only other sign of life was a hawk.

''It's not far, now,'' Timmy said.

The sun relinquished its reign to scattered stars. Blue gave way to gray and gray gave way to black. The stiffening breeze rustled the grass, and brought with it the distant yip of a coyote.

Dunn was grinning, as at a secret only he knew.

Small squares of light blossomed. Timmy whooped

and slapped his thigh, exclaiming, "I told you! We're safe now."

Jesco did not share the younger man's confidence. Only three windows in the ranchhouse were aglow. No lights showed at the bunkhouse or any of the other buildings.

"It's awful quiet," Timmy remarked as they neared the corral. "Where is everyone?"

"On their way to the DP," Jesco hazarded a guess. Kent Tovey had finally shaken off his grief, and was about to make the worst mistake of his life.

"There must be someone," Timmy said, and gigged his weary horse toward the bunkhouse.

Jesco veered for the main house. Ordinarily, a few servants would be washing the supper dishes and tending to other duties. Dismounting, he tied both sets of reins to the hitch rail, climbed the steps, and knocked.

"You're wastin' your time," Dunn said. "Right before I left, I heard Tovey tell Clayburn to send the servants into San Pedro for their own protection."

Jesco tried the latch. The door was unlocked. He opened it a few inches and called out, "Anyone here?" The silence mocked him.

"Told you, you lunkhead."

It was not long before Timmy came running up, breathless and agitated. "Not a soul! Not a livin' soul! The bunkhouse is empty. The cookhouse stove is cold. No one anywhere. We're alone!"

Jesco came down off the porch and unwrapped the reins. "We need fresh mounts." He shifted on his heels to lead the two animals toward the stable.

"What for?" Timmy asked.

"Use that noggin' of yours, boy," Dunn taunted. "There's just the two of you. How long before my friends figure it out?"

"Who cares?" was Timmy's retort.

"I swear," Dunn said. "You're so dumb, you couldn't teach a hen to cluck."

As if to prove him right, a rifle boomed, and lead smacked into a porch post. From out of the surrounding darkness came a harsh shout, "That was just a warnin'! Throw down your guns and throw up your hands, or we'll turn you sons of bitches into sieves!"

Chapter 23

The Rio Largo had always divided the ranches, a natural barrier that conveniently defined their common border.

Kent Tovey sometimes thought that the only reason the Circle T ended up with more land than the DP was because there was more land north of the river than south of it. Kent would not have minded if it were the other way around. The land did not matter as much as the river.

Without the Rio Largo, neither ranch would exist. It not only ran through the heart of the valley, it *was* the valley's heart, its very sustenance. Without the life-giving nourishment of the ever-flowing water, the lush green grass would brown and wither. Without the Rio Largo, there would not be enough graze to feed a herd of goats, let alone huge herds of cattle.

So Kent always thought fondly of the Rio Largo, and looked forward to those occasions when he had an excuse to ride along its banks or cross over to visit the DP.

But not today.

Kent dreaded the crossing. Once on the other side,

the Circle T hands would be in what had become enemy territory. The friendship, the good graces of the Pierce family, had been replaced by implacable hatred. How else to explain Nance's murder? Julio was to blame, but Julio would never act without the knowledge and consent of his brothers. The Pierces were as tight-knit as a hill clan. Dar had seen to that; he raised them to depend on one another, to be loyal to the family as well as the brand.

Kent missed Dar. Almost as much as he missed Nance. Many an evening, he and Dar had sat sipping brandy or whiskey and sharing stories of their early years and their dreams for the future.

Dar had entertained the hope that his sons would take over the DP, once Dar was ready to hang up his spurs and spend his days in the rocking chair in front of the hearth. Dar had been getting on in years, but it would have been a decade or more before he was ready to put himself out to pasture. Now he would never get to enjoy those waning years, and the sense of accomplishment that came from a man making a success of his life.

Kent had always been proud of his own success. The Circle T was no small thing. It had taken near superhuman perseverance to wrest a working ranch from the forces of nature and the financial pitfalls that conspired to destroy his dreams. Disease, poor markets, bad winters, all had brought him to the brink of ruin at one time or another. Always, he stuck it out, and in the end he had a ranch that was the envy of the territory.

Now the Circle T teetered on the brink again. This time, the forces arrayed against him were his former friends. The hands he once shook so warmly had stabbed him in the back.

Kent could forgive most any affront. He would have been willing to overlook harsh words spoken in the heat of anger. He would even have excused a few shooting affrays, if worse came to worst. But he could never forgive them for Nance. She had been everything to him. As the Rio Largo was the valley's heart, so was Nance his. To lose her was worse than losing an arm or a leg. It was like having his heart cut out. Hers had been the pulse that beat for both of them, and with her gone, he felt lifeless and drained.

"Sweet Nance," Kent said softly as he led his punchers toward the glistening ribbon that was the Rio Largo.

"Did you say somethin', Mr. Tovey?" Clayburn asked.

Embarrassed, Kent shook his head. He must get over his grief. He needed all his wits about him when he confronted the Pierces. He already had worked out what he would say. They must hand over Julio. That was first and foremost, a condition on which he would not relent. Then they must give their word that all hostilities would cease, and from that day on, never cross north of the Rio Largo without informing him of their intent beforehand.

Kent had explained his terms to Clayburn earlier, and his foreman had looked at him askance, and commented that in his estimation the Pierces were getting off too easy.

"What else would you have me do?" Kent had responded. "Wipe them from the face of the earth?"

"I reckon that wouldn't do, either," Clayburn had said. "I'm just glad it's your decision and not mine."

Life was all about decisions. About making the right one at the right time, because the wrong one invariably resulted in regrets. Kent did not have many regrets. At the top of his list was being unable to have children. He had no heir. He'd always assumed he would die before his wife, since women generally lived longer than men, and leave the ranch to her. Now she was gone. There was really only one other person he could leave it to. Only one person with a blood tie who was worthy to take over the Circle T.

Kent gave a toss of his head. He would handle that after he settled with the Pierces.

"Look yonder, Mr. Tovey," Clayburn said.

Kent spied movement at the middle crossing, men milling about on the Circle T's side of the river. A lot of riders, nearly all wearing wide-brimmed sombreros, and others on foot.

"Do you reckon it's the DP outfit?"

At the question, grim murmurings spread. The punchers were eager to avenge Nancy.

"It must be," Kent said. His eyes narrowed. They appeared to be moving bodies. The logical conclusion was that the bodies were his own men, caught by surprise and gunned down. "Who did you send to guard that crossing?"

"Timmy Loring."

Kent's breath caught in his throat. Surely fate could not be so cruel, he told himself. But then, fate, being fate, had no regard for humankind. "Only Timmy?"

"One man for each crossing, exactly as you told me," Clayburn said.

Kent glanced over his shoulder at the punchers

strung out in his wake. Only two were missing.
Allowing that one of the bodies was Timmy's, where
did the rest of the bodies come from? Had Timmy
given a good account of himself before the vaqueros
filled him with lead? Timmy wasn't Jesco, but when
a man's life was in the balance, he liked to take as
many of his enemies with him as he could.

One of the vaquero's yelled and pointed at them.

Kent slowed. The Circle T outnumbered the DP,
but he would not throw away the lives of his hands
needlessly if he could help it.

"My God! Are those women?"

At Clayburn's exclamation, Kent looked again. He
recognized Steve Pierce by Steve's clothes. Armando
was next to him. Nearby sat two hourglass figures
in riding habits, holding quirts. "Dolores and Trella,
the sisters."

"What in hell are Steve and his brothers thinkin'?"
Clayburn said. "Females shouldn't be involved in
this. It's not right."

"They always stick together," Kent reminded him.

"Range wars should be left to the menfolk. It's
bad enough without women dyin'." Clayburn caught
himself, and said sheepishly, "Sorry, Mr. Tovey."

"That's all right," Kent lied. The remark had
seared him like a sword. *Nance. Oh, Nance.*

"How do we handle this?"

They were almost within rifle range. The Pierces
and their vaqueros were scattering in among the
trees.

Kent raised an arm, and brought his small army
to a halt. He reached back for his saddlebags, and
then remembered he did not have his telescope.

Which reminded him. "Where is Jesco when we need him?"

"I don't rightly know," Clayburn admitted. "Shonsey saw him run from the stable to the corral and light a shuck west. Shonsey hollered, askin' where he was headin', but Jesco didn't answer. By the time Shonsey fetched me, Jesco was out of sight."

"Damned peculiar," Kent said. Jesco was usually as dependable as the seasons. He shrugged. "Oh well. He'll show when he shows. We can get by without him." He said that for the benefit of the men behind him, waiting expectantly for their orders. "Have everyone dismount."

Jack Demp was fidgeting like he had ants in his britches. "We could charge them, Mr. Tovey. Like the cavalry."

"Across open ground, and right into their gun sights?" Kent shook his head. "We would be slaughtered. No, we'll stay out of range and wait to see what they do." He slid down and stretched, glad for the reprieve from riding. He was not as spry as he used to be. These days, an hour in the saddle, and he ached in places he did not normally hurt.

Clayburn was issuing instructions. "Floyd, you and Charley take care of the horses. The saddles stay on, in case we need them in a hurry. Shonsey, get a fire goin' and put coffee on. Somethin' tells me we'll be here a while." Clayburn pointed at three punchers, one after the other. "Mel, Carver, and Tilden. I want you to take your rifles and crawl fifty yards closer to the river, to keep an eye on things. Stay down, so they don't spot you. Mel, you go to the right. Carver, to the west. If they try to sneak up on us, give a holler."

The cowboys hustled to obey.

Kent began to pace, to relieve the stiffness in his legs. It was a good thing they had come along when they did. If he were still back in the parlor, moaning over his loss, the Pierces could have surrounded the buildings under the cover of darkness, and in the morning, when his hands filed from the bunkhouse to the cookhouse for breakfast, picked them off as easily as clay targets.

Kent shuddered. He must not make that mistake again, not let his grief affect his judgement. His men depended on him, and he must not let them down.

"Poor Timmy must be dead," Clayburn commented. "Odds are they caught him nappin'."

"Another life they must answer for," Kent said. The last one, if he had anything to do with it.

"I never thought I'd live to see the day," Clayburn said. "Steve Pierce is a good friend. Or was. Armando and me got along well, too. Maybe my grandpa was right."

"Your grandpa?"

"He was a cantankerous old cuss. Soured on life from the day he was born. Nothin' was ever good enough. No one ever measured up." Clayburn paused. "Anyway, he never had any friends, never seemed to want any, so one day when I was about ten, I asked him why. He laughed and said that they weren't worth the bother. That friendship was only skin deep, and given half an excuse, so-called friends would turn into enemies. I never believed him."

Kent refused to believe it, too. He hunkered down, plucked a blade of grass, and stuck the stem between his teeth. The sun was about to set. Once it did, he would give the order to close in.

"I've heard of feuds like this," Clayburn went on, "but never taken part in one. Always figured all the killin' was senseless. But after what they did to Mrs. Tovey—" He glanced down. "There I go again, shootin' off my blamed mouth. Maybe I should sew it shut until this is over."

"I can't stop thinking about her, either," Kent admitted. But he had to, for all their sakes. He stood back up. The three sentries were well out in the grass, wriggling on their stomachs like oversized lizards.

"Do you reckon maybe Steve and his brothers planned this all along?" Clayburn asked. "To take over the entire valley, I mean? Julio never was too happy about you layin' claim to the other half."

The possibility stunned Kent. He had taken it for granted that Dar's sons shared Dar's outlook, and that there were no hard feelings. But now that Clayburn mentioned it, he recalled a few comments the brothers had made. Little things, like Steve saying how the DP could triple its income if they owned the north half as well as the south. Or Armando, commenting that if it had been up to him, he would have fenced off the entire valley long before Kent came. Or Julio, always so touchy about the Mexican half of his heritage, always so critical of everything and anything from north of the border. Had their true feelings been there in front of him the whole time, and he had been too blind to see it? Kent took the blade of grass from his mouth and crushed it. His stupidity had cost Nancy her life.

"They didn't keep us waitin' long," Clayburn said.

Kent glanced toward the Rio Largo. A vaquero on horseback was heading their way, holding a trimmed branch with a strip of white cloth tied to the end. "No one is to shoot. Spread the word."

"Yes, sir."

The vaquero was smiling. The fading sunlight gleamed off silver conchas on the man's belt, hat, saddle, and bridle, and his saddle horn and stirrups looked to be part silver.

"That's the one they call Hijino," Clayburn said. "I don't know much about him. He's new."

Bristling with weapons, Demp and Shonsey and other hands formed a semicircle around Kent and the foreman. "I'd like to see him try somethin'," Demp said. "We'll send him back belly down."

"No shooting," Kent stressed.

Hijino had his arms out from his sides. He passed Tilden, who rose on his knees and covered him. As casually as if he were enjoying a Sunday ride, Hijino came on until he was ten yards out, then drew rein. "*Buenas tardes*, Señor Tovey."

"What I can do for you?" Kent demanded.

"The *patrón* sent me. Steve Pierce. He would like to parley, as you gringos say. He will ride out halfway to meet you. Him, Armando, and one vaquero. They will be unarmed, but the vaquero will not. Señor Pierce says that you may bring two men with you, but only one may be armed. All they want is to talk."

"Don't trust them, boss," Jack Demp urged.

"Steve Pierce gives his word, señor," Hijino said. "Julio's death has shaken him. He loved his brother very much."

Kent was incredulous. "Julio is dead?" He glanced at Clayburn. "Why wasn't I told?"

"This is the first I've heard of it, Mr. Tovey."

Leaning on his saddle horn, Hijino said, "What do I tell the *patrón*? Will you meet with them under a flag of truce?"

"Don't do it," Shonsey said. "I don't trust them."

All eyes were on Kent. He sensed that he was about to make a decision that could decide the outcome. Would it be more bloodshed, or peace? "I have no choice. Fetch my horse."

Hijino's smile widened. "You will not regret it, señor."

Chapter 24

Timmy Loring was scared witless. They had been caught in the open, framed in the square of light from a window. He was about to do as they had been commanded, when John Jesco exploded into motion. Before Timmy could quite comprehend what Jesco was up to, he had seized Dunn, hauled him off the horse, and pushed him toward Timmy, bellowing, "Into the house! Use him as a shield!"

Timmy's Colt was in his hand, but he did not remember drawing it. Jamming it against Dunn's spine, he backpedaled. Dunn started to twist away. "I'll blow a hole in you as big as an apple! I swear!" Timmy warned.

Off in the dark, rifles spat flame and lead. Slugs whined to Timmy's right and left. Several struck the porch, and sent slivers flying.

Jesco answered them. He drew his Colt and banged off three shots with incredible swiftness. Timmy thought Jesco was shooting wildly but then someone cried out, "I'm hit!" It dawned on him that Jesco had fired at the muzzle flashes, with remarkable effect.

Timmy nearly stumbled on the top step, but he gained the porch, and pulled Dunn after him. A rifle banged near the corral, and he fired back. Then he was at the door. Reaching behind him, he opened it and kicked with his boot. The door slammed wide. Another instant, and he was inside, still hauling Dunn after him.

Jesco backed inside, squeezing off another shot as he cleared the threshold. Pressing his back to the wall, he reloaded, his fingers flying.

Timmy had never seen anyone reload so fast. He was glad Jesco was there. No one else could have done what Jesco did, and hold the seven cutthroats at bay long enough to make it indoors.

"You're only delayin' things," Dunn snarled. "Both of you are as good as dead."

"Shut your mouth." Jesco spun the cylinder, then twirled the Colt, cocking it as he did, and trained it on the outlaw. "Or you can die here and now."

If looks of raw hate could slay, Dunn's would have reduced Jesco to bleached bones.

More lead peppered the front of the house. A slug drilled the window to the left of the door, and a vase on a table crashed to the floor.

"Stop firin', damn it!" came a roar from outside. "We don't want to hit Lafe by mistake!"

"Is that Saber?" Jesco asked.

Dunn nodded.

In the sudden silence, Timmy could hear his ears ringing. "What now?" he whispered. Were it up to him, they would slip out the back. So what if they were on foot. The important thing was to go on breathing.

Jesco sidled to the window, but did not show himself. "Saber? Can you hear me?"

"Of course," came the gruff reply.

"Leave, now. One at a time, at a gallop. Or I shoot Dunn."

Timmy felt Dunn move, and tensed, then realized Dunn was indulging in quiet mirth.

"Do you really expect him to do what you want, cowboy? You don't know him like I do. The only person he cares about is himself."

Saber's answer proved Dunn right. "Go ahead and curl him up if you want. But me and my pards ain't goin' anywhere."

"Told you," Dunn said.

Jesco cupped his left hand to his mouth. "Mr. Tovey and the rest will be back soon. You don't want to be here when they do."

Cold laughter wafted on the breeze. "I wasn't raised in a turnip patch. Your boss is likely off across the river, swappin' lead with the Pierces. The boy and you are on your own, and that's an awful big house."

"What does he mean by that?" Timmy wondered.

Dunn responded instead of Jesco. "You can't cover all the windows and doors. Sooner or later my friends will find a way in, and that will be that."

Jesco glided toward the stairs. As he went past Dunn, his right arm streaked out. "I told you to shut up."

Like a tree felled in a forest, Dunn pitched to the floor and did not move. His other temple was bleeding from a gash wider and longer than the first.

"That should keep him out of our hair for a

while," Jesco said. "Go check the back door. Be sure the bolt is thrown. I'll be upstairs but I won't be long."

Timmy shriveled inside. The rear of the house was dark, not a lamp lit anywhere. He moved slowly down the hall, groping with his left hand. He vaguely recollected a small table somewhere past the parlor. Suddenly his boot made contact. He drew back, skirted it, and continued to the inky rectangle in the kitchen.

Timmy froze. Was it his imagination, or was a cool breeze fanning his cheeks? He envisioned the back door open, a killer lurking just inside, ready to blast him into eternity when he came close enough. Then a curtain rustled, and he saw that the window over the counter had been cracked a couple of inches to admit fresh air.

Grinning at his silliness, Timmy entered. He had only taken a few tentative steps when he froze a second time. He had heard movement! There could be no mistake. The sound came from over by the back door.

Crouching, Timmy licked his suddenly dry lips. He strained and strained, but could not spot whoever was waiting to do him in.

Timmy yearned to shout for Jesco, but it would give him away. His skin crawling, he crept forward. First one foot, then the other, careful not to scrape his soles or otherwise betray where he was.

There it was again! This time, Timmy glimpsed a shadowy shape low down to the floor. Lying flat, he figured, to be harder to hit. He tried to swallow, but

now his entire mouth was dry. Never in his whole
life had he been so afraid.

The shadow moved toward him.

Timmy's hand began to shake. He grasped the Colt
in both hands, but he still could not hold it steady.
To add to his shame, his teeth began to chatter. He
had to grit them to make them stop.

In the gloom, the outline of a pale face appeared.
Timmy saw the eyes and the chin, but he could not
make out much else. He did not need to. All the
servants were gone, all the punchers, too. It had to
be one of Saber's bunch.

Taking a deep breath, Timmy prayed to the Almighty to guide his aim, and stroked the trigger. In
the confines of the kitchen, the blast was unnaturally
loud. So was the screech that punctuated the shot.

The shadow leaped high into the air, did a somer-
sault, and came down hard. It tried to rise, and
collapsed.

Timmy cocked the hammer as boots drummed.
Jesco called his name, but Timmy did not reply. He
must make sure. Easing closer, he listened for breathing, but heard none. He was about to shoot again,
when he saw that the sprawled shape was smaller
than a person would be. Much, much smaller.

Jesco burst into the kitchen, a lamp held over his
head, filling the room with its glow. "I'll be
damned!" He stopped short. "What did you go and
do that for?"

Timmy rose to his knees, his chin on his chest,
ashamed of himself. "It was dark. I thought it was
one of Dunn's friends."

"With whiskers and a tail?" Jesco stood over the body and felt for signs of life. "As dead as Mrs. Tovey. It's a good thing she's gone to her Maker, or she would be mighty upset. She was right fond of this cat."

Luck once again favored Hijino.

The sun was almost gone. Steve and Armando had delayed going to meet Tovey, thanks to an argument with their sisters. Little did Dolores and Trella realize, but they had sealed their doom.

"Enough is enough. We must go, or Kent Tovey will think we are up to something," Armando said.

Trella stepped in front of him, her hand on his chest. "Please! One last time I beg you to reconsider. I have a bad feeling about this."

"As do I," Dolores said.

Steve moved past them to his horse. "We are taking Hijino. The rest of the vaqueros will have us covered."

Roman nodded. "That we will, *patrón*. At the first sign of treachery, we will shoot them from the saddle."

Trella would not relent. "What will talking to them accomplish? How can you trust them, when they have killed Mother and Father and Julio?"

"And Berto," Paco said. "Do not forget Berto."

"I must learn why," Steve said. "I must hear it from Kent Tovey's own lips."

"You are a fool," Trella said.

Dolores clasped Armando's hand. "We do not want to lose the two of you, too. Take us with you."

Hijino stiffened. If the women went along, he

could not carry out his plan. "It is too dangerous, señorita," he made bold to interject.

"Don't worry," Steve Pierce assured his sisters. "Kent will respect a flag of truce. He will grant us that much."

"You speak of him as if he were the man we once believed him to be," Dolores said. "A man of honor and decency. But he has proven he is not."

"You are jumping to conclusions." Steve stepped into the stirrups. "Now out of our way."

Armando strode to his horse and mounted, the saddle creaking under him. He smiled down at Dolores and Trella. "Have confidence in us. We are not idiots. We will not let anything happen." He palmed his revolver and handed it to Paco.

Steve gave his Colt to Roman. "Remember, no one is to shoot unless I do this." He made a chopping motion with his arm.

"*Sí, patrón.*"

Trella stamped a small foot. "Don't go! You never listen to me because I am the youngest, but this time you should."

"You are adorable when you are angry, sister," Steve said, and gigged his mount toward the cowboys.

Armando flicked his reins and caught up with Steve.

Tingling with expectation, Hijino followed. He loved a good challenge more than anything, and this promised to bury him unless he did it just right.

"I did not say anything back there," Armando remarked to Steve, "but I hope you are right. I do not share your respect for Tovey."

"We will make this quick," Steve said uneasily, as if he were having second thoughts. "It's getting dark."

Three riders came to meet them. One was Kent Tovey. The second was Clayburn, the Circle T's foreman. Both were unarmed. The third rider, Hijino was delighted to see, was Jack Demp. He suppressed a laugh. The stupid gringos were playing right into his hands.

Midway between the two forces, they reined up. Hijino contrived to knee Blanco slightly past Steve and Armando, and near Demp. He rested his right hand on his silver saddle horn, and smiled.

Clayburn started right in. "It took you long enough. What kept you? This was your idea, remember?"

"Now, now, Walt," Kent Tovey said. "The important thing is that they want to talk. Maybe we can settle this without more bloodshed." He paused. "But first I need to know something. I saw your vaqueros moving bodies. Was one of them Timmy Loring?"

"Who?" Armando said.

"It was Julio and some of our vaqureos," Steve said. "Now I want to know something, Kent. I want to know how you could turn on us after so many years of being our friend?"

"I'm still your friend," Kent Tovey declared. "May God strike me dead if I am lying."

Armando flushed with anger. "You can sit there and say that? With our father and mother and our brother dead?"

"I had nothing to do with their deaths," Kent said.

"Nor am I entirely convinced you had anything to do with my wife's."

Hijino grinned at Jack Demp. Beads of sweat peppered the cowboy's brow below his hat brim. Demp was nervous, and kept placing his hand on his hip and lowering it again. *A man should not be so highstrung*, Hijino thought. Tricking Demp would be child's play.

"We liked your wife, señor," Armando assured Tovey.

"Nancy was our mother's best friend," Steve added. "We would never harm her."

Clayburn glared from one brother to the other. "Well, someone sure as hell did, and if it wasn't you or your vaqueros, then who?"

"I can not answer that," Steve admitted. "But if we agree to end hostilities, we can sit down together and try to piece things out."

The moment for Hijino to act had come. Suddenly straightening, he raised his hand toward his hip, and exclaimed loud enough for those at the river to hear, "Do not touch that *pistola*, gringo!"

Jack Demp, startled, blurted, "What?"

"I will warn you only once!" Hijino cried.

Blinking in confusion, Demp unwittingly did exactly as Hijino was hoping he would do; he reached for his Colt.

"No!" Hijino shouted. He drew and fired, just as Demp's fingers closed on the revolver. Hijino shot him in the head. The cowboy never stood a chance. "Watch out! It is a trick!" he yelled at Steve and Armando. Then he sent a slug into Kent Tovey's chest.

"No!" Steve Pierce bawled.

Hijino swiveled to shoot Clayburn, but Kent Tovey's horse shied and came between them. Before he could apply his spurs, the cowboys and the vaqueros began firing, each side seeking to protect their own. Rifles blasted in a ragged volley. A slug creased a furrow in Hijino's shoulder. Swinging onto Blanco's side, he reined around and raced for the river. He looked back and saw Steve Pierce and Armando trying to flee. Both were hit, repeatedly. Armando fell. Steve succeeded in turning his mount, only to have a slug rip through his throat.

Hanging from his saddle, his shoulder throbbing from his wound, slugs whizzing all around, Hijino chortled with glee.

Everything had worked out exactly as he wanted.

Chapter 25

As soon as Jesco was sure the doors and the windows were secure and no one else was in the house, he blew out the lamps.

"I'd rather have the light," Timmy said.

"Would you rather be shot?" Jesco countered. They were in the hall. Bending, Jesco grabbed hold of Dunn by the leg, and dragged him into the parlor. "Mrs. Tovey always kept a butcher knife in the top drawer under the kitchen counter. Run and fetch it for me."

"You're not fixin' to cut him up, are you?"

"He deserves to be, but no," Jesco said. "In the hall closet you'll find some blankets. Cut one into strips, so we can tie this hombre to a chair." The young cowboy jangled off, and Jesco glided to the parlor window. Glass crunched under his boots. It had been shot out, and wind rustled the curtains.

Removing his hat, Jesco risked a peck. Something was going on over at the stable. The double doors were open, and several outlaws were moving about. The rest were well hidden. He did not see them anywhere.

Backing away, Jesco replaced his hat. He turned just as a broad shoulder slammed into his gut. A human battering ram lifted him off his feet and slammed him into the wall.

In the dark, Dunn's features were demonic. He unleashed a punch, snarling, "Now I've got you, you son of a bitch!"

Jesco jerked his head aside, and Dunn's knuckles cracked against the wall instead of his jaw. Dunn howled, and recoiled, enabling Jesco to plant a boot in the other man's gut. He kicked with such force, Dunn catapulted backward as if he had been fired from a cannon. He crashed into a chair, and both went down. Dunn scrambled to his knees, only to meet a right cross that caught him on the chin.

Jesco could have shot him. Lord knew, Jesco wanted to. But he owed it to Kent Tovey to try and keep Dunn alive. Dunn must answer for Nancy. Jesco swung again, but the killer threw himself back. Jesco immediately closed in, and had his legs swept out from under him.

Jesco came down hard on his back. A hand clawed for his throat, another at his Colt. Jesco swung and connected, but only a glancing blow. He lunged onto his knees.

Dunn sprang, and they grappled. Desperation lent Dunn extra ferocity. His fingers closed like a vise on Jesco's throat. His knee drove at Jesco's midsection. Jesco twisted aside to avoid the knee and sought to pry the hand off his neck, but Dunn's fingers were like railroad spikes, digging deep, choking off his windpipe.

Jesco pushed, but could not throw Dunn off. He

rolled to the right, then to the left. Dunn growled, and bunched his shoulders to apply more pressure. He was denied the chance. A revolver thudded against his head, once, twice, three times, and Dunn collapsed on top of Jesco.

"Did I do good?" Timmy Loring asked. He held his Colt aloft, ready to strike again if need be.

"Took you long enough," Jesco joshed. Pushing the limp weight off, he slowly rose. "That is one tough hombre."

Together they lifted Dunn into a chair. Jesco let Timmy wrap the strips binding Dunn's arms and legs, but he tied the knots himself.

"What do we do now?"

"Nothin' at all," Jesco answered. "We sit tight, and wait for Saber to make the next move."

Timmy anxiously glanced at the window. "Shouldn't we try to pick a few of them off?"

"In the dark?" Jesco shook his head. "All we have to do is stay alive until Mr. Tovey gets back."

"Is that all?" Timmy asked dryly.

"Think, Tim, think. They won't go after the rest of the outfit if we keep them busy here. With Dunn our prisoner, we hold the high card." Jesco touched a sore spot on his neck. He was painting a rosier picture than the situation called for. The part he left unspoken was that Saber's pack of curly wolves were not about to wait out there twiddling their thumbs.

"Want me to make some coffee?" Timmy asked.

"Sure, and while you're at it, bake a pie and go out on the porch and dance a jig."

"That's a no, I take it?"

A noise outside drew Jesco to the window. Something was moving toward the house from the stable. At first he thought it might be men on horseback, but then the shape acquired detail and substance. It was the buckboard, the tongue up, the bed piled high with hay. Saber and his men were pushing.

"They're not thinkin' what I think they're thinkin'," Timmy said at his eblow. "How can we stop them?"

"We can't," Jesco said. "But we can up the ante. Follow me." In the next room was a gun cabinet. Lined up on a rack were two shotguns and four rifles. Jesco handed a double-barreled shotgun to Timmy, and claimed one for himself. Boxes of ammunition were stacked at the bottom. "Ever fired one of these?"

"Can't say as I have, no." Timmy was fiddling with the release to break the shotgun open.

Jesco held up a shell. "These are buckshot. Both barrels at close range can pretty near blow a man in half."

"I heard someone say once that a shotgun is the next best thing to a cannon," Timmy mentioned.

"They have a kick," Jesco warned. "Keep the stock tucked to your shoulder and a firm grip on the fore end or the recoil will knock you on your backside." He crammed shells into his pockets and gave the rest to Timmy. "Hurry. We don't want them to start the frolic without us."

They reached the window in time. The buckboard had stopped twenty yards out.

"Where are they?" Timmy whispered.

"Behind it."

In confirmation, a torch flared to life, then a second, and a third. Each was tossed onto the hay. The buckboard promptly began moving again, gaining speed, as flames rapidly climbed the mound in the bed.

"Stay put," Jesco commanded. He ran to the front door, wrenched it open, and darted out. Thumbing back the shotgun's twin hammers, he skipped to one side. Out in the dark to the left, a rifle blasted, and a slug bit into the wall. Jesco crouched next to a post. He ignored the shooter and concentrated on three pairs of legs visible under the end of the buckboard.

The front of the house was lit up as bright as day. Another rifle boomed, from the other side, and the post shook with the impact. The crackle of flames and the rattle of the buckboard nearly drowned out a third shot that struck the porch at Jesco's feet.

By now, the buckboard was less than twenty feet away. Jesco leveled the shotgun at two of the legs, and let loose with one of the barrels. At that range, the shotgun could shred flesh like a grater shredding cheese. A man shrieked and fell, flopping about like a fish out of water.

The buckboard lost momentum. Someone beyond the ring of flickering light roared, "Keep pushin', damn your hides, or I'll shoot you myself!"

The other two men behind the buckboard put their shoulders to the tailgate. Jesco could see the crowns of their hats. Rising, he aimed below the top of the nearest hat, and fired.

Wood and hay burst outward and upward. A hole the size of a cantaloupe appeared about where the man's head must have been. The outlaw was flung to the earth, and did not move. That left one man to push, and he lost his nerve. Breaking away, he sprinted to the man Jesco had shot in the legs, and, bending, sought to drag him out of the light.

Jesco switched the shotgun to his left hand, and swooped his right hand to his Colt. He had no compunction about shooting them in the back. But their friends awakened to their peril. Rifles and revolvers banged, forcing Jesco to fling himself flat. When the firing stopped and he looked up, the pair had melted into the night.

The burning hay had ignited the buckboard, but the buckboard was not close enough to do the same to the house.

"You'll have to try somethin' else!" Jesco shouted, hoping Saber would answer and give his position away, but the wily killer was too smart to fall for the ploy.

Jesco crawled to the door. Once inside, he rose and kicked it shut. He found Timmy over by the parlor window.

"I reckon you taught them!"

Jesco set him straight. "I was lucky. If they'd had men at both ends of the porch, they'd have caught me in a crossfire." He began reloading the shotgun. It had repelled them once, it might do so again.

"Will they give it up?"

"Not likely," Jesco said. "We know too much." Saber *must* kill them, no matter what it takes. "Go take a peep out back. I wouldn't put it past them to try somethin', thinkin' we'll be watchin' the wagon burn."

The man Jesco had shot in the head lay where he had fallen. Dead, Jesco figured, which whittled the odds a little. He heard a groan behind him, and said without turning, "Have a nice nap?"

"Bastard," Dunn spat. "How long have I been out?"

"Long enough for your friends to try to burn us out, and for one of them to learn the hard way that buckshot means buryin'."

"Crow while you can. We have a powerful hankerin' to be rich, and you're all that's standin' in our way."

"I wouldn't count the rest of the Circle T hands and the DP out just yet," Jesco said. "Kent Tovey is no tree stump. He'll figure it out, and when he does, there will be hell to pay."

"He won't figure it out in time. In a day or two, this whole valley will be ripe for the pluckin'."

Jesco looked at him. "If you put half as much effort into makin' money honestly as you do makin' it dishonestly, you'd have more than enough to get by."

"I don't see you with your own spread and money galore in the bank," Dunn retorted. "The problem with livin' honestly is that it leads to the poorhouse."

"Why, you're a philosopher."

"Go to hell."

"But there are worse things than bein' poor," Jesco said. "Like losin' your honor and self-respect."

"God. You should be a parson. Where's the honor in nursemaidin' cows? Where's the self-respect in forty a month and found?"

"If you don't know by now, you never will."

Timmy cat-footed into the parlor, saying, "No sign of anyone out back. I bet we could sneak off without them noticin'."

"You would lose the bet," Jesco said. "There's bound to be at least one waitin' for us to try. Step foot out the back door, and you're worm food."

Dunn's teeth showed bright in the dark. "Don't listen to him, boy. You go ahead and do as you please."

From somewhere between the house and the stable came a harsh bellow, "Are you awake in there?"

"We're playin' checkers!" Jesco replied.

Saber was not amused. "You've killed a pard of mine and about near crippled another. This is your last chance to come out with your hands over your heads. You have one minute."

"It must be the bull," Jesco shouted back.

Silence lasted for all of ten seconds, then Saber yelled, "What bull, you damned nuisance?"

"The one that kicked you in the head when you were little and addled your brains. Why else would you think we'd give up?"

Timmy chortled and slapped his leg. "That's tellin' him!"

Through the shattered window came the ratchet of rifle levers being worked. Whirling, Jesco threw himself at Timmy and tackled him, bearing him down as the night exploded in gunfire. It sounded like five or six firing at once. Slugs ripped through the wall, through the front door, through what was left of the glass pane. Slivers flew every which way. A lamp disintegrated with a loud crash. A pillow on the settee spewed feathers. A portrait of Nancy Tovey's mother fell off the wall.

Forty or fifty rounds were expended before the firing ceased.

Jesco raised his head and nudged Timmy, who had his arms over his. "Are you all right?"

"No." Grimacing, Timmy groped low down on his left leg. "I've been hit. I can feel blood."

"Let me have a look-see."

Enough light spilled inside from the still burning buckboard to reveal a half-inch-deep furrow above the young cowboy's ankle. The lead had missed the bone, and even as Jesco examined the wound, the bleeding slowed to a few drops.

"You'll live."

Timmy pointed. "It doesn't look like he will."

Dunn was slumped in the chair. His chest rose and fell erratically, as if he were having difficulty breathing. A pair of spreading stains on his shirt explained why.

"Well, this is fittin'." Jesco poked the killer in the shoulder, and Dunn slowly lifted his head.

"I hate you."

"You're the one chose the life of a lobo," Jesco said. "Us honest folks don't generally get shot to pieces by our friends."

"I can't tell you how much I hate you." Dunn let out a long breath. "It wasn't supposed to end like this. I was goin' to have more money than I knew what to do with." He coughed, and swore, and coughed some more, ending with a gasp that abruptly choked off.

Jesco felt for a pulse. "And then there were six."

"What do we do with him? Just leave him there?"

Scratching his chin, Jesco glanced at the window. "I hate to see a good body go to waste."

Chapter 26

Hijino always had luck. He was lucky at cards, lucky with the ladies, and particularly lucky when he was in situations where it was shoot quick or die. He counted it luck bordering on a miracle that he reached the strip of woods along the Rio Largo alive. A hailstorm of slugs sought his life, yet he and Blanco made it.

Hijino raced in under the trees, past vaqueros who were firing in a mad frenzy at the gringos. He went almost to the river, then drew rein and swung down while Blanco was still in motion, yanking his Winchester from its scabbard as he alighted. Turning, he had taken barely six steps when Trella flung herself at him. In near hysterics, tears streaming down her cheeks, she beat on his chest with her small fists and screamed in his face.

"What happened? What in God's name happened?"

Dolores and Paco and Roman were running toward them.

"Didn't you see?" Hijino responded. "The cowboy, Demp, went for his *pistola*. I yelled at him not to, but he would not listen. Then the rest of the gringos started shooting."

"Steve and Armando!" Trella wailed. "My brothers are dead!"

"I am sorry," Hijino said. "I could not save them."

"Mi hermana," Dolores said, enfolding Trella. "It was not his fault. There was nothing he could do."

Trella wailed louder, and tried to push loose.

Paco was furious. Ordinarily the mildest-mannered of men, he swore luridly, and jabbed a finger at the gun smoke wafting over the grass. "We will kill them for this! Every last one! They made fools of us! They honored our white flag so they could kill Armando and Steve."

Roman did not say anything. His eyes were hidden by the wide brim of his sombrero, but he appeared to be staring at Hijino.

"Tell me what you would have me do, and I will do it," Hijino said to Paco, playing his part.

"Help the others. Shoot as many as you can before it is too dark to see."

"Sí." Filled with secret delight at how he had tricked them, Hijino threaded through the trees in a crouch. Slugs whistled and buzzed among the branches and boles, clipping leaves and bark and branches. Flattening, he snaked to a trunk wide enough to offer some protection.

A vaquero to his left raged nonstop with every shot. "Damned stinking gringos! Damned rotten *bastardos!*"

Inwardly smiling, Hijino sighted at the center of a gray mushroom, and fired. "Shoot at their smoke!" he hollered. Someone came through the woods and joined in. He knew it would be Roman. A glance confirmed it. "We will give them hell!" he declared.

Roman merely nodded.

Does he suspect? The hairs at the nape of Hijino's neck prickled. But Roman would not act unless he was sure. That was the great difference between Hijino and men of honor. They always needed a reason to squeeze the trigger; Hijino did not. They always had to justify killing; Hijino killed for killing's sake. They were good men, decent through and through; there was not a shred of decency anywhere in Hijino's being.

So Hijino was wary, but not overly worried. He would deal with Roman when the time came. Until then, he did as the rest of the vaqueros were doing, and emptied his rifle at the cowboys, twice in succession. He had to pretend to be as outraged as everyone else.

The twilight darkened into the black of night, and Paco shouted for the shooting to stop.

"I wonder how many of them we got?" a vaquero said.

"I saw one fall for sure," another mentioned.

"I hit one in the head when he popped up to shoot!" a third exclaimed. "I saw his hat go flying."

Boots crunched, and Paco materialized out of the gloom. "Roman, the señoritas would like to talk with you. You, too, Hijino."

More cause for Hijino to be delighted. He was more than a simple vaquero now. He was part of the inner circle. Trella's doing, he suspected. She had succumbed to his charms with all her heart.

The sisters were with the horses. Dolores was pacing, her arms across her bosom. Trella sniffled and gazed glumly into the water. When she saw Hijino, she rushed over and embraced him.

"I am sorry for hitting you. It was wrong."

Hijino graciously excused her. "You had good cause. It is I who am sorry for not saving your brothers."

Paco cleared his throat. "The important thing is to decide what to do next. I think the señoritas should return to the rancho."

"I am in charge now," Dolores said. "My place is here with the vaqueros, as it would be if I were Steve or Armando or Julio."

"With all due respect, Señorita Pierce," Paco said, "you are a woman, and they were not. You hamper us by your presence."

"How?" Dolores demanded.

"If the cowboys attack, the men will think of you first, and their own lives second. They will not be as careful as they should."

"That is silly," Dolores said, but not unkindly.

Paco shrugged. "It is the nature of things, señorita. They hold you and your sister in the highest esteem, and would gladly throw their own lives away to save yours."

"I do not like it. I do not like it one bit. Women should not be treated differently than men." But Dolores sighed, and said resignedly, "Still, I would not be the cause of more men dying than must. My sister and I will go back and await word."

"*Gracias*. It is for the best."

Dolores put her hand on Paco's arm. "I appoint

you the new caporal. You take Berto's place. Roman and Hijino are witnesses, and will spread the word. The men are to listen to you as they would listen to Trella or me."

Flushed with pride, Paco said, "I am grateful beyond words."

"You have earned it."

"Then my first order is this." Paco turned to Hijino. "You will accompany the señoritas to safeguard them. Stand guard at the house. If the cowboys slip past us, their lives will be in your hands."

"I will protect them with my dying breath," Hijino glibly lied. Once again, his luck served him well.

"You need Hijino here," Dolores said. "You need his skill with pistols."

Paco disagreed, much to Hijino's amusement. "His skill is best served protecting you. Should we fall, he must take Trella and you to San Pedro. From there, you can take the stage south. The Chavez rancho is only ten days' travel. They will look after you."

"What you say makes sense, but I do not like it." Dolores glanced at her sister. "How about you?"

"Hijino is fine with me," Trella said. "He has my utmost confidence. He will keep us alive if anyone can."

Roman broke his silence to say, "He had better."

Paco clapped Hijino on the back. "Then it is settled. Off you go. Watch over the señoritas every minute."

"Never fear," Hijino said. "They are in good hands."

* * *

"Sons of bitches!" Shonsey the cook pounded the ground, then shook his fist at the vegetation lining the river. "Those yellow scum! Shootin' unarmed men!"

"Simmer down," Walt Clayburn urged the fighting-mad cook. "They won't get away with what they've done. Don't you worry."

Kent Tovey heard them as from a distance, even though they were on either side of him. He was on his back on a blanket. They had removed his blood-drenched shirt and bandaged him as best they could, but it would not delay the inevitable.

Strangely enough, Kent felt no pain. None whatsoever. He always thought people who were shot were in agony. All he felt was weak, so weak he could barely keep his eyes open. But he must. He could not die yet. There were things to say. "How bad off are you, Walt?"

"They winged me, is all," Clayburn responded. "I managed to get you out of there. I just wish I had done it sooner."

Kent sought to soothe his guilt. "You did all you could. How many others besides Jack Demp have we lost?"

"Two," Clayburn said. "Kyle and Vintnor. Kyle got too close to the trees, and Vintnor tried to help him."

"Lousy greasers," Shonsey spat.

"Don't talk like that," Kent said. "Until a few days ago, they were our friends. I can't understand how it all went so wrong. So terribly, terribly wrong."

"They only pretended to be friendly," Shonsey said. "Deep down, they always hated us. They resented you for claimin' half the valley, and they resented the rest of us because we're not Mex."

"Dar Pierce was not bigoted," Kent said.

"It's not him I'm talkin' about," the irascible Shonsey growled. He started to say more, but Walt Clayburn cut him off.

"That's enough. Go see that the wounded have been tended to."

Grumbling fiercely, the cook slunk off.

"Sorry," Clayburn said. "He hasn't seen your wound. He doesn't know." The foreman coughed. "You should let me send a rider for the buckboard."

"I wouldn't last two miles," Kent said. Another strange thing: He did not feel sad or upset. Maybe because without Nance, life had lost a lot of its meaning.

"What do I do when you're—?" Clayburn stopped. "I mean, who will be in charge? Who takes over the ranch? Your brother back east?"

"Floyd couldn't run a chicken coop without help. Remember when he came to visit? You had to saddle his horse for him."

Clayburn chuckled. "Some of the men did wonder how he got around without a diaper."

"I have a will," Kent said. "But I left the ranch to Nance."

"Oh," was all Clayburn said.

"Go to my horse," Kent directed. "You'll find paper and a pencil I use for tallies in my saddlebags. Bring them here." He listened to the jingle of spurs, and closed his eyes. *Only for a few moments,* he told himself. He was tired, so very, very tired. *I'm coming soon, Nance.*

It had been a good life, Kent reflected, until this madness. He could look back with no complaints. His childhood had been largely tragedy free. When he was seventeen, he met Nancy. When he was nineteen, he married her. To say he was happy was to say a bear loved honey. For her sake, he started the Circle T. For her sake, he toiled day in and day out, year in and year out, but the funny thing was, as hard as it had been, the time flew by because he had been doing it all for her.

That was the secret to life, Kent reflected. To live it for someone else, and thereby make it worth living.

Kent shivered. He had grown cold inside. He dearly needed a fire, but it was out of the question. A creeping black cloud began to numb his mind, and with a gasp, Kent opened his eyes and rose on his elbows. It took every ounce of remaining strength he possessed. *That was close!* Kent realized. Another few seconds and it would have all been over. "Clayburn?"

"Right here, boss." The big foreman knelt. He had brought the saddlebags. "Which one is it?"

"Look in both." Kent did not have the energy to do it himself. It was not long before paper rustled and a pencil was carefully placed in his hand. "You'll have to hold the paper where I can see it."

Writing proved near impossible. Kent could not hold the pencil steady for more than a few seconds. Fortunately, a single line sufficed. But it took him over fifteen minutes. He signed it, then said, "Read it for me, please, so I know I got it right."

Clayburn hunched over the sheet, moving his lips

as he read, "I, Kent Ezekiel Tovey, do hereby bequeath the Circle T and all my possessions and those of my wife, Nancy Herbert Tovey, to Timothy Asher Loring—" Clayburn stopped in astonishment. "You're leavin' it all to Timmy?"

"He's my sister's boy," Kent revealed. "I told you about her once."

Clayburn smacked his forehead. "Loring! I plumb forgot, it's been so long. So he's hers? Why didn't you say so when he first showed up?"

"He didn't want to be treated special because he's related to me," Kent said. "It was important to him that he be considered just like all the other hands."

"I'll be damned," Clayburn said. "I respect him for that. So will the men when they hear."

"Look after him, Walt. He's a good boy, but he doesn't know enough yet. Help him. You and Jesco both."

"Jesco," Clayburn said. "We could use him."

"He must be off with Timmy somewhere." The blackness started creeping over Kent anew.

"I'll find them. I promise."

"Give that paper to my lawyer. It should be legal. Tell Timmy to bury me next to Nance. And Walt?"

"Sir?"

"Let the men know that no rancher has ever been prouder of an outfit than I've been of them. I mean that."

"You made it easy to be loyal to the brand," Clayburn said.

Suddenly an oath blistered the night air, followed by a gunshot. "They're attackin'! Look to your guns!"

Shots boomed on all sides as the night burst with thunderous fireflies. A man screamed. Then a horse neighed.

Clayburn dropped flat, and drew his Colt. "Did you hear that, Mr. Tovey? They've snuck up on us! I have to move you! We have to get you out of here."

There was no answer.

Chapter 27

"Are you sure this will work?" Timmy Loring asked, making no attempt to hide how nervous he was.

Jesco removed Dunn's hat, and jammed his own hat on Dunn's head. They had already taken off Dunn's shirt and replaced it with his. "The only thing I'm certain of in this life is being born and dying. Everything else is a roll of the dice. Including this." He wrapped his arms under Dunn's. "Lend a hand."

"He weighs a ton," Timmy complained.

"Corpses generally do." Grunting, Jesco sidestepped to the chair, which they had positioned near the shattered window—but not so near that those outside could see it.

"I suppose he does look like you from the waist up," Timmy said. "The two of you were about the same height."

"Where's that broom I had you fetch?"

Timmy scooted over to where he had left it propped against a wall. "Here. But won't they notice?"

"Not as dark as it is. Do exactly as I told you, and

you'll be fine." Jesco stepped behind the chair, pried at the cuff of Dunn's left sleeve, and fed the broom's handle into it, across Dunn's back and into the right sleeve. The effect was to give the impression that Dunn was holding his arms out from his sides. "See?"

"I don't know." Timmy was still skeptical.

"Get ready," Jesco said, and moved aside so Timmy could come crouch behind the chair. "Just remember to keep your head down."

"What will you do for a shirt and a hat?"

"I can go without for now." Jesco edged to the left of the window frame and called out, "Saber? Are you still there?"

"Where in hell else would I be?" was the rejoinder. "What do you want, cowboy? Unless you're ready to throw down your guns and come out, we have nothin' to talk about!"

"Would you talk for ten thousand dollars?" Jesco shouted.

"How's that again?"

"Kent Tovey doesn't much like banks. He always keeps a lot of cash on hand for payrolls and such, in a safe in his bedroom. I bet you didn't know that."

"No, I didn't. Why are you tellin' me? Seems to me you would want to keep a thing like that secret."

"I'll toss the money out to you if you'll give your word that you and your men will light a shuck."

Brittle mirth greeted the proposal. "How stupid do you think I am? Why in hell are you bein' so generous?"

"For my friend's sake," Jesco replied. "He took a stray slug. I've done all I can, but he needs help. I have to get him to San Pedro, or he'll die. What do you say? Ten thousand dollars just to ride off?"

"I'd like to oblige you," was Saber's answer. "But there's a little matter of trust. I don't trust you not to shoot whoever comes over there for the money, and you can't trust us not to jump you when you're on your way to San Pedro."

"It's a chance I'm willin' to take if you are." Jesco waited expectantly. Everything depended on the outlaw's greed. He thought he heard whispering. Evidently, they were talking it over.

"Sorry, mister. No deal. But thanks for the information. After we buck you out, we'll help ourselves."

"I'll burn the house down before I let you get your hands on it."

"All that money?" Saber was appalled.

"Why don't we talk it over face-to-face?" Jesco offered. "You come to the porch. I'll come to the window."

"And have you fill me with lead the moment I show myself?" Saber snorted. "Not likely."

Jesco added the frosting to his bait. "I'll show myself first. With my arms out from my sides and my hands empty. How would that be?"

"I suppose that would do." Saber tried to sound as if it were of no consequence, but his tone betrayed his bloodlust.

"Give me a minute."

"Take as long as you want."

Jesco darted back to Timmy. "You heard. He fell

for it. Count to a hundred, real slow, to give me time. Then push the chair to the window. Whatever you do, don't show yourself."

"What if they don't shoot?"

"They will."

"What if all he really wants to do is talk? He'll wonder why you don't say anything."

"It won't come to that." Jesco ran to the hallway and down it, to a room on the left. Nancy's piano occupied a far corner. Past the piano was the window. He had tested the latch earlier, and it did not make noise. Nor did the window as he slowly slid it open high enough for him to slip over the sill. Just as quietly, he closed it behind him.

The night air was cool on Jesco's face. Drawing his Colt, he padded toward the front of the house. He had only gone a few feet when he sensed danger. He whirled, thinking as he did that it was his nerves and nothing more, of how silly he would feel when he saw no one was there.

But someone was.

Steel glinted in the starlight. An inky figure was almost on top of him. Jesco had the illusion he was being attacked by a set of clothes. Somehow he got his hand up and caught a wrist, establishing that his assailant was flesh and blood. The illusion was due to the man's skin, which was as black as the night.

Jesco was slammed against the house. His own wrist was seized. Why the black had not shot him was anyone's guess. Maybe the man enjoyed carving others up. Or maybe the black wanted to take him alive in order to inflict a long, slow, agonizing end.

Jesco considered himself strong, but the black proved stronger. The knife inched toward his neck. Exerting every sinew, he bent his back into a bow.

It did no good.

Another few moments, and the steel would bury itself in his throat.

In the dark, a stone's throw from the front of the house, four figures lay with rifles to their shoulders. A fifth man, skinny as a rail, was on his back facing the house, his legs crudely bandaged, a pistol in his hand. Nearby was a sixth figure, his head half blown away.

"What's takin' that cowboy so damn long?" Twitch groused.

"Be patient, cousin," Saber said. "For ten thousand dollars, we'll give him all the time in the world."

Twitch swore, but not too loudly. "You don't really believe he'll hand it over, do you? It has to be a trick."

"We'll find out soon enough," tittered the third man with a rifle. "And if he shows himself, he's maggot bait."

"Watch that itchy trigger finger of yours, Fritz," Saber cautioned. "No one is to fire unless I do. Is that clear?" He glanced at the skinny man with the bandaged legs. "How are you holdin' up, Harvey?"

"The bleedin' has about stopped," the wounded man said. "But I hurt like the dickens."

"At least you're breathin'," Saber remarked, with

a meaningful glance at their former companion, who had taken the brunt of the shotgun blast in the head. "We can't say the same about Lutt."

The last of them now spoke. He was burly and filthy and missing several front teeth. "That damned cowboy has to suffer for what he did. We need to take him alive and do to him as the Comanches did to my grandpa. Cut out his eyeballs for starters, then chop off his nose and ears."

Saber grinned. "You sure are a bloodthirsty cuss, Caleb. I'd like nothin' better. But you saw that cowboy unlimber his hardware. He's slick as axle grease. Takin' him alive might cost a few of us our lives, and with Lutt dead and Fritz barely able to walk, we're runnin' short."

"Speakin' of runnin' short," Twitch said, "where in hell did Creed get to? That darky is never around when we need him."

"I wouldn't call him that to his face, were I you." Saber rose on his elbows to scan the yard. "He's supposed to be keepin' watch out back in case those cowboys try to give us the slip."

They fell silent, waiting. Finally Saber raised his cheek from his rifle, and remarked, "You're right, cousin. It's takin' a lot longer than it should. It makes no sense. It was the cowboy's idea."

"You can't ever trust a cow nurse," Twitch said. "They're sneaky as hell."

Saber nudged Caleb with his boot. "Work your way up to the house and have a look."

"Why me?" the burly outlaw objected. "Why not your cousin or Fritz?"

"Because I want you to do it," Saber snapped, furious that his decision was being challenged. "Unless you would rather that you and I have us a little talk of our own after this is over."

"No," Caleb said quickly. "Those talks of yours end too permanent for my likin'. I'll go."

Saber came close to shooting Caleb anyway. Questioning his judgment had become contagious. It hinted that whoever disagreed thought they could do better at leading. The next step from thinking they could do better was wanting to take over, and the next step from there was to bury a knife in his back or blow his brains out. It wasn't easy leadin' a pack of cutthroats. Saber must always watch his back, and never, ever show a sign of weakness. At the slightest hint, they would pounce. "Where the hell is that cowboy?" he grumbled.

Timmy Loring was in a predicament.

He had counted to one hundred, slowly, exactly as Jesco told him to. Then he started to slide the chair toward the window. It was harder than he reckoned. Dunn weighed over two hundred pounds. To make things worse, the wood floor was not as smooth as it appeared to be. Where the boards joined were slight ridges. Each time the chair came to a ridge, the legs caught. Timmy had to lift first one front leg and then the other, then push the chair until the rear legs caught. Then he had to do the same with the rear legs.

It was taking forever. But another five feet should do it. The chair would be close enough to the window for the killers to see Dunn.

Timmy was sweating profusely. His clothes stuck

to him like a second skin. A bead of sweat dripped from his forehead down the bridge of his nose and fell to the floor with a tiny, wet *spat*. He pushed the chair, only to have it snag, yet again.

Lying flat, Timmy extended both arms, and gripped the right front leg. He started to lift. In his haste, he misjudged, and the chair leg rose higher than he intended. Without warning, the chair tilted in the other direction. Frantic to keep it from crashing to the floor, Timmy gripped the rung between the legs, and pulled. He pulled too hard. The chair rocked onto its rear legs. Rocked, and tilted in his direction.

Timmy flung out both arms but he was a shade too slow. The chair, and its enormously heavy burden, fell on top of him. The sound was not as loud as it would have been had the chair struck the floor, but it was still much too loud for Timmy, and he glanced at the broken window in fear that the killers had heard.

Nothing happened. No one shouted to ask what was going on.

Relieved, Timmy pushed against the chair, but it wouldn't budge. He pushed against Dunn, but Dunn's body had shifted as it fell, and lay across his back, and he could not get enough leverage. The best Timmy could do was raise his right shoulder a few inches.

"No, no, no." Timmy tried again, pushing with all his might. It made no difference. He was pinned.

Timmy's heart hammered. He had to right the chair and place Dunn back on it. Jesco was counting on him. Clenching his teeth, he pushed and pushed and pushed, and met only failure.

Timmy took stock. Maybe he was going about it all wrong. He figured he could roll out from under the body and stand up, but he had barely begun to roll when something snagged, and he could roll no farther.

If it isn't one thing, it's another, Timmy lamented. He slid his hand between his body and Dunn's, his skin crawling at the contact, and discovered his revolver had somehow become entangled in Dunn's shirt. Or, rather, Jesco's. He tugged, but it did no good. He sought to slide the Colt from its holster, but it would not come out.

"This can't be," Timmy said, fighting panic. He braced both hands flat on the floor, and attempted to rise. He might as well have attempted to stand with the world on his shoulders.

At his wits' end, Timmy sank back down. "What else can go wrong?" he whispered, and happened to glance at the side window.

A face was peering in.

Timmy couldn't stifle a gasp of dismay. The parlor was dark, but the man might catch sight of him and the fix he was in. Again he attempted to wrest his Colt free, and couldn't.

The face at the side window disappeared.

Breathing a sigh of relief, Timmy allowed himself to relax. He would lie there a while, gather his strength, and try again. He imagined Jesco out in the dark somewhere, impatiently waiting for him to carry out their plan. The outlaws were bound to shoot at Dunn in the mistaken belief it was Jesco. Jesco would know right where they were, and pay them back in kind.

Timmy glanced up.

The face had returned. The man tugged, but realized the window was latched. Undaunted, he raised a rifle to smash the pane.

Awash in helplessness, Timmy wanted to shriek in frustration. All he could do was lie there and hope that his death was a quick one.

Chapter 28

John Jesco could not stop the black man from burying the knife in his neck. The black was too strong. With the certainty came action. Rather than continue to pit his sinews in a lost cause, Jesco shifted to one side, and twisted. The blade nicked his neck, leaving a razor-thin red line, and sank into the wall. Before the black could pull the weapon free, Jesco drove his knee between the man's legs.

The black staggered but did not go down. Recovering, he yanked out the knife and stabbed at Jesco's chest, but Jesco skipped aside.

Apparently deciding enough was enough, the black man suddenly reversed his grip from the hilt to the blade, and threw the knife at Jesco's throat. Jesco automatically ducked, and saw that the black was going for his pearl-handled revolvers.

Jesco tackled him, wrapping his arms around the other's so that the black could not complete his draw. They sprawled on their sides. Jesco swung his right fist at the black's jaw, swung with all his might, but in the dark, he struck the man's neck instead. The black man arched upward, his revolvers forgotten as he bucked and gurgled and vainly clutched his crushed throat.

It was hard to say which of them was more surprised. Jesco rolled onto his knees and drew his Colt, but he did not shoot.

The black man made sucking noises. The whites of his eyes showed as he fixed them on Jesco in disbelief. "Not like this!" he croaked. "It can't be like this!"

But it was. Another minute, and the convulsions stopped. Jesco felt for a pulse and confirmed there was none. He did not feel particularly elated. Whoever the black man was, luck had beaten him, plain and simple luck, not anything special Jesco did. Straightening, he turned toward the front of the house and received yet another unwelcome surprise.

Another man was coming around the front corner. Jesco hunkered down in order not to be seen and watched the skulker slink to the side window. He had a rifle. Rising on the tips of his toes, he pressed his face to the pane.

Jesco had a good shot, but the blast would forewarn the others. There was a better, quieter way. He holstered his Colt, and groped about for the knife. It lay at the base of the wall.

The outlaw was trying to open the window.

It felt strange using a knife. Jesco never carried one, had never killed with a blade until now. He much preferred the crack and buck of his Colt. A slug through the head or the heart was always fatal, but a knife was an iffy proposition, like shooting someone in the guts. Sometimes it killed them outright, and sometimes it didn't.

Foiled, the outlaw raised his rifle to break the glass.

Jesco was only a few feet away when the man apparently sensed him, and spun. The man started to level his rifle at the same instant Jesco lunged. Steel rang on steel. The blade glanced off the rifle's barrel, and once again, a fluke favored Jesco. The knife was deflected downward, into the man's groin. It sliced through his pants and his flesh as if they were not there.

The man bleated and dropped the Winchester. Tottering, he cupped himself, then turned and bolted past the front corner of the house, screeching, "I've been stabbed! I've been stabbed!"

Jesco sprang to the corner. Stealth was no longer called for. Drawing his Colt, he called out, "Fill your hand!"

To his credit, the man tried. He stopped and turned, his splayed, bloody fingers dropping to his revolver.

Jesco shot him. One was all it took, smack between the eyes. The man's head whipped back, and he melted to the earth like so much wax. Beyond him, rifles spat flame and thunder. Lead thwacked against the house, and narrowly missed Jesco's cheek. He replied with thunder of his own, three swift shots, then backpedaled and commenced reloading.

"Surround him! Cut him off!"

The shout and the sight of shadowy forms flitting toward him galvanized Jesco into shoving his Colt into his holster with two cartridges still to be replaced. Spinning, he felt on the ground for the Winchester. Finding it took only a moment. Then, jamming the stock to his shoulder, he centered a hasty bead on an onrushing silhouette, thumbed back the hammer, and applied his finger to the trigger.

The rifle did not go off.

Belatedly, Jesco realized its previous owner had not fed a cartridge into the chamber. He remedied the oversight with a flip of the lever, and banged off the shot. Several rifles cracked in cadence as Jesco dodged around the corner. He felt something fly past him, but his skin was spared.

Jesco had a decision to make. Should he stay and fight it out or stay on the move and make them come to him? The fact he was outnumbered decided the issue. He turned and ran, glancing over his shoulder to ensure he did not take a bullet in the back. He forgot about the dead black, and the oversight proved costly.

Running at full speed, Jesco tripped over the body. He tried to stay upright, but pitched onto his stomach, absorbing most of the fall with his hands. His ankle spiked with pain. He rolled as a rifle blasted, and heard the slug tear into the dead man. Flat on his back, he sought the shooter, but no movement registered.

The night became deathly still.

Jesco slowly sat up, with his back to the house. He set down the rifle, and hastily finished reloading the Colt. It was now a game of cat and mouse. He was unsure how many were left. Definitely three, perhaps four. They would expect him to stay close to the house, so he cautiously made off into the darkness.

Thirty feet out, Jesco squatted. The silence rubbed on his nerves. He would as soon they all came at him at once, to get it over with. The yard, the corral, the stable were deceptively peaceful. He decided to crawl toward the front of the house and provoke them into giving themselves away.

The wavering yip of a coyote reminded Jesco of the world past the buildings. He wondered where Kent Tovey and Clayburn and the rest of the punchers had gotten to, and hoped to heaven they weren't attacking the DP. Too many lives had already been lost to hatred and greed.

To think that once the two ranches had been like peas in a pod. It said a lot about human nature. About the dark depths that lurked in the hearts of even the innocent and decent. About the dangers of jumping to conclusions, and letting emotion warp reason.

Jesco never considered himself all that savvy, except about cows. He could handle a revolver better than most, but that was the result of practice, not insight. Human nature was pretty much a mystery to him. He wasn't joking when he told Timmy that the only two certainties in life were being born and dying. The rest was a muddle, a maze of right decisions and wrong decisions and decisions that seemed right at the time, but turned out to be wrong later. The best a person could do was pick a course and stick with it, the rest of the world be hanged.

Jesco had picked his course. He was a cowboy. He would always be a cowboy. A cowboy's life was not as grand, say, as being president. Riding night herd could not begin to compare to riding herd in the country. Nor was their much money to be had. The few cowmen who became rich were the exceptions, not the rule. But cows were what Jesco liked, and cows would do him until his turn came to be planted. Which he hoped was later rather than sooner.

A sound snapped Jesco to the here and now. He stopped and listened, and presently the sound was repeated—a stealthy scrape and soft rustle, as if someone was crawling through the grass . . . in his direction. Lowering his chin to the ground, he waited. Soon, heavy breathing testified to the other's exertions. Whoever it was, he was making enough noise for two or three men.

Jesco thought it had to be a ruse. No one would deliberately be so loud. Then it hit him, who the crawler must be. Silently setting the Winchester at his side, he drew his Colt, his thumb on the hammer.

The seconds passed on tortoise feet. Then the grass parted, framing a thin face. In the man's left hand was a rifle, which he was holding by the barrel. He crawled another foot or so, and stopped in surprise. "Fritz, is that you?" he whispered.

"No, it isn't," Jesco said, and cocked the Colt.

"You!" the man let go of his rifle and thrust his hand out in fear. "Don't shoot, mister! For God's sake, haven't you done enough to me? I may be crippled for life."

It was the outlaw Jesco had shot in the legs with the shotgun. "If you're lookin' for sympathy, you're barkin' up the wrong tree. You were tryin' to burn the house down, and me along with it."

The man defended the deed. "I was only doin' what I was told. Besides, you stopped us. No harm done, except to me and Lutt." He licked his lips. "Everyone calls me Harvey."

Jesco scoured their vicinity, but did not spot anyone else. "You can try with the rifle or a six-shooter if you have one."

"Please, mister. I'm hurtin', hurtin' powerful bad." Harvey's fear was thick enough to cut with a blunt table knife.

"Whenever you're ready."

"God Almighty." Harvey rose on his elbows and looked about him. "All I want is to leave this place alive." And just like that, he threw back his head and bawled, "Saber! Over here!" Simultaneously, he grabbed his rifle and swung the muzzle up. He almost made it.

Jesco cored him through the forehead. The blast had not yet faded when Jesco sprang into motion. Holstering his Colt, he rolled to his feet, snagged the rifle on the move, and flew toward the house. It occurred to him that he should check on Timmy. Something had gone wrong with their plan; the rustlers had never opened fire on Dunn's body.

A shape hove up out of nowhere and a rifle boomed. Jesco returned the favor, emptying the Winchester, and it was the shape that crumpled, not him. He ran on, to the same side window he had slipped out of. It was open a few inches, and he was sure he had closed it. Worry lanced through him. He opened it high enough to hook his leg over the sill.

"Timmy?" Jesco whispered in the stillness of the room. The Colt firmly in hand, his elbow molded to his side, Jesco crept down the hall to the parlor. By then his eyes had adjusted. The first thing he saw was the overturned chair, and what appeared to be two bodies intertwined beside it. He took a bound, and was brought up short by the abrupt blaze of a lamp.

From behind the settee rose a lanky man in a buckskin jacket. He was holding the lamp. In his other hand was a Colt, pointed not at Jesco, but at one of the two sprawled figures on the floor.

Another man came out of the shadows near the front curtains. He had feral features and a vivid scar down the right side of his face. His Colt, too, was trained on one of the figures. "Do anything hasty, cowboy, and we give your young friend a new set of ear holes."

Timmy was pinned under Dunn, his arms outspread, completely helpless. "Sorry," he said.

"How in the world?" Jesco exclaimed, relieved to find him alive. Then, to the man with the scar, "Let me guess. You're Saber."

"What gave you the clue?" The outlaw leader nodded at the window. "I heard a lot of shootin' out there. My other lunkheads?"

"Won't be stealin' any cows."

"Damn."

"Your scheme has failed," Jesco told him. "There's only the two of you left."

The man holding the lamp snickered. "That's what you think, mister. There's still Hijino. By now he's probably wiped out the Pierces."

Saber glowered hotly. "Shut your mouth, damn it, Twitch. You talk too much. You always have."

"Two or three, it doesn't matter," Jesco said. "There's not enough of you to steal the herds."

"Not now, no," Saber said. "But those critters

aren't goin' anywhere. I can send out word and in two or three weeks have enough men to replace those you've turned into maggot bait, plus extra." A smug smile curled his scar. "All you've done is delay things a mite."

Twitch raised the lamp higher. "We have you over a barrel," he gloated. "Drop that smoke wagon, or else."

Jesco looked at Timmy. If he set the Colt down, they were as good as goners. So long as he held onto it, they had a prayer. "No."

"We'll plug him," Twitch threatened. "Me or Saber, one or the other. So help me."

"Go ahead," Jesco said, sidling to the left so he could watch both of them without having to turn his head.

"What?" Both Twitch and Timmy declared in disbelief, with Twitch going on, "You don't care if we bed him down permanent?"

Saber swore luridly. "Of course he cares. But he's got more grit than I gave him credit for."

"I'll shoot the first one of you who fires," Jesco vowed. He was tense from head to toe with apprehension over what he had to do.

"We have us a standoff," Saber said. "It's what I get for thinkin' this cowboy was no different from any other."

"I'm just a puncher," Jesco said to keep them talking. He was staring at them, but he was seeing the arroyo, and the scores of broken bottles. All that practice was about to pay off, or get him and Timmy killed.

"No cowpoke could do what you've done," Saber

said. "I always figured my boys were a match for fifty of your kind."

"You figured wrong," Jesco said, and shot him in the chest. Quick as thought, he shifted and fanned off two shots at Twitch's face. Twitch's right eye exploded, and his nose spouted crimson. In the same split second, another shot banged, and a slug dug across Jesco's ribs.

Saber was still on his feet. "You're mine!" he roared.

They fired simultaneously. It was Jesco who went on firing, fanning his Colt until it was empty.

Tendrils of gun smoke hung thick in the air. The thrashing and mewing ended, and as Jesco reloaded, he walked over to the bodies and nudged them to be certain.

"What about me?" Timmy impatiently asked.

Jesco twirled the Colt into his holster, and grinned. "I should leave you there. The boys can use a good laugh when they get back."

Timmy Loring had learned a lot of cuss words at the Circle T.

Chapter 29

Dolores was a talker when she was mad, and *Madre de Dios*, was she mad now! Hijino listened to her go on and on, while secretly yearning for the moment when he could shut her up forever.

"We need more vaqueros! Lots of them!" Dolores was saying to Trella. "An army of vaqueros to crush the Circle T. To kill all the cowboys and burn all their buildings to the ground."

The three of them were riding abreast under the star-sprinkled heavens. The Rio Largo was miles behind them—the rancho less than a mile ahead. A stiff breeze from off the mountains fanned the long hair of the two women, and the manes of their horses.

Trella was deep in the grip of sorrow. She had barely uttered three words since leaving the river. Hijino had made bold to lean over and touch her arm a few times, playing his part of the devoted protector, but she did not respond. Now, to Dolores's proposal, she merely nodded.

"You must snap out of it, *mi hermana*. The fate of our rancho depends on us. Everything father and mother worked for, all their years of sweat and toil, will be for nothing if we do not keep our heads and do what must be done."

In acute misery, Trella softly asked, "How could it come to this? How could our happiness be so quickly crushed?"

"You dwell on the past," Dolores criticized. "On what we have lost, not the steps we must take to ensure our future."

Trella looked at her. "How can you? Do you not have emotions? Our parents are dead. Our brothers, dead. The loss is almost more than I can bear."

"Snap out of it, I tell you," Dolores said harshly. "We will be dead, too, if you do not. We must plan, and plan carefully. We must foresee every contingency. Such as the one I fear the most."

"What can be worse than what has already happened?"

"More proof you are not thinking clearly. For as terrible as things are, for all our loss and our sorrow, things *can* get worse." Dolores paused. "They can get very bad indeed, if Paco and Roman and the rest of our men at the river are wiped out by the cowboys."

"Paco will not let that happen."

"A fantasy, sister. Do you think Father let himself be shot? Do you think our brothers let themselves be murdered? No. Bad things happen whether we want them to or not. We must be realistic. The cowboys outnumber our vaqueros. Unless Paco is very clever, the cowboys will win."

The starlight bathed the tears glistening in Trella's eyes. "We should not have left them there."

"On the contrary. The cowboys would have given chase, and you and I would be caught in the fight."

Dolores swiped at a stray lock of hair that had fallen over her eyes. "The best we can do is pray for Paco and the others. By now they have either driven the cowboys off, or met their end."

"They were safe enough in the trees," Trella mentioned. "The cowboys could not get at them."

"Paco was not going to wait for them to try. He planned to attack them as soon as we were safely away. Paco felt it better to strike first, with surprise on his side, than to wait for the cowboys to move against him. Paco is a good man. I have faith in his judgment, but I had faith in our father and our brothers, too."

Hijino smiled at her comment. He had met a lot of people with faith. They were always surprised to find out that faith did not stop bullets. His only faith was in his *pistola*, and the speed with which he could draw it.

"I don't know if I can go on without our loved ones," Trella was saying.

"Quit being silly," Dolores snapped. "We *must* go on. Our father saw to it that we know as much about ranching as any man. We can run the DP, the two of us. We will take over the valley, and not let a single gringo set foot in it without our permission. We will not make the same mistake our father did."

"Do not speak ill of him."

Dolores sighed. "I loved him as much as you. But it was unwise to let Kent Tovey move in."

"How could Father have foreseen that Tovey would betray him? None of us can predict the future."

"*Sí*. But we mold the future by the decisions we

make in the present. The decisions you and I make over the next several days will determine our futures twenty years from now."

Hijino shut out their prattle. It was all for nothing, only they did not realize it. He glanced from one lovely woman to the other, supremely delighted at the capricious whim of circumstance that had delivered them into his hands. He did not know which one to kill first. Or how. The how was important. He had time on his hands, so there was no need to rush. He could indulge himself. It would be great fun.

All the vaqueros were at the river, but there were the servants to deal with. Hijino ticked them off in his head: the cook, the two maids, the old man whose name Hijino could not remember, and who did the gardening and other odd jobs and slept out in the woodshed because he liked being by himself. That made four.

Ordinarily, at that time of night, the casa would be dark, but every window was lit when they arrived. The servants were too overwrought to sleep and came out to greet them. The old man took their horses to the stable. The cook scurried to the kitchen for food and drink for Trella and Dolores. The maids hovered over them like anxious hummingbirds.

Trella invited Hijino in. He stayed in the background, savoring the sweet nectar of anticipation. *Where to begin?* he asked himself. Or, rather, with whom? So many possibilities presented themselves.

Dolores excused herself to freshen up, saying, "We will meet in the kitchen in twenty minutes, sister." She ignored Hijino as she went out.

Trella slumped in a chair, a portrait of despair. "I am tired. So very tired. But I could not sleep if I wanted to."

"Me either," Hijino lied. "*Con permiso*, señorita, but I left my rifle with my saddle. I should get it in case, as your sister says, the worst comes to pass."

"Whatever is best," Trella said wearily. "But hurry. I want you by my side, tonight and ever after."

The sweet look she gave him would melt most any man. Hijino smiled and said, "You flatter me, señorita. I am but a humble vaquero." Then he got out of there before he laughed in her face.

The stable doors were open. The old man was stripping the saddle blanket from Trella's mare, and grunted in greeting when Hijino entered. "A terrible time, eh? I feel sorry for those poor girls."

"I, as well," Hijino said, standing under the hayloft.

"Would that I were younger!" the old man said with great passion. "I would teach those gringos. In my day, I was an hombre to be feared."

"I bet you were." To Hijino's left was the ladder that led to the loft. He casually moved toward it.

The old man draped the saddle blanket over a stall. "You would not think it to look at me, but I was formidable. I fought Apaches. I fought the Navajos. They were everywhere then."

Propped against the ladder was a pitchfork. Hijino stood next to it, and folded his arms across his chest.

"I rode with Señor Pierce before he started the DP," the old man said, as he led the mare into a stall. "He was young, but I knew he would make something of himself. You can always tell with the good ones."

"How about the bad ones? The killers?"

The old man patted the mare, then moved toward Dolores's mount. "Killers are not always bad. Roman has killed, but he is a man of honor. The truly evil ones are those who snuff out life as you or I would snuff out a candle."

Hijino took hold of the pitchfork's long hardwood handle. "Maybe they do not see themselves as evil. Maybe they only do what they like to do, and to them that is good."

"Bad can not be good," the old man said as he undid the cinch. "A deed is either one or the other."

"So Roman has shot men down, but he is good? Does that mean I am good, too, if I have done the same?"

"It depends on why you did it," the old man asserted. "Roman has only killed in self-defense."

"If I were to bury this pitchfork in your back for no other reason than to watch you die, would that be bad, then?"

"What a strange question. Most assuredly, it would be bad."

By then, Hijino was close enough. "In that case, I am perhaps the most evil person you have ever met." The metal tines met with no resistance as he drove them into the old man's back, between the shoulder blades.

With a loud gasp, the old man stiffened and tried to turn, but was held in place by the pitchfork. "In heaven's name, why?" he bleated.

"Were you not paying attention?" Hijino asked. Grinning savagely, he twisted.

The old man cried out. Blood spurted from his nose and the corners of his mouth. He reached behind him to try and grab the handle, but could not. "I do not understand," were his last words. He fell on his stomach, the handle jutting into the air.

Whistling to himself, Hijino dragged the body into an empty stall. Not that he expected anyone to come looking. But better safe than prematurely dead. He closed the stable door and strolled up the path to the house. Instead of going in the front, he walked around to the rear door. Through it, he saw the cook at the stove. She gave a start when he entered.

"Señor! You scared me half to death! Next time you should knock, eh?"

Hijino played the gallant. "I am most sorry." A counter was midway between the stove and table. Walking over, he leaned against it. "You are afraid?"

"Who would not be? Those awful cowboys could show up at any moment." She was a stout woman with wisps of gray at the temples, and always wore an apron over her dress.

On the counter lay a butcher knife. Hijino placed his right hand beside it, and remarked, "You must have faith in the vaqueros."

The cook came toward the table. She had already set out plates and glasses and silverware. "I have faith in God, señor. The Lord is the only one who can truly protect us from harm."

"Then he must be asleep," Hijino said, and thrust the butcher knife into her abdomen. She was as shocked as the old man had been, and opened her mouth to cry out. "No, you don't," Hijino said, clamping his other hand over her fat lips even as he slit her open from hip to hip. She died on her feet, with her intestines oozing out. He lowered her under the table and left the knife buried in her belly. Before moving on, he wiped his hands on a towel.

Hijino was halfway down the hall when a maid appeared at the other end. He stopped and leaned against the wall, his arms folded across his chest. "What is your hurry?" he asked, as she came hurriedly toward him.

"I am to bring the coffee for Trella." She was a young thing, still in her teens, the granddaughter of the old man in the stable. Her name was Carona, Hijino remembered. "Excuse me, señor." She shifted to slip past him.

"And if I don't?" Hijino's hands were on her throat, and he was forcing her to the floor before her brain accepted the reality. She frantically clawed at his arms and tried to gouge his eyes, but he drew his head back. When it was over, the impressions of his thumbs and fingers were buried deep in her flesh. He dragged her into a room, closing the door as he went back out.

The second maid was with Dolores. Hijino heard their voices before he came to the bedroom. Dolores was in a chair, the maid fussing over her hair. They did not notice him.

"Hurry, Rosalita. I told them twenty minutes, and it has been more than that. I am worried about my sister. In her state, she might do anything."

A small table was near the doorway. Hijino leaned

against it and folded his arms across his chest. "Do not worry, señorita," he said. "I would not let sweet Trella harm herself."

The two women glanced over, and Dolores said sharply, "What are you doing here? You should be with Trella, watching over her."

On the table were knitting needles and a roll of yarn. Hijino lowered his arms, saying, "It is important we talk, you and I, señorita. It is about your sister, and for your ears alone."

"You may go, Rosalita," Dolores told the maid. "Help Jimena in the kitchen."

"*Sí*, senorita."

Several vaqueros were fond of Rosalita, but she was much too plump for Hijino's tastes. She had big thighs and big buttocks, big arms and big eyes. Those eyes were fixed on him as she smiled, and went to walk past. Whether she saw his hand move, he would never know. He drove the needle into her left eye as far as it would go, curious how she would react, since he had never stabbed anyone with a knitting needle before. All she did was say, "Oh!" and collapse.

Dolores was glued to her chair. Hijino reached her in one bound and lanced another needle into her throat. His knee on her chest, he covered her mouth and nose so she could not breathe. She bucked upward, and when she could not dislodge him, she seized his wrist, but could not pry his hand off. Gradually, her struggles weakened, and as life faded from her features, he leaned down and whispered in her ear, "Give my regards to the rest of your family."

Trella was still in the parlor, still slumped in the chair. "There you are, Hijino. What took you so long? And where is everyone else?"

"Here and there," Hijino said.

She had another question. "What is that in your hand?"

"A ball of yarn."

"I can see that, silly. But what are you doing with it? Have you taken up knitting?" For the first time that day, Trella smiled.

Hijino halted in front of her and gently placed his other hand on her chin. "Open wide."

Chapter 30

"That's not a good sign," Timmy Loring said.

Buzzards circled in the azure sky. The Rio Largo was a glistening blue-green ribbon visible through gaps in the vegetation that fringed its banks.

John Jesco rose in the stirrups. He smelled smoke. Wisps rose from among the trees. He was about to gig his mount when he spied a long row of bodies laid shoulder to shoulder. Bodies of cowboys and vaqueros, both.

"Look at all of them!" Timmy exclaimed.

A puncher named Johnson appeared, his leg bandaged, a shovel in hand. He shouted something over his shoulder, and as they brought their horses to a stop, Walt Clayburn strode tiredly out to meet them.

"Thank God. I was beginnin' to think the two of you had met your Maker. Most everyone else has."

"Is that Shonsey?" Timmy asked, pointing at the old cook, aghast at the hole in Shonsey's forehead. "And next to him, Jack Demp?"

"Only five of us are left," Clayburn said. "We've been diggin' graves all mornin', and we're not half done. It will take a month of Sundays for the blisters to heal."

Jesco swung down. "Mr. Tovey?"

"Wrapped in a blanket in the shade. He asked to be planted next to his wife. We'll take him back tomorrow." Clayburn removed his hat, and wiped his sleeve across his heavily perspiring face. "You should have been here. We needed you."

"I had problems of my own." Jesco briefly recounted his clash with the would-be rustlers.

"Damn, you were lucky," Clayburn declared.

The next body to be buried was that of a vaquero, a handsome man, shot multiple times. His hands were on his chest. So were a pair of pearl-handled, short-barreled Colts.

"How many did Roman take with him?" Jesco asked.

"Six, damn him. He was hell on wheels. We put bullet after bullet into him, but he wouldn't go down until he was shot to ribbons, and when he did go down, he didn't stop shooting until he took enough lead to sink a sternwheeler. I never saw anything like it."

"Any get away?"

"The two sisters left early on with that one they call Hijino. Another vaquero lit out after the scrape. He was hurt, but he made it to a horse, and I didn't have it in me to shoot him in the back." Clayburn stared glumly at the row of bodies. "I never want to shoot another person as long as I live."

Jesco climbed back on the bay.

"Where do you think you're goin'?"

"To finish it."

Timmy Loring turned to his mount, saying, "Wait for me!"

"No, you don't." Walt Clayburn snagged the younger man's arm, and shook his head. "You're stayin', sir."

"Let go, you big ox," Timmy said. "And since when do my betters address me as sir?"

"Since you became the new owner of the Circle T." Clayburn produced a folded sheet of paper. "Read this. It will explain." To Jesco, Clayburn said, "He's Tovey's nephew. Kept it a secret so we wouldn't treat him special."

"This is Kent's last will and testament!" Timmy marveled. "My God. He's left everything to me. How could he do that? He never mentioned anything to me."

"Kin is kin," Clayburn said.

"Wait a minute." A gleam came into Timmy's eyes. "If I'm the new rod, then I give the orders. So I can go with Jesco if I want."

"No, you can't," Clayburn responded. "Mr. Tovey didn't write it down, but he told me to look after you, to point out when you're makin' mistakes, and keep you out of trouble. Well, it would be a mistake for you to tag along. You're liable to get yourself shot, and then the Circle T won't have any owner at all."

Timmy's features betrayed the inner struggle between his immaturity and his new responsibilities. "Very well," he reluctantly relented. "My first order as the new big sugar is for Jesco to hunt down the last son of a bitch to blame for all of this and kill him dead as dead can be."

"I reckon I'll like havin' you as the new boss,"

Jesco said. He meant it. Loring was green as grass, but he was sincere and eager to learn. There was also the fact that it hammered the final nail into the coffin of Timmy's wish to become a leather slapper.

Jesco forded the river, and rode south at a measured pace. He had a lot of miles to cover, and it wouldn't do to arrive at the Pierce spread with the bay exhausted. He thought about the sisters. He never knew them that well. He had swapped pleasantries with the older girl once at a rodeo. Dolores was always friendly, but the younger girl, Trella, tended to put on airs. Not that he resented her for that. People were entitled to their delusions.

When the adobe buildings finally hove into sight, Jesco drew rein, and verified he had six pills in the wheel. He spun the Colt forward and back, flipped it and caught it by the grips, and spun it some more. Satisfied that his hand was limber, he twirled the Colt into its holster, and rode past the outbuildings and the stable to the grand house.

No one came to greet him. No shouts rang out. A lathered horse stood near the portico. To the southeast were tendrils of dust.

Jesco dismounted, and started for the door. In the shadows lay the body of a vaquero. The man had been shot twice in the chest, older wounds rimmed by dry blood—wounds from the river battle, Jesco suspected. A third wound was fresher. Someone had put a pistol to the man's forehead and blown his brains out.

Out of habit, Jesco went to the door and knocked. There was no response. *Surely not*, he told himself. *Not the sisters, too.* But then he realized Hijino had no way of knowing about Saber and the others. No way of knowing that killing Dolores and Trella would be pointless.

Jesco opened the door, and pushed. The hall was narrow and cool. His spurs jingled, but he did not take them off. The parlor was the first room he came to. He blinked, and blinked again, his stomach churning. Trella had put on airs, but she hadn't deserved *this*. Steeling himself, he went over and pulled her dress down around her ankles.

He went from room to room. The slaughter sickened him. Out of respect, he covered each body with a blanket. He hesitated before covering the cook. Her insides seemed to cover half the floor. Careful not to step on her innards, he swung a blanket so it covered her face and chest. The smell got to him. The sweetly sickening reek of fluids that were supposed to be in a human body, not out of them. Jesco went out the back door and leaned on the post, breathing deep.

Jesco repeated Timmy's orders. "Hunt down the last son of a bitch to blame for all of this and kill him as dead as dead can be." Squaring his shoulders, he went around the house to the bay and climbed on. There might be other bodies, but they could wait. The important thing was that Hijino not get away.

The dust to the southeast had been a clue. The killer was bound for San Pedro. Maybe it was where Hijino was to meet with Saber.

Jesco felt drained of emotion. The ordeal of the past twenty-four hours was like an avalanche waiting for a crack in his self-control to bring the full horror crashing down on him. He understood Walt's loathing. There was only so much killing a person could take. A normal person, anyway. Those like Hijino were not normal. They were monsters in human form. Outwardly, they were just like everyone else, but inside they were twisted into something unnatural.

Or were they? The notion startled him. Could it be, Jesco wondered, that the violent side of human nature was as normal as the peaceful side? He shook his head in annoyance. Such pondering was better left for those who enjoyed wrestling with questions no one could ever answer. The truth of it was, normal or not, there must be an accounting. Hijino must not get away.

Usually, the lights of San Pedro brought a smile to Jesco's lips. He always looked forward to a few drinks, and the company of friendly doves. Not tonight. He rode into town as somber as a tombstone.

Only a few people were out and about. At that hour, the general store and most of the other businesses were closed. A notable exception was the Lucky Star. Laughter and voices mingled with the tinny music of the piano and the clink of poker chips.

Jesco reined up at the hitch rail, next to a white horse with a saddle that gleamed with silver. The white horse and saddle were caked with dust. Dismounting, he wrapped the reins around the rail, then went through his ritual with his Colt.

At the batwing doors, Jesco paused. For a weekday night, the place was crowded. The bar was to his right, the tables to his left. All the tables were occupied. At most, card games were under way.

Jesco pushed on through. Something in his manner, or his face, caused those near him to take one look and back away, or whisper to those next to them. He walked past the poker tables to a table in the far corner. The sounds around him faded.

It was a few seconds before the spreading quiet made the man at the table look up from his meal. A sombrero hung down his back by the chinstrap, and he had been bent over a plate of beans, wolfing them with a spoon. He wore as much silver as the white horse. Smiling, he waited for Jesco to say something, and when Jesco didn't, he asked, "Do you want something, señor?"

"You."

His eyebrows knitting, the man lowered the spoon. "Do I know you, señor?"

"I know you, Hijino. Timmy Loring described you to me. He saw you kill Julio Pierce and those vaqueros."

"Is that so?" Still smiling, Hijino placed the spoon on the table, and sat back in the chair.

"I've been to the Pierce ranch. I saw Dolores. I saw Trella. I saw what you did to the cook and the others."

Complete silence gripped the saloon, save for the tick of the brass clock above the bar.

Hijino folded his arms across his chest. "You saw all that, yet you came after me? You heard about Julio, yet still you came?" His smile widened. "Either you are loco, or you have a death wish."

"Whenever you are ready."

Puzzlement etched Hijino's face. Suddenly he straightened. "Ah! I have it now. You are the one they call Jesco. You have saved me the trouble of finding you when my friends and I—"

"They're dead."

"Who is?"

"Saber. Dunn. All the rest. I killed them, just as I'm about to kill you." Jesco watched Hijino's right hand. The eyes did not always give a man away. The hands, though, did.

"All of them, señor? I find that hard to believe. They are not as fast as me, but it would take more than one hombre to slay them."

"The pleasure was mine, and no one else's," Jesco reiterated.

"The best lawmen in several states and territories have tried to do what you claim to have done, and could not. How do you expect me to believe you?"

"I don't care whether you do or you don't," Jesco said. "The important thing is that it's just you now. You and me."

"Saber? A man with a scar here?" Hijino touched his cheek.

"Dead."

"Twitch? He wears a buckskin jacket, and his mouth is never still."

"Dead."

"Creed?"

"Was he the black, or one of the others?"

Hijino had it, then. He finally believed. He did not swear. He did not indulge in insults. Incredibly, all he did was lean back and laugh. "This is wonderful. Most wonderful."

"You're the one who is loco," Jesco said.

"You do not understand, señor. I live for moments like this. For the challenge. There is no challenge in killing old men with pitchforks or women with knitting needles. I did that for amusement."

"Stand up."

"Hear me out, señor. *Por favor*. You see, real challenges have been few. I have yet to meet my equal. They say you are quick, like me, and that delights me, because maybe, just maybe, you will prove them right. Too many times I have met hombres who were supposed to be quick, and they were turtles."

Jesco suspected the *pistolero* was stalling. Hijino knew Jesco had walked into the saloon primed to draw. By talking, by dragging it out, Hijino hoped to blunt his mental edge.

"Nothing to say, eh?"

"Let's do it," Jesco said.

"Very well." Smiling, always smiling, Hijino slowly rose, and just as slowly pushed the chair back with his foot. He lowered his hands to his sides and wriggled his fingers, then stood stock-still. "I am ready when you are, señor. How should we do this? Have someone count to three? Or perhaps have someone drop a glass, and when the glass hits the floor, we draw?"

"Just you and me."

Their eyes met and locked.

Jesco emptied his mind of everything, save that moment. When Hijino's hand flashed down and out, his own was a mirror image. It was his Colt that boomed first, a fraction of a heartbeat before Hijino's. He felt a searing pain even as Hijino rose onto the tips of his toes, and the taunting smile was replaced by astonishment. Then Hijino crashed onto the table, upending it, and both smashed onto the floor.

Jesco gingerly probed his shirt. The slug had taken a chunk of flesh above his hip. He was bleeding, but he would live. He walked to the bar, the onlookers scrambling out of his way. The bartender slid a bottle across, and Jesco treated himself to a long swig. "I'm obliged," he said, and walked out. It wasn't until he went to unwrap the reins that he realized he was still holding his Colt. He slid it into its holster, forked leather, and rode out of San Pedro without looking back.